For Debbie Reynolds
with love from your Australian friends
the Delaney family.

June 1966

*Pastures
of the Blue Crane*

H. F. Brinsmead

# Pastures of the Blue Crane

ILLUSTRATED BY
*Annette Macarthur-Onslow*

*London*
OXFORD UNIVERSITY PRESS

Oxford University Press, Amen House, London EC4

GLASGOW  NEW YORK  TORONTO  MELBOURNE  WELLINGTON
BOMBAY  CALCUTTA  MADRAS  KARACHI  LAHORE  DACCA
CAPE TOWN  SALISBURY  NAIROBI  IBADAN  ACCRA
KUALA LUMPUR  HONG KONG

First published 1964
Reprinted 1965

*Acknowledgements*

The lines from 'The Gardener' taken from *Collected Poems and Plays of Rabindranath Tagore* are reproduced by kind permission of the Trustees of the Sir Rabindranath Tagore Estate and Macmillan & Co. Ltd., London.

Like some ragged owlet With its wings expanded,
Nailed to some garden gate or boardin'
Thus will I by some men All my life be branded,
Never was it true this side of Jordan.   [*Page 105*]

Take off your old coat and roll up your sleeves,
Life is a hard road to travel I believe.   [*Page 221*]

PRINTED IN GREAT BRITAIN BY
WESTERN PRINTING SERVICES LTD., BRISTOL

# I

Melbourne was drenched in sunshine. Winter was past, with its grey days of fog, its biting winds and sad rain, and November had come again; the city was sunlit, its grey cathedral towers soft against a water-colour sky, its parks bright with young leaves, and in Collins Street the multi-coloured umbrellas were open again above the pavement cafés, close to the bright splash of colour that was Jonas's Fruitshop.

But around the corner in Spring Street were the beehive buildings of solicitors' offices, and these, for the most part, never changed from season to season.

The room where Ryl waited on a hard chair pushed against the wall was a sombre place. Not so different, thought Ryl, from the headmistress's office at school. There was the old-fashioned desk, the panelled walls hung with framed Company certificates with impressive red seals, the filing cabinet and glass-fronted bookcase filled with weighty tomes. Ryl noted that dust still gathered on the

I

shelf under the window, just as usual. Twice a year for thirteen years, she had sat on this chair—and always there was the dust on the shelf. Once when she was six, and writing was a newly-acquired art, she had spelled out her name on that shelf, with one finger. Ryl Merewether. She remembered how Miss Adams from the prep. school had reprimanded her for the unmannerly incident, and wiped out the name with a perfectly clean handkerchief.

That was the first year that Ryl had been at Rushton College. It was her first real school, after a succession of 'holiday homes for children', where pre-school infants were gathered beneath the protective but impersonal wings of trained nurses and retired ladies of academic background.

The first time that Ryl had sat here her legs had been far too short to reach the floor, and she had thrust them straight out in front of her—her feet encased in sturdy brown brogues, a remarkably small distance from the edge of the plain frock that was her best. A plain dress, the forerunner of a long series of school uniforms that had since been her fate. She looked down now at the blue checked skirt that would be the last of its line.

'One more week,' thought Ryl, mentally speaking to the dress as though it were an enemy, 'one more week, and I'm going to tear you up into tiny pieces! I'm going to cut you up with my nail scissors, and I'm going to—'

The door opened in the far wall, and Mr. Herbert—senior partner in the firm of Herbert and Harrow, Solicitors—came into the room.

He, too, at the sight of the girl, remembered the first occasion she had sat waiting for him in this office. He remembered how small she had been, and how composed. There had been a hardness about the face that was incongruous with so young a child. He remembered his feeling of amazement and dismay on reading the letter which accompanied her. In it, her father, Robert Merewether of New Guinea, had consigned her to his care.

'You will'—so it ran—'enter her in some good school, see that she has everything required, and that her fees are regularly paid.' He gathered that the child's parents had separated, that the father found New Guinea unsuitable for her upbringing, and so had decided to send her to Melbourne. Also, he gathered that Mr. Merewether intended to ignore his daughter as far as possible, that

2

she had no relatives or family friends to help her, and that, at the age of three, she was expected more or less to make her own way in the world!

Mr. Herbert's first thought was that he could not accept this assignment, but finally, with some reluctance, he had become Amaryllis Jane Merewether's legal guardian.

Of course, no 'good school' would take so young a child. For the first few weeks Mr. Herbert and his wife had themselves played host and hostess to her, and they had noted that she never asked for her father. It was hard to tell whether she was unhappy. She was so self-contained, so stoical. She seemed never to have been a child. Then Mr. Herbert had placed her in a holiday home for young children, and Ryl had embarked upon a life of group activities and juvenile regimentation into which she had never quite fitted. Biannually for the next thirteen years, she had seated herself on the same straight-backed chair in Mr. Herbert's office. Her legs had grown longer, the skirts above had changed through a succession of ginghams and tartans. The heavy black hair became plaits, then a shoulder-length bob. The green eyes still dominated the face, which was still small, and in expression somewhat grim.

For years Ryl had been the only child to remain at boarding-school throughout holiday periods. She had learned to win herself invitations from various likely schoolfellows by sheer force of personality, and the judicious habit of present-giving—for spending money had never been one of her problems. So it was that from an early age she had learned to be calculating, self-centred (for who else was there to think of her?), and yet not without flashes of charm. As far as Mr. Herbert knew, her father kept their correspondence to the low level of one letter per year—a duty letter which Robert Merewether wrote to his daughter on the occasion of each birthday, and to which she replied briefly.

She had been unable to avoid learning good manners, and could produce them upon demand—so now she rose, and solemnly held out her hand to Mr. Herbert. He took it, and looked down into her face, wondering if the girl had in her one shred of emotion, one grain of spontaneity. He had no idea.

Before him was a tall stick of a girl in the neat uniform of Rushton College. She was used to being likened by her classmates to the definition of a straight line—'length without breadth'. But the

3

curve of shining black hair beneath the brim of her school hat held a certain suggestion of elegance, and the small-boned face with its green eyes could, thought Mr. Herbert, be oddly beautiful, were it not for the cold, somewhat repellent expression.

Then she smiled. Strangely, he could not remember having seen her smile before. It was a disarming one, slightly crooked, showing a dimple. Mr. Herbert was surprised and pleased by it.

Then he remembered why she was here, and what he must tell her. The very day when, after thirteen years, the girl seemed human, was the day he must tell her of the death of her father—and read his will.

The door opened again, and the clerk ushered a third person into the room. Ryl's back was turned towards him. He stood in the doorway, absorbing and understanding slowly, as an old person does, the strange room and its occupants. Mr. Herbert studied him over Ryl's shoulder.

He saw a rosy-faced, stoutish old gentleman of seventy-odd years, dressed in a manner unfamiliar to the decorous office, with its air of well-being. Mr. David Merewether had changed into what he called his 'other clothes', but the brown suit, worn with a striped shirt with no collar or tie, made no pretence of having any other origin than the Salvation Army bag. His face, with its beetling white eyebrows, was pink and cleanly-shaved, for the old gentleman had spruced up for the occasion, and his boots, shabby as they were, shone with the deep rich glow that only comes with years of polishing. They were the way Mr. David Merewether—otherwise Dusty to his friends—thought a pair of boots should look. These new-fangled shoes and desert boots were not his idea of footwear. No matter what the shortcomings of the rest of his clothes might be, Dusty's boots were a credit to him.

'Mr. Merewether?' Mr. Herbert released Ryl's hand, and turned to his new client. It struck him that at some past time the old fellow's eyes must have been identical with those of the girl.

'Won't you sit down?' asked the solicitor.

Dusty lowered himself stiffly on to a chair.

On hearing her surname used unfamiliarly, Ryl had swung around, and stood staring at the new-comer. For his part, the old man's eyes were fixed on the girl's face with an odd expression. Even when Mr. Herbert had given him time to collect himself,

4

and begun with introductions, he gave no sign of listening, but continued to regard her unwaveringly, shadows of emotion passing across his time-blurred features.

'Mr. Merewether,' began the solicitor, 'I'm glad to know you. I believe you've already heard the—the sad news.'

'Ah,' said the old gentleman.

'I'm sorry not to have made your acquaintance before. You understand Mr.—my client—your son—never mentioned—mm. Now this young lady—I'd like you to meet—'

'Ryl.'

It was the old gentleman himself who filled in her name. He said it softly, tonelessly, almost like a sleepwalker. Mr. Herbert stared.

'That's right. Amaryllis. But I understood you'd never met your grand-daughter?'

'No. I never had.'

Ryl moved uncomfortably.

'You call this—person—"Mr. Merewether",' she said. 'Who is he?'

Mr. Herbert cleared his throat.

'My dear, this is Mr. David Merewether. He's your grandfather. Your father's father.'

Ryl looked staggered.

'A grandfather?' She sounded incredulous. 'A—? But where could he have come from?'

Dusty answered for himself, in a voice just as sulky as the girl's.

'From Trafalgar Street, Carrum, miss—if you want to know. Seeing that's where I live!'

She opened her lips as though with a retort, then closed them again. They glared at one another. Then—

'How do you know my name?' she asked.

Dusty dropped his eyes. He cleared his throat.

'I had a girl once. A daughter. You're the spitting image of her. Ryl, her name was. You just look like her. Fooled me into saying her name.'

'Oh.'

'But,' said Mr. Herbert, 'you knew you had a grand-daughter?'

Dusty put an aggrieved expression on to his round pink face. 'Not until yesterday. Never knew a thing about her. Until that young fellow came to me yesterday, from the police, to tell me—

5

about Robert being dead. He told me Robert was dead, and that there was a young girl. And here she is, it seems. The young fellow from the police said I was to come to this office to hear Robert's will, and that she'd be here, too. And seems he was right.'

The girl leaned forward, questioning.

'What's this he says? He's saying my father's dead! He can't be!' Then uncertainly—'Can he?'

Mr. Herbert nodded slowly, watching her eyes. But her face was a pale mask, devoid of emotion. She remained detached while he confirmed Dusty's words.

'Yes, I'm afraid it's true, Amaryllis. Your father was killed. It happened in a timber accident, in New Guinea. It's dangerous work, timber milling. I want you to know you have my deepest sympathy. I'll be happy to do all I can for you. As a friend, you know, my dear, not just as a solicitor.'

A long silence hung in the room. At last it was broken by Mr. Herbert.

'Would you like to go home now, Amaryllis? I have your father's will here, but perhaps you'd rather not hear it today. One shock is enough.'

But Ryl raised her head. Her eyes were steady. She said, 'I'm all right. You'd better read it and get it over.'

To Mr. Herbert the stoicism of these two bereaved people seemed almost grotesque.

He took the document from his desk drawer, and spread it out in readiness, then settled in his chair, while Ryl and the old fellow faced him under the uncompromising, business-like row of framed certificates. Their eyes, both green and slanted, one pair old, one young, seemed to give him only grudging attention. Mr. Herbert mumbled rather unintelligibly through the opening gambit of legal phrases, then coming to the core, became more coherent:

'The whole of my estate and such moneys as remain after the payment of my just debts I wish to be divided equally between my father David Giles Merewether and my daughter Amaryllis Jane Merewether.'

He skimmed through another maze of wordage, stopped, and looked up from the page to the two people opposite him. They were aloof from one another, with an unseen wall of coldness between them.

'Now,' he said, 'it seems that Mr. Robert Merewether owned

6

property in New Guinea valued at about twenty thousand pounds. Then he had shares worth about ten thousand. These assets can be fairly easily divided. They're investments as they stand. I won't have much trouble putting the New Guinea timber business into the hands of a company. As Amaryllis's guardian that's what I'd advise. Have you any objections, Mr. Merewether?'

Dusty looked straight over the solicitor's shoulder without meeting his eye.

'Do anything you like with it. I never asked for no part of it. I've got me pension. I don't need no fortune of Robert's.'

Mr. Herbert concealed his exasperation. What a difficult pair they were, he thought with a sigh.

'Still, Mr. Merewether, you've got part of it, whether you want it or not. Anyway, I'll get along with the arrangements, as you've no further suggestions.'

He sifted once more through the pile of papers under his hands.

'Then there's one other thing. It seems Robert also owned a property in this country—though it's a dubious asset. It's a farm up in North New South Wales. At a place called—' he consulted his papers—'Bundoora, in the shire of Murwillumbah. Evidently not far from the Terranora Lakes. I had trouble finding it on the map. It must be one of those places with nothing but a post office.'

Dusty took his eyes off the middle distance and looked at Mr. Herbert for the first time.

'What's that? Did you say Bundoora?'

'Rings a bell does it, Mr. Merewether? Do you know the place?'

Dusty moved creakily.

'I was born there,' he said. 'Left the district when I was a lad of fifteen or so, and never been back. You say Robert bought a place there?'

'It seems so. The records show that he bought it in 1946, just after the war ended. But he never lived there. It's been in the hands of a share farmer. A Mr. Bradley. He grew bananas on it, and ran cattle. It's valued at eight thousand, but these are old figures. I've been in touch with a solicitor at Murwillumbah, trying to learn something about the place. They seem to think it's devalued over the years. They say it's run down and useless. Only fit to cut up and sell as building blocks or some such thing. But it's so out-of-the-way, no one would ever buy them. The share

7

farmer didn't get much of a deal, apparently, from Robert Merewether—no offence, mind—and bought himself an adjoining property twelve months ago. So that this farm has really been on the market for twelve months. But there've been no interested parties.'

The old man was shaking his head and tut-tutting to himself like a sleepy hen.

'Well, I'm blessed,' he muttered. 'I'm jiggered. A farm at Bundoora!'

'You're surprised, are you, Mr. Merewether?'

'I remember now,' said Dusty. 'Robert'd been talking about taking a trip back up north, after he got out of the army. He was posted up there during the war. Of course I used to talk to him about Bundoora when he was a little feller.' Dusty stopped rather suddenly. For the first time his face became a little distorted, like a leaf in a stream when the current ripples over it. Then he went on, 'I used to tell him what a great place it was. Then, when he went up there during the war, he saw it for himself, and he reckoned it was a dead-and-alive hole, nothing but a backwater.' The old gentleman looked fierce, as though remembering the cause of an argument. 'He didn't like it! My old boyhood home! He didn't like it!'

'Then why did he want to take a trip back there?' asked Mr. Herbert.

Dusty took a handkerchief, clean but unironed, and blew his nose. He took a long time about it, putting the handkerchief back into his pocket with great deliberation.

'Suppose he had his reasons,' he muttered at last.

'Well, whatever they were, he bought a farm of sorts,' said Mr. Herbert. 'I suppose I ought to go up and take a look at the whole thing.'

'There were only a handful of properties that made up Bundoora,' said Dusty in his fruity voice. 'I wonder which of 'em Robert bought?'

Mr. Herbert looked again at his sheaf of papers.

'It only identifies it here as "the Masterton property". The Murwillumbah solicitor tells me it's actually the only one left in the district. The rest have been absorbed into surrounding postal divisions, or all but one. Or it may even be in the Terranora zone.'

He raised his eyes, and the look on Dusty's face arrested him.

8

'Why, what is it, Mr. Merewether?'

Dusty slapped his stout knee, and exploded into a wordless exclamation. 'But that's the place where I was born!' he cried. 'The Masterton place! Why, my dad sold it to Bill Masterton! It was him that sold it to Masterton—don't you see? I lived there! I lived there meself!'

At last something had roused the senior Merewether into some display of emotion. Now his eyes were twinkling and gleaming. Mr. Herbert could see the remnants of a strong dynamic personality in the glowing pink face. It was like sudden candlelight in a darkened window.

Mr. Herbert smiled. 'It certainly is an amazing coincidence,' he said.

'1946, hey?' pondered Dusty. 'Then Robert must have gone there straight after he left Melbourne. He must have gone there and bought the old farm. Now, fancy him doing that! And him and me had just had words, and all.'

'Well, he didn't stay there long, apparently,' said Mr. Herbert. 'He must have gone to New Guinea almost straight away.'

'He'd been there with his unit when the war was on, too,' said Dusty. 'He liked New Guinea. Liked the timber there. He said he'd go back after the war and go into the timber industry.'

'He did very well out of it,' agreed the solicitor. 'But as to this Bundoora property, it needs looking into. I've a lot of work to do, but I suppose I'd better make a trip up north, and see what's to be done about it.'

He looked unhopefully at his clients. One old man and one young girl. Neither particularly like a business person. He was searching in his mind for a deputy for the task when suddenly Ryl spoke.

'I want to go,' she said.

The two men turned to her as though they had forgotten that she had a tongue. A skinny, long-limbed child she looked, sitting on her straight-backed chair in her school uniform. A far cry from an inspector of properties.

'I've just sat for my matric.,' she said. 'There's nothing more for me at school. A time's come when I've got to leave it, whether I've anywhere else to go, or not. They say I'm too young for University. Even if I wanted to go there—which I don't particularly. I don't know *what* I want to do! You and my father'—she

9

glowered at poor Mr. Herbert—'did it ever occur to either of you that you couldn't *always* get rid of me simply by shoving me into some school?'

There was soft venom in her voice that, the solicitor realized with a pang, made her more human than ever before. It made her a person with feelings and rights, to be hurt or soothed, overridden or considered.

'Yesterday,' said Ryl, 'there was nowhere. Nothing for me. Nothing. I didn't want to go back to—him. To New Guinea. Why, I didn't even *know* him! To me he'd have been just another stranger. And there's no one here in Melbourne who wants me particularly. The girls at school have their own lives to live. So—well, there was just nothing, that's all. Now—all at once—it seems that there's actually a place that belongs to me—or half, anyway.' She tossed a baleful, sideways glance at the old man. 'Then why can't I at least *look* at it? Why must it be sold out of hand? The one place where I have some sort of claim?'

Mr. Herbert cleared his throat, feeling for words with which to stem her tirade.

'Certainly, it's on the market, but you wouldn't want to keep it? What would you do with it?'

10

'There's plenty of money, from what you say. Then why can't I go and look at it, and *see* if I want to keep it? Maybe I could stay there for a while, and have a chance to think about what to do next. I can look after myself. Goodness knows I always have.'

Dusty broke in quickly:

'While *you* decide if *you* want to keep it! And what about me, hey? I was born there.'

They glowered at each other.

'I reckon I'll take a dekko at it meself, first of all,' announced Dusty grandly. 'I can tell you if it looks the same after—let's see now—fifty, fifty-five years. And it don't seem half that time, that's the funny thing! I've got as much right to it as she has!' He turned aggrievedly to Mr. Herbert. The solicitor, watching the sulky, belligerent expressions on the old face and the young, was again aware of the likeness between them.

The old gentleman thrust out his jaw.

'I don't suppose I've really got any pressing business in Melbourne. Me only dependant is Jones—that's me canary—and I'll take him along for the ride!'

Mr. Herbert looked from one to the other. He knew that Dusty was a pensioner, living in poor circumstances. Right enough, the old gentleman had nothing to lose. As for the girl, her soft, bitter little voice had suddenly shown him the bleak wastes of the unknown that made up her future. 'Let her go if she wants,' he thought. 'Let them both go and make their own mistakes, and enjoy them.'

Though as to enjoying anything together, he could not really see that happening! He could not really imagine that they would want to share even a brief tenancy of this hypothetical farm—the girl with her expensive boarding-school snobbery, the old man with his Salvation Army suit, and shirt with no collar. Really, he reflected, there was something most prickly and difficult about the pair of them!

'Then will you both go?' he asked, deliberately sounding casual.

Ryl tossed her head and glared scornfully at Dusty. She could hardly stop him from going. And she had no intention of letting him stop her. Dusty returned her look from beneath his ferocious eyebrows. Then suddenly his face dissolved into a lop-sided, shame-faced grin. Not unlike the girl's crooked smile of a while ago.

11

'Oh, what-the-hell, I may as well buy it!' he said. 'I'll go with her. What about you, Ryl? You game?'

She thought, 'When he smiles he looks rather nice. He's an old wreck and could do with a complete overhaul—his clothes are terrible, but he's—well—he's got something!'

She turned to Mr. Herbert.

'I suppose if he must come I can stand it,' she said.

It was hardly a gracious invitation to share her company. But Dusty took it in his stride. In fact, to him the speech sounded not so out of place. They were much the words he would have used himself.

# II

Dusty left Mr. Herbert's office in the city building, and walked to Flinders Street Railway Station. He had his pensioner's tram concession ticket, which entitled him to travel for half price—'But why not walk for nothing at all,' he thought. 'What are legs for? People don't walk enough, these days. Why, when I was a boy—'

He showed his train pass at the ticket barrier, and made his slow and stumping way on to the train which would take him to the outer suburb of Carrum. This was where he lived. He rented a remarkably battered caravan on the property of a small-time market-gardener, and was even given a small piece of land where he was able to grow a dozen head of lettuce, a row of silver beet, and a pumpkin vine. Dusty was somewhat concerned that this unexpected trip to the city had interfered with his washing day. He had grown used to his routine. Nations could make war, tidal waves could sweep the world—but Dusty counted these things as none of his business. What really shocked him was to have to postpone his washing day. He thought about it as the train rattled from station to station, and finally brought him to his destination.

Dusty stumped along the track by the railway line, and let himself into the market-gardener's field through the rickety back gate. He made his way through the rows of cabbages, through a gap in a thorn hedge, and so to his own corner. Jones, the canary, was clamouring to have his cage moved into the sun, for shadows had crept around his place against the wall while his friend and master had been absent.

Dusty hastily moved the cage, talking to the bird as usual.

'All right, all right. No call to shoot off your beak, you yellow larrikin!' Then he added, 'You missed me, uh, you son of a gun—didn't you, then? You missed me. You didn't have no one to talk to, did you? Well, I'm back now. You can never guess where I've been, mind. I've been talkin' about taking a trip, that's what! How would you like a trip, hey?'

The canary trilled loud and long. It may have been the prospect of travel—or then again it may have been the fresh patch of sunshine which warmed him.

Dusty went into his caravan, making his way through the daily-renewed obstacle race in which he lived. First he must stoop to avoid a low-watt electric light bulb which hung from the middle of the ceiling, then he must step over the pile of newspapers which was not only his education and entertainment but also his extra winter bedding, then sidle past the ancient radio cabinet, which also served as sideboard and dressing-table—and so around the bed-end, bedecked with a rag-tag array of nondescript brown garments which constituted his work-day clothes. Here Dusty changed into this familiar garb, carefully hanging the garments he was wearing—his 'other clothes', sacred to Sundays and pension days—in their place.

He decided there was just time to do the washing before lunch. Out in the yard was the half kerosene-tin which he used to carry water from the tap by the fence. Dusty filled this, and carried it inside, placing it on the small wood stove at the end of the caravan. He took sticks from a box on the floor, and lit a fire under the water. When it was hot he carried it into the yard, placing it on the rickety bench close to Jones's cage. Then he collected the piece of yellow soap, and tucked up the sleeves of his work-day shirt, which was khaki in colour and a real bargain from the Red Cross Opportunity Shop for half-a-crown. ('Only,' thought Dusty, 'no one calls it half-a-crown, these days.') Dusty collected his meagre assortment of soiled garments. There were some socks with large holes in them, as well as darns executed in strange colours with his own hands. There was a sheet which he had patched with the tail of his last 'best' shirt, and sundry shapeless objects which had started life as undergarments.

By the time he had pegged these things on to the string clothes-line, both Dusty and Jones were more than ready for lunch. There, in the cupboard, was a cold chop. 'A cup of tea will do me good,' thought Dusty. Not a fresh cup, of course, with tea at two-and-four the half pound. Ah, no, but there was always some left in the pot from breakfast, and it tasted a treat, warmed up on the stove. Couldn't tell it from fresh. Hardly, anyway. Hardly tell it. And tomorrow was the big day. Tomorrow it was hot lunch at the Pensioners' Soup Kitchen. 'Ah, yes,' he thought.

14

And then, 'Maybe it'll be the last hot lunch with the pensioners.'

It was no use. Dusty had to admit it. He had forced himself to be occupied and busy, ever since he had come home from the interview in the solicitor's office. But it was no use pretending. All the time his mind had been in the past, nagging at him,

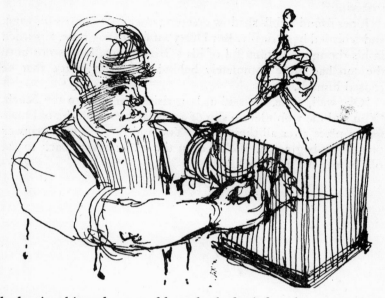

badgering him, about problems he had tried so long to forget. Dusty stood in front of Jones's cage, his shoulders hunched.

'Jones,' he whispered. 'He went back. Robert went back. We'd just had that quarrel—aw, you wouldn't remember—but I do— little as I want to. Robert went back to the old place. Now why do you reckon he did it? For me? Or for the girl? Or for—'

Dusty lowered himself to the bench in the sunshine.

'A grand-daughter,' he muttered. 'Lucky she's not like her mother, anyway. Ah, I was crooked on her. Why did Robert have to get mixed up with her, that's what I could never make out! She finished it, between Robert and me, that's what she did. She finished it. We never did get on, as you might say—but she was the end of everything.'

The old man sat staring ahead into the afternoon sun, that retreated westwards, away from the dingy caravan in the corner of the cabbage-field.

15

'Not that she could help it, I suppose,' he said to Jones, after a long period of silence. 'I suppose she couldn't exactly be blamed. But why—that's what I could never make out—why did he have to go and marry *her*, of all people? Why couldn't he marry some ordinary sort of girl, like all the other young fellers was marrying?'

Jones found a chill shadow creeping once more across his cage, and whistled hysterically. But Dusty sat for a long time, absorbed in his thoughts, unmindful of his surroundings. It was not until the sun had gone completely behind the thorn hedge that he roused himself.

'Oh, well, mate,' he said at last, rising stiffly from the bench. 'You and me won't let no slip of a girl lay hands on the old Masterton place after all these years. You and me will have to pack our carpet-bag again. We'll be on the move again. Back to the old home. We'll go back.'

# III

Miss Donahue, science mistress of Rushton College, stood on the edge of Platform One at Spencer Street Station. She was wishing the northbound train would go. The Spirit of Progress was there too, hissing and grumbling, an express train eager to be off into the evening.

Miss Donahue had come because it had seemed cold and sad that no one should be there to see the last of Amaryllis Merewether.

The girl had been, if not the most popular boarder, at least the one of longest possible standing, and after all these years at the school a decent good-bye was due to her. So Miss Donahue had come with Ryl in the taxi from Bourke Road, shepherding the porter with the brand-new luggage, and suffering the indignities of peak-hour crowds with reasonably good grace.

'It's lucky, Amaryllis,' she said breathlessly, tacking a laboured course along Platform One, among throngs of travellers and their friends and relations—'It's lucky you're going before the school holidays begin. I hate to think what this station will be like then!'

Down where the first-class carriages began, Ryl touched her sleeve.

'There's—Mr. Merewether.' She spoke the name awkwardly, for she hardly knew how to call him.

Dusty stood like a moth-eaten and overweight Napoleon beside a battered carpet-bag and a roll of grey blankets tied up with new rope. Again he was spruced up and dressed in his 'other clothes'. But this time with a new shirt, and new, though badly-knotted, tie. These improvements were at Ryl's suggestion—or rather, command.

'If I'm to travel with you,' she had said, 'you'll have to get a new shirt. And a tie to go with it.'

'This,' Dusty had retorted, 'is a good shirt, but they don't seem to make spare collars for them these days.'

17

'Then you'll have to buy one *with* a collar, the way they've been for the last thirty years! And you can put that one in the dustbin!'

'What, throw away a good shirt like this! Ah, they don't make shirts like this any more.'

'Thank the Lord,' said impious Ryl.

'I wore it on me weddin' day,' continued Dusty.

'And slept in it ever since, by the look of it. Mr. Herbert, *you* buy him a shirt, for gosh' sake! With some of all this money you've been talking about.'

Dusty had begun to bluster.

'By gee, she's starting to give orders already! I'll wear what I like, miss, and you can lump it or go somewhere else—'

But Ryl had left him standing with the solicitor while she was already in the lift, with an expression that proclaimed her willing to challenge grandfathers unlimited, as well as gravitation itself.

As Mr. Herbert arranged finances with the old man he could see the shadows again, passing across his face like ghosts of dead emotions. He fancied he saw a little hurt there, but amusement, and even a touch of pleasurable anticipation.

That Ryl had consented to travel with him at all remained a kind of wonder. There was plenty of antagonism between them. And yet in spite of it they accepted each other more naturally than the solicitor had expected. It must, thought he, be true that blood is ultimately thicker than water. He guessed that these two stubborn and arrogant people were both more lonely than he could imagine, and at the bottom of their hearts pleased to find themselves with kith and kin, no matter whom.

Miss Donahue at that first meeting was not so dismayed by Dusty's appearance as hints along the school's grape-vine had prepared her to be. For, of course, word had leaked out somehow that Amaryllis Merewether had discovered a grandfather who lived on his old age pension in some queer circumstances. Amaryllis, the proud and aloof, had one solitary relative at last, but one to cause her pride to fall.

Certainly Dusty looked far from well groomed. But still, on a warm spring evening at Spencer Street Station, not out of place. He had a kind of air about him. Those boots, like rich old mahogany. But his luggage made Miss Donahue wince. She preferred to avert her eyes from the blanket-roll, wrapped in some nameless

18

textile and looking like a swagman's 'bluey'. But strangely enough, Ryl, so crisp and smart in her new clothes, gave no sign of disapproval of him. She made the introductions.

'Miss Donahue, this is Mr. Merewether.'

Dusty jostled his hat, and gave a winning smile. He nodded to Ryl.

'My friends call me Dusty,' he told her. 'You may as well do the same. Can't keep calling me "Mr. Merewether" all the time.'

Somewhere a bell began to ring, and a voice called over the loudspeaker, urging visitors to leave the train.

'We'd better go.' Dusty picked up his impedimenta. He added darkly, 'They made me put Jones in the guard's van. My word, they'd better treat him right, or I'll have their blood!'

'Oh, never mind, he'll be all right. Come along.'

Ryl half helped, half pushed the back of his brown coat, and so encouraged, Dusty boarded the train. She turned to her teacher.

'Miss Donahue, thanks for coming.' Unexpectedly, the girl's eyes filled with tears. She leaned forward and brushed an awkward kiss against the older woman's cheek. The teacher was surprised and touched, and returned the kiss.

'You'll write to us, won't you, Ryl? You'll keep in touch?'

But already the cold mask was back in place, and Ryl's moment of regret for her childhood was over.

'I might,' she said. 'If I have time.'

She had flung a dash of cold water over the other's sympathy. But this was Ryl's pattern.

'Very well, Amaryllis,' murmured Miss Donahue. 'There goes the final whistle.'

'Oh, yes—I'd better go on board.'

Ryl climbed the step. Dusty had already gone into the carriage. The train shifted its weight, about to start—and, suddenly as ever, Ryl smiled and was human again.

'I won't wait,' said the teacher, 'or I shall never find a cab. Good-bye, Ryl.'

'Good-bye.'

They waved to each other, and the train began to pull away from the platform. Then the one familiar face was lost in the crowd, and Ryl turned to enter the carriage, presenting her back to Melbourne, the years of childhood, and her life at school.

19

In the carriage she saw Dusty, and went to him, sliding into the window seat next to his. The passing platform outside, and all the people on it were drained of colour by the coming night. They seemed to pass in a slow stream, like sea creatures in shadowy water. Ryl thought of a newsreel she had once seen, pictures taken from an underwater observatory. Here in the train compartment she felt herself to be in such a place—a place apart, from whence she could peer with curiosity into the depths of some other dimension. Venturing into this unknown sphere, danger would surely overtake her, but from her underwater tower she could watch life drifting around her, and be safe, and apart.

It was a feeling that brought with it a strange calmness, a kind of peace. Although Ryl had not been aware of it, she had never in her life come to any island of peace, or tower of safety. Always she had been on guard, on the alert in a mood of self-defence. Always it had been Ryl against the rest of the society in which she lived. Her native character was independent, and she had kept aloof from the ties of others, a lone wolf. The price of her independence had been an ever-present loneliness, like a nagging tooth. And now suddenly, this nagging small ache, this tense guardedness, was gone.

She realized with surprise that it had been dispelled by the presence of the stout, gnome-like figure at her side. Dusty was both a new experience and a new possession. She had seen such old men before—weeding the school garden, perhaps, or sitting on a park bench outside St. Paul's Cathedral. But she had scarcely regarded them as human, they were so unlike the people with whom she mingled. Perhaps it was because of this that she found Dusty's company so restful. There was no need for any façade, no need to pander to his presence. Yet, this strange relative had been given or bequeathed to her in some way by the dead father whom she had hardly known. Perhaps it was accident or perhaps design that had brought the two of them together. She wondered which.

The train was moving slowly along the platform, gathering speed into its stride, putting away its association with the evening city. A chapter of her life was receding, a chapter of impersonal kindness, houses that were not homes, thoughtless cruelty. Sitting near the rushing window, she felt bird-like in flight, a bird migrating from nowhere to nowhere on blind wings. A poem came into her mind, Indian poetry by Rabindranath Tagore:

20

'Ah, where is the sunny, green shore, where is your nest?
Bird, oh my bird, listen to me, do not close your wings.'

Dusty turned to her, breaking into her almost self-pitying thoughts.

'Well, my girl, pleased to be going?'

'No. No, I don't think so.'

'Sorry to be going?'

'No. Not sorry, either. Certainly not sorry.'

Dusty nodded wisely. 'Ah,' was all he said.

Now the light outside was fading. Cars were switching on their headlights, and orange squares began to appear in the dark hulks of railside buildings. The city was behind them. Away to the left were open fields and dark cyprus hedges, to the right the suburbs had become nothing more than a nest of glow-worms in the pale evening.

'How does me new shirt suit you?' asked Dusty. 'The price I paid for it! And no quality in it, mind you. It'll never be the shirt me old one was.'

Without thinking, the girl reached across and straightened his tie.

After a while Ryl made her way to the dining-car. Dusty had brought sandwiches with him, and refused to indulge himself in a formal dinner.

'That's nothing but a waste of money,' he grumbled to her.

'But we have plenty of money!'

'You wouldn't talk like that if you'd ever had to go without! I won't waste good sandwiches. I made them with the last of my corned beef. The people in Russia would think they were a real banquet!'

'Then send them to the people in Russia, and come and have dinner with me!'

But Dusty would not be talked out of his economy.

When Ryl returned to the carriage, he was asleep. She shook him gently.

'I think I'll go to bed now. You look as though you may as well do the same,' she said.

'Go to bed? What are you talking about? You mean you've got one of those sleeping-berths?'

21

Ryl was exasperated.

'Of course I have! And so have you! Mr. Herbert booked them for us!'

'Well, I don't need one! I've got my blankets! Fancy wanting a sleeper! At your age! The kids are all milksops these days!'

'Oh—Dusty! Anyhow, we *have* sleepers—so there! Let me see your ticket!'

She perused his ticket, while he muttered darkly, 'I've always travelled second-class before! There's nothing wrong with second-class travel! It's a ridiculous waste of money!'

'Well, I didn't ask you to travel with me!' retorted Ryl. 'In fact, I didn't ask you to come at all! It says here that your sleeper is the one next to mine! Good night!'

She flounced off, while Dusty called after her, 'You didn't ask me to come, but I'm coming anyhow, Miss Hoity-Toity! I've as much right to come as you have, and come I will!'

Their tenuous thread of companionship was broken, at least for the moment, and they had no good nights to spare for each other.

Morning came, and the monotonous forward roll of the train which had given background to her sleeping now stirred the girl to early wakefulness. From her pillow she watched the red, rolling plains with wonder, and the echoing emptiness of the New South Wales sheep country. It was quite new to her, for her childhood world had been small in spite of its far beginnings. She had a few vague and tattered memories of New Guinea, and the boat trip to Melbourne. But mainly her memories were only of schools, of city and suburb, and a few bright ones of holidays in the Dande-nongs and Gippsland. But the heart of Australia—even its distant fringes such as she now glimpsed from the train—was quite new to her, and different.

She saw wheat crops tawny as a tiger's coat, with occasionally a harvester or header waiting for the day's work to begin. Red earth roads ran beside the metal tracks for short distances, coming from the plains, and returning whence they came. Wheat-silos stood black against the sunrise like castles of enchantment. 'Rapunzel, Rapunzel, let down your hair,' thought Ryl. A flock of white cockatoos rose into the bright-coloured sky. Horses came down to drink at a still, reflecting dam, in a hush that could not be

22

broken even by the train's passing. It was the first time she had felt herself part of a new-waking day.

The guard came with a cup of tea, and Ryl drank it, wondering how Dusty was faring, and if he too had been given tea. She dressed as fastidiously as possible in the cramped carriage. She cleaned her teeth, and went to sit again in the observation car, where Dusty sought her out just before odd houses began to break up the horizon.

'Did you have a good night?' she asked him.

'Fair enough, fair enough.'

The train wailed into the mist-dappled lowlands, and factory buildings loomed by the rails, and a highway, keeping pace with them, became beaded with traffic. Soon Sydney reached out to take them into its sprawling suburbs, with their atmosphere of shabby devil-may-care. They passed through Strathfield, noisy and casual. Red roofs stretched as far as the eye could see—which was not too far—and stations flashed past in a whirl of bricks, soot and metal, then the interstate express came roaring into Central Station by the crossword puzzle of shining rails, tunnels and hoardings, and all the noises of a city in full swing.

Dusty took up his raffish burdens and they climbed down the high steps on to the platform with sailors' legs, to stretch them with the long walk to the dining-room, and breakfast. A state of armistice prevailed.

They were to spend the day in Sydney, waiting for the departure of the Casino express.

Unexpectedly, it proved to be one of the happiest times that either of the oddly mated travellers had ever known. The old fellow was more child-like than Ryl in his wonder as they rode on the Mosman ferry, ate sandwiches at the zoo, and waffles and maple syrup at Hillier's. There was the taxi-driver who whistled 'Funicule, Funicula', and shouted abuse at a garrulous bus conductor—'La, la, la, you pulla da head in—a—sport!' The waitress who called them both 'love'—the small coloured newsboy who sold them an evening paper. These things would stay in Ryl's memory, making an amalgam of pleasure that was Sydney.

Then the neon signs blinked on and off, on and off, in the warm dark, and they made their way back to Central Station. The new train welcomed them, leashed to the long asphalt causeway that seemed to the girl like a magic carpet.

23

And they were on the move again.

This night was different. Ryl lay in her sleeping-berth and the train rocked beneath and around her with a different rhythm, more leisurely and gentle. It seemed to come from the warm moist air, with its soothing touch of the North. The girl in the railway compartment slept, tired from the active day, and felt the gentle air through her dreams, smoothing the discontented lines from her face, moulding away the hard set of her mouth.

Then another day. The tough country was gone, the bare sheep stations of southern New South Wales. Now came tracts of blue-green bushland, patches of grass-tree scrub, and the darker green of semi-tropical jungle. The train rushed by billabongs quilted with water-lilies and mauve hyacinths. On the tablelands, the great gum forests dwarfed it to toy size, as it wound through the country of the Great Divide, that wall of mountains that runs parallel to the Australian coast for more than a thousand miles.

At Casino on the tableland, where scarlet-blossoming trees lined the station yard, they left the express, and boarded an ancient rattling steam-train. From here the way led always down—making for the narrow green strip of country that lies between the mountains and the sea. This was the land of the Northern Rivers, and great bridges carried the train across the Clarence, the Manning and Macleay, their banks lined with mangrove swamps, and ferries plying slowly across the yellow waters. There were times when the odd little train would stop for no apparent reason in the midst of wild, impenetrable jungle, a frenzy of lantana, groundsel, wild passion vines and tree-fern, with no sign of a railway station in sight.

'Maybe they're boiling the billy,' said Dusty. 'Selfish right through, these railway workers, why can't they treat us to a mug of their tea?'

'I can do without tea,' said Ryl, 'but what wouldn't I give for a long, long shower!'

It was hot. Dusty shed his new tie and loosened his collar. He had long since folded the shapeless brown coat and somehow squeezed it into his carpet-bag. Throughout the journey he constantly visited the guard's van, and reported that the canary Jones was in good spirits, even enjoying the mountebank life. Their common discomfort sealed the truce of yesterday, as they shared a

24

carriage with a large and joyful family from Sydney. There were five children, a plump mother, who sat tirelessly knitting some bulky garment in spite of the dust and heat, and a tough, nut-brown little man, the father of the brood, whose good temper was indefatigable.

'Ah, I reckon you Melbourners aren't used to being warm,' he told Ryl. 'We don't think anythink of this! Just a pleasant day, where we come from!'

'I quite like it, really,' said Ryl.

'Good on yer, mate,' he encouraged her. 'That's the spirit.' He became communicative. 'We're off on a holiday to Surfer's Paradise. I've been telling your grandad. It's costing us a packet, of course. Gee whiz, you spend money like water with kids, so help me. Fish and chips all the time—peanuts and pop—no end to it!'

The children certainly did appear to be steady eaters.

'I'm on the buses,' he went on, 'and I've got my long service leave and my bonus, and we're gonna blue the lot—hey, Mum? We'll blue it in a fortnight, and no trouble at all—won't we, Mum? No trouble at all—here, have a banana.'

'No thanks, really.' Ryl declined the proffered paper bag.

'While we're up north here, we're gonna eat bananas all the time and expense be blowed—hey, Mum?'

Mum addressed her youngest child, George.

'George, tell the girlie what you learned at school, come on then, love. Tell her the one about "Mary, Mary".'

The child's father gave him a proud slap on the side of the head.

'Ah, the things he learns at school!' he cried fondly. 'He's the bright one, this one—he's that quick, mind you! First morning at school he picked up a dirty word, spare me days!'

The whole family laughed with pride.

'Come on, George,' encouraged Mum. 'Tell the girlie about "Mary, Mary".'

'He's a caution,' said the father. 'Smart as paint.'

Ryl listened and watched as though they were a variety show. She had never met such people before.

The ancient, soot-encrusted train wound down, down, ever downwards to the plains and the sea, the temperature increasing as it went. It was mid-afternoon and the thermometer registered almost 100 degrees. Byron Bay appeared around the hills, with its smell of whaling station—then rich, green swamp-lands with rank elephant-grass eight feet high, and ti-tree forest, and lush undergrowth to make cover for countless water-birds and snakes.

Then came cuttings between sharp hills, and a strange outline of mountains, light blue against the sky, Ryl's first sight of the Numinbah Range.

At last the old steam-engine came wheezing to a halt in the croton- and fern-swathed station of Murwillumbah.

26

# IV

'Well, now.' Dusty mopped his glowing brow with an enigmatic khaki handkerchief. His thick white curls, defying the comb, had become hardened with dust, and today his chin was unshaven.

Still, his eyes gleamed with a rousing light. Tired as he was from travelling, his years felt gentle upon his shoulders before the long-forgotten challenge of adventure.

'Well, now, I'll get Jones out of the guard's van and I'll get all that stuff of yours, and then we'll find a shop where we can buy some bread and a few pounds of chops. And then we'll find the bus. The guard says it goes past Bundoora.'

Ryl had never for a moment thought of food, or the providing of it.

'It's still miles to Bundoora,' she said. 'Can't we buy things there? Can't we have a meal at a restaurant?'

Dusty shook his head sagely. 'We won't be buying anything much at Bundoora. It can't have changed that much since I saw it last.'

'But golly, that was fifty years ago! If it hasn't changed I'll be surprised, for one.'

But Dusty was firm. 'Not from what Mr. Herbert said, it hasn't changed. There just might be a bit of a shop there—and then again, there might not. It's better to be sure than sorry. We're not like Jones, you know, who can live on a bit of bird-seed that 'ud fit in me coat pocket. We'll get food here. Bread and tea and chops.'

Ryl muttered that the way he described food, bird-seed might be a more attractive diet at that.

The feckless family for Surfer's Paradise were already filing into a bus with the rest of the train's passengers. The rough little locomotive had done its duty in humping them over the range, and now handed them over to road transport. The highway followed the river flats and the shining sea to the state border.

'We'll miss the bus,' Ryl pointed out.

27

'Bus or no bus, we've gotta eat!' cried Dusty. 'You don't even appear to realize that food doesn't grow on dinin'-room tables!' He added as an afterthought, 'And they call that education!'

It was true and could not be gainsaid that Ryl had never before had to trace food to its origin, as it were. She tossed her head, and picked up her overnight bag.

'Then I'll see to the luggage—and your old canary—and I'll try and find a car for us, because we'll have missed the bus anyway! Probably a good thing, too. A car will be much better. And you can go and buy whatever you call food. Seeing you're an expert on the subject!'

She stalked off in the direction of the guard's van, feeling that she had called Dusty's bluff and guarded against starvation at the same time.

It took some time to find a porter to move the luggage, which was too heavy for the girl to carry. By then the bus, as she had predicted, was disappearing in a cloud of dust and petrol fumes. Ryl noticed a taxi passing by at break-neck speed, and hailed it. With a screech of tyres it made a U-turn and circled back to the railway steps.

'Can you drive us to a place called Bundoora?' she asked the driver.

A voice answered her from under the sun shield.

'Sure. Not many calls to Bundoora! It's quite a way, you know!'

'Yes, I expect it is.'

'Anyhow, it so happens that I'm just going off shift, and I live there myself. So I can take you, and take myself home at the same time. It'll make it a bit cheaper for you.'

She could see Dusty returning, a pair of stubby legs beneath a large cardboard box in which his food purchases were stowed.

The driver got out, took the load from the old gentleman and put it in the boot of his car, then followed it with Ryl's cases. Dusty's meagre contribution of luggage served to fill up the corners of the back seat.

'I don't know what you'll ever do with all that junk,' the shopping expert grumbled to Ryl. 'A person can only wear one lot of clothes at a time, so what's the use of having cases and cases full? Just means more things to get dirty!'

He climbed in with his carpet-bag, and Ryl took the front seat beside the driver.

28

Out of the town, cottages and houses, paintless and brown, straggled along a flower-scattered wayside beneath shouting scarlet blossom of poinciana-trees and sweet, pale frangipani. By one house, tall on stilted piles, an Indian woman in a faded pink sari was picking cannas. A white goat with twin kids watched golden-eyed from the top of a pile of fruit boxes. Children trailed indolently home from school.

Then the road was walled by ten-foot sugar-cane, and roofed with cobalt sky. To the left the cane-break fell away, and there was the river, where boats were tied, and an old black man sat fishing. In days to come, she was to grow used to this fact, that wherever the river was, there was a coloured fisherman. Sometimes the road was lined with wine-coloured crotons, or jacaranda-trees, or giant bamboo.

If the sheep country had, two days ago, touched Ryl with a sense of freedom and adventure, this warm, rich land of rivers and lush growth touched in her some other chord. Perhaps it was only because she was travel-weary, but it seemed to the girl that slowly a feeling of peace never before known was welling within her—release from all tensions and fears, relief from all past cares of living. It was as though she were quite separated from her past. Just as truly as the Melbourne schoolgirl had stood apart from the infant orphan from New Guinea, so now the schoolgirl stepped away from her, leaving her disengaged, free—empty of the old life, unfilled by the new....

As for Dusty, sitting stoutly on the back seat, he kept up a muttered commentary to whom it might concern.

'Well, well, well. Old Tumbulgum, hey? Old Tumbulgum. Two new houses. And a milk-bar. Well, well. That's movin' with the times, so help me. Two new houses. The old 'uns look the same, though. Fifty-odd years since I saw them last. Cane-fields grown a bit in places. In some places gone altogether. They've got tram tracks in the cane-fields now, I see. Wonder what became of the bullock teams? And old Chindera. There's the pub, under the poinciana. It fair covers the place. More tree than pub now. It was planted the same year that I left the district, come to think of it.'

So Dusty put aside the years with their dower of disappointment and failure, and took up an old garment long forgotten—

a garment of homecoming. It was edged with a little sadness, but still cut from a fabric of peace....

They turned from the highway on to a cobbled ferry siding. The tub-sized vessel inched towards them over the river, and they drove on board, the only customers for its skipper. On the far bank a notice read—'WARNING TO SPEED-BOATS. BEWARE OF SUBMARINE CABLES.' But the message stood tip-tilted among tall grass, wild cane-grass, as though its presence were unnecessary and it only lounged there for want of other employment.

'You're up for a holiday, I suppose?' the cab driver asked Ryl.

Ryl had been furtively studying the boy. His features were high-boned and chiselled, his skin smooth and brown, his eyes very dark. Ryl thought she had never seen such a good sun-tan. The hands on the steering wheel looked different somehow from the hands of any other boy she knew. They were, she thought—well, very fine-boned, almost delicate. And brown. He wore a white towelling T-shirt, long white socks, white shorts and a yachting cap. His feet were encased in white leather shoes. He looked wonderfully clean and cool, and undefinably foreign somehow.

'Sort of,' she told him. 'We may be here for a month or two, really.'

He smiled, showing very white teeth.

'But you're surely not going to stay at Bundoora?'

'Yes.'

'Then you must be friends of the Bradleys. Bundoora's so small that it's practically non-existent. The Bradleys *are* Bundoora, you might say!'

'No, we're staying at a farm. It's empty at present.'

'What! Not the old Masterton place?'

'Yes, that seems to be what it's called. How did you guess?'

'It's the only other farm there. Easy, you see!'

'It's a queer address, just "the Masterton place". But you seem to know where it is.'

'Oh, sure. "The Masterton place"—it is a funny name for a property, I guess. It's just always been known as that, even though it changed hands when I was knee-high to a grasshopper. The Bradleys have lived there ever since I can remember. Though I believe they didn't own it. Only worked it.'

30

'Yes, I know,' said Ryl. 'My father owned it. Now—we do. Me—and—Dusty. We both do.' She indicated the old gentleman in the back.

'Gee, do you really! What do you know!' The boy showed surprise, as well he might, for neither of the two looked at all like a North Coast farmer.

'Our name's Merewether,' said Ryl. She volunteered the information, for the boy had said he lived at Bundoora, and he might as well know to whom he was speaking during their stay.

'This is my grandfather.' She nodded towards Dusty. It was a queer feeling to be saying those words: 'This is my grandfather.' She could hardly believe she had said them. But they sounded quite well. 'My grandfather.' She had to stifle a desire to repeat them out loud, just to hear the sound of them again. Dusty, too, from the corner of his eyes, slanted like Ryl's, had a secret smile, in spite of his set mouth and studied indifference to the conversation.

She said, 'We're just coming to look at the place. It's up for sale. But we thought we might as well take a look at it.'

'Then you haven't been here before?'

'No.'

'No, if you had we'd have met, most likely. It's such a small place that everyone knows everyone.'

'Hey,' put in Dusty. Then: 'You may be here for only a month, miss, but I won't say that for meself. It's great to see this district again, that it is. I'm beginning to think I might stop here after all. I might not budge, once I'm back.'

She tossed him a glance over her shoulder.

'Huh!' she said sceptically.

'Anyhow,' said Dusty, 'the district hasn't changed that much. I could still find the place meself—I think. Isn't it all a picture? Old Bundoora. It's up at the top of this ridge, isn't it, son?'

'That's right. Say, do you know it?'

'I do that. I lived here when I was a youngster.'

'That's amazing,' said the boy, suitably impressed. He added, 'We'll be neighbours. I don't live far away. Just down the hill a bit towards Terranora. No distance, as the crow flies.'

'Yes?' Ryl did not really sound interested in this piece of news. She watched the road sloping upwards from the river. 'The first thing I'll do,' she said, 'will be to think up a more suitable address.

31

I'm not going to live at "the Masterton place". If the houses aren't numbered I'll have to think of a name for it.'

'Numbered!' said the boy. 'Little do you know!'

The car was protesting because of the steep escarpment, and he changed into a lower gear. The way was flanked by a tall, cut-away bank on one side, and on the other by a precipitous slope crowded with verdure—cane-grass, milkweed, broad-leafed castor-oil plant and cotton-trees. Now they emerged on to the crest of a long razor-backed ridge. To the right, far below, lay a patchwork of cane-fields, severed by the silver river and stretching to distant sand-banks and the sea. To the left were green pastures and banana plantations with here and there an isolated house, sloping to a winding system of lakes and inlets—and again, at last, the sea. Straight ahead the road took a dog-leg bend, and on the corner was a drunken wooden gate. A shabby weather-board cottage huddled beneath huge Moreton Bay fig-trees, and beyond it were grassed slopes that ran down again to the river—and beyond— again, the sea. Ryl stepped out of the car as it came to a halt, and stood taking in the three-fold vista.

'Golly!' she said.

The boy was at her elbow, pointing—'See—'way south, that's Brunswick Heads. And straight ahead there's the lighthouse at Kingscliff—and there's Fingal; there's a lighthouse there, too, for the fishing-boats. Then, bearing north, there's Coolangatta— can you see that headland with the pine-trees? That's Green-mount. And the closer one with the cliffs, that's Point Danger. Then past Coolangatta you can follow the line of beach—see— right round the coast to Surfer's Paradise.'

Ryl was impressed in spite of herself. She had never thought it possible to find such a view. It was like an aerial view from firm ground. The boy said, 'Now turn round and see what's behind you!'

She did. At their backs, to the west, the razor-back ridge merged into a tumble of valleys and folds, which ran pell-mell into an almost sheer mountain face—or so at this distance it seemed. A jagged range loomed and towered suddenly out of the narrow broken coastal plain of downs and deltas. In the middle distance she could distinguish the even green of banana plantations, steeply clinging to the wild foothills. Then sheer cliffs rose in buttressed walls.

32

'Golly!' said Ryl again.

Their guide looked smug, as though he personally had designed the view.

'That table-topped crag—that's Springbrook,' he explained. 'And that high, timbered part that rises out of the last valley, that's Numinbah. That's wonderful country. Wild as mountains can come. Red soil—grow anything, if a chap could tame it. Some of the best bananas grow there, but they have to use "flying-foxes" to gather them, the hill-sides are so steep.'

Dusty was bouncing on his heels like an excited brown bear.

'Well, my oath,' he muttered over and over. 'My oath.' He filled the simple phrase with a wealth of emotion. 'It's the same place. The same old place. Same view—hardly changed a bit. Same place where I was born and bred. Well, well, well. . .!'

But Ryl was not used to creature discomfort, and now her much-travelled condition asserted itself.

33

'If I can't have a shower at once, or even sooner, I'll die—I'll just die!' she announced.

She turned to the driver.

'Let's get the luggage out of the car.'

Suddenly she felt bone-tired, tired to the point of exhaustion.

It was the first time she had ever arrived at an empty house, where no one had prepared a room for her and a meal, and where gracious living was not already going on in full swing.

She knew with horrible surety that she was the only person who would be likely to put gracious living into any kind of operation. Under any circumstances she would not have known where to start. But in this crazy wreck of a house! What, she thought, could you do?

Then the bright voice of the cab driver brought encouragement.

'Oh, I forgot to say,' he smiled. 'My name's Perry Davis. I live just around the hill a bit, down towards the lake. Actually, my grandfather's and my banana patch must join your banana patch. See? Down that-a-way!'

He pointed left, down the hill-side.

'And there's the Bradleys' new house—see, the brick one on the other side, towards the river. They'll be your closest neighbours. They're great people, too. And I'll be pretty close. So if you ever want help of any kind—I mean, if there's anything I can do—'

He gave a gesture to finish the sentence.

Ryl looked over the paddocks to the brick house. It looked trim and new, and a contrast to the old place they were about to enter.

'Our Melbourne solicitor told us to talk to the Bradleys,' she said. 'He told us they'd look after us while we're here.'

'Look after us be blowed,' grumbled Dusty. 'I can look after myself.'

'Me, too, of course,' agreed Ryl. 'But still, they'll be useful.'

She sounded a high-handed young duchess.

'If they were expecting you to come, they'll have left the door-key somewhere,' said Perry.

But Dusty, walking on ahead, called back, 'The key's in the door. It seems like Mr. Herbert must have wired them that we were coming. They seem to have left the place ready for us.'

34

Perry dumped Ryl's two big suitcases on the flagged porch, and went back to the car for the packing-case in which, at Mr. Herbert's suggestion, Ryl had brought a pair of new sheets and blankets. At this time Ryl had no practical ideas of her own and had not grasped the fact that she would not be cared for by the ravens.

She was realizing with pain that this crazy old building in its setting of beauty was to be quite literally her home for some weeks. Not some shining new motel, not some serviced flat or hotel room. This place. She almost panicked.

'Golly!' she breathed. 'Golly! Do you think the inside's as bad as the outside? Do you? I can't look!'

Perry seemed to understand.

'Take courage!' he grinned. 'Never say die!'

'Oh, I won't. But glory, I do hope there are plates and cups and things, otherwise whatever will we do? Though what we'll put on them I can't imagine.'

'I'll soon tell you what we'll put on 'em,' declared Dusty. 'Chops and bread and a cuppa tea. What else would you want to put on 'em?' He added, 'We'd better let you be on your way, boy.'

'Oh, I'm in no hurry. But you'll be O.K. now. The fare's a pound.'

A look of horror made Dusty's jaw drop. Ryl gave him a withering look, took a pound note from her bag and passed it to Perry.

'Thanks.' He slipped it in his pocket. 'Don't forget—if ever you need anything.'

'I'll have to go into Murwillumbah to see the bank manager there,' said Ryl. 'Dusty should too—Mr. Herbert said so. And I've just realized that I'll probably have to buy some things. Is there a bus? I'll go into the town tomorrow if there is one.'

'There is, but I'm doing afternoon shift tomorrow on the taxi run. I could call and pick you up on my way in. About one o'clock. No charge, mind. On the house. Be my guest.'

'What would you want to go shoppin' for?' asked Dusty scornfully. 'And I'm in no hurry to see this bank feller. I'll go when it suits me.'

'Well, there *will* be things to buy!' declared Ryl.

'What things? I bought tea and bread and bird-seed. What more would we want?'

35

Ryl had been on the point of refusing Perry's offer, for she had an instinctive mistrust of all proffered friendships. But Dusty's grumbling opposition changed her mind. She tossed her head at him.

'Only about a million things, that's all!' she told him. 'To start with, I have a pretty good idea that those blankets of yours are only fit to be burned after this trip! And I'm not going to live on chops and bird-seed. So there!' She graciously inclined her head to Perry. 'Thanks very much. One o'clock. I'll be ready.'

'Good. See you then.' The boy loped to the car. He called back over his shoulder, 'There's a sort of general store just down the hill about half a mile away. You can get lots of things there. You cut across the paddocks to it. It's on the Terranora Road.'

With a wave, he turned the car and revved the engine.

But as he drove away, Ryl saw with a slight shock why it was he had that odd foreign touch. As he turned the car he put up a hand and removed his yachting cap, tossing it on to the seat beside him. Probably the heat prompted him to discard it. But in that moment Ryl noticed his hair. Hair? No, it was wool. The crinkly black wool of the South Sea Islander. . . .

The house was like nothing she had ever seen before. The front door, which was close to ground level, was surrounded by a rough, flagged area and roofed by a rickety pergola which was kept from falling down only by a mass of vines. There was a creeper with pink trumpet flowers, a strange lush-leafed plant with huge yellow blossoms, and a monstrous philadendron, whose creamy-speckled leaves were as large as dinner plates. Crowding against the whole was the inevitable poinsequoia in blazing flower. On the opposite side of the building was a jacaranda, in full, feathery leaf, with the last of its blue flowers falling.

The door opened into a living-room which had once been a verandah, for its south side and far wall consisted of windows and a french door. The door was brushed by the red giant flowers of the poinsequoia. The floor was made up of bare boards which time and sunlight had rendered to an even silky grey colour, which even Ryl found not unpleasant.

This room opened into a kitchen, also long and narrow, and with the jacaranda branches looking in over the sink at the far end. A bedroom opened off the right-hand kitchen wall, also fash-

36

ioned from a glassed-in verandah. A ramshackle bathroom jutted to the left, forming a lean-to wall at right angles to the front door. A second bedroom was to the left of the living-room. From it, a glass door faced the eastern sea, and gave on to a tall flight of steps which led down into a jungle of monstrous leaves. The french windows of the living-room opened also on to the same steps. On either side of the house, at a short distance, were dark Moreton Bay fig-trees, huge and hung with elk-horn ferns.

By and large, the house seemed to have been built in a series of afterthoughts, each room starting as a verandah, only the second bedroom being the original building. The bathroom had clearly been the last, and most haphazard addition. Still, the design was not without advantages, inasmuch as each room was filled with light and air. The panoramic view dominated every corner, a living mural.

'I want this room!' said Ryl, entering the bedroom, the original one, off the living-room. It was the larger of the two. However, Dusty was quite satisfied with the lesser room. In fact, there was no part of the house which he would criticize.

'Just look at it!' he cried in admiration. 'It's a real dream 'ome!' He gazed about at the unlined walls, discoloured with age and lack of paint, and at the bare, pewter-tinted floors. Ryl prowled from room to room.

'It's the most frightful dump I've ever seen,' she called. 'I'd just never realized there could be such a dump! The whole thing looks as though it might fall down any moment!' She peered in the bedroom and continued, 'At least there are beds of a sort, with more-or-less mattresses.'

She prodded the lumpy flock mass of Dusty's predetermined bed. It was true that each bedroom contained a small wooden bed with—as she called it—a 'more-or-less' mattress, and a solid chest of drawers. The living-room was entirely empty, while the kitchen retained a cheap wooden table, some shelves holding odd crockery and cutlery, and a rusty, one-fire stove. But it was when she came to the bathroom that Ryl really gave tongue.

'Oh no! I can't bear it! This really is the bottom of the barrel!'

Her usually low, hard little voice rose to a disconsolate and childish wail, then cracked suddenly. Dusty finished hanging the canary's cage over the kitchen window.

'There you are, Jones, me boy. How d'you like that, huh? You'll

37

get your fill of sunshine now, old cock. Sunshine to throw away; you can play ducks and drakes with it and good luck to you.'

Then he rolled unhurriedly to the bathroom doorway, and stood looking in.

The lean-to floor was made of the same smooth but untrimmed stones that were laid outside the entrance to the house. Its walls and roof were of undressed wooden slabs, doubtless the home of many varieties of millepedes and spiders. Its sole furnishing was a rusty tin bath, with a board resting across it which in turn supported a tin dish. An iron tap projected from an extra large crack between two slabs, and hung from the wall at an angle calculated to direct the water almost into the bath, but not quite.

Ryl, in her limp linen frock, a travesty of its former self, looking like some Left Bank waif, dirty even by Dusty's standards, was perched on the edge of the bath. Tears made snail tracks down her grubby cheeks. With a hopeless gesture she reached out and turned on the tap. It made an asthmatic hissing sound, coughed out a few drops of rusty water on to the stone floor, and relapsed into silence. Ryl again buried her face in her hands and abandoned herself to loud weeping.

# V

'No shower,' sobbed Ryl. 'Nothing! I won't even be able to have a bath! Simply for ever.'

She palmed her eyes with grubby hands.

For a moment Dusty stood gathering his ideas together. All this, he saw, was because she couldn't have a bath, or a shower or whatever, in a bathroom with all tiles and everything left, right and centre, and fancy plumbing and so forth. 'Spoiled brat. Though she'd had a long trip, mind. A bit tuckered out myself,' he thought. 'She does look as though a good scrub wouldn't do her any harm. Ah, she's only a bit of a kid when all's said and done, in spite of her airs and graces.'

Aloud he told her, 'Now come on there, buck up and be a man about it. It's no tragedy—no tragedy at all! I'll look around the place and find a bucket or a hose or something, and I'll get some water in the tub for you out of the kitchen tap. You'll get your bath, don't worry. I'll even have one myself.'

He stumped away, sounding elephantine on the bare floors. She heard him thump, thud, thump, thud, slowly down the steps from the french windows. Ryl enjoyed her cry in peace for a few more minutes. Then he was back in triumph.

'Hey! There's a shower if you want one. It's out under the tank stand, near the jacaranda tree, right next to one of the Moreton Bay figs. They must have put it there so as to get some water pressure. Want to take a dekko at it?'

She blew her nose, and walked with him to the kitchen window. Outside, partly concealed by foliage of the trees, was a large tank stand on a stilted platform. The long piles were nailed about with fibro cement sheeting, to form a primitive shower-room.

'Oh gosh, what a dump,' she said. She turned, droop-shouldered and gangling, all poise collapsed, to get her toilet things and clean clothes from her luggage.

$\cdot \qquad \cdot \qquad \cdot \qquad \cdot$

39

Gingerly, Ryl in her sprigged brunch-coat, incongruous as the proverbial lily on the dust heap, pushed aside the canvas curtain that served as door under the tank stand. Inside the scantily-enclosed space were a few untrimmed paving-stones, making a floor beneath an old-fashioned shower. An empty sardine-tin was tacked to one of the piles by way of a soap holder. Waste water was obviously intended to flow away through an open trench in the red soil, which was at least prettily overhung with ferns and banked on one side by tree roots. An ancient rake stood in one corner.

She hung her new white bath-towel on a nail, thoughtfully provided for the purpose, her brunch-coat on another—then standing naked and defenceless and huddled into as small a package as possible, turned on the tap. Cold water gushed out in more than adequate quantities. In fact, its 'pressure', of which Dusty had spoken with approval, all but knocked her off her feet. That and its icy temperature combined to send the air rushing out of her lungs. Instead of being white and exhausted with the heat, she now clung to the wobbly wall, hair plastered and streaming, blue with cold, and gasping for breath under its onslaught. At last, regaining her presence of mind, she was able to turn back the tap. A very small turn reduced the flow of water to a faint trickle; there was something sarcastic about it. But thankful for respite from the deluge, she took the chance to lather her hair with shampoo and her person with French soap. Then, taking a deep breath, she turned the tap again, and wrestled with the good water pressure.

It was twenty minutes later that a very clean Ryl, wrapped in a very wet brunch-coat, climbed back up the tall steps whose supports stood among a forest of monstera plants. She went through the glass door into her room, deep-littered with luggage and far-flung clothes. She really did feel better. After all, the shower with its strange challenge was stimulating in its own rough way. Voices came from the kitchen.

'Who's he talking to?' she wondered, as she pulled on a shirt. Then—'Where are my thongs? Where the *heck* are they, in all this mess? Whatever will I do with it? Oh, who cares, I'll go without them.'

Barefooted, she padded along the empty living-room.

40

In the kitchen there was a pretty grey-haired woman dressed in a T-shirt and blue jeans. There was a large tray on the table, with a cloth over it. The woman turned to her with a blue-eyed smile.

'Well, hullo, my dear! So you're the little Miss Merewether! I've just been introducing myself to your grandad! Mr. Herbert wired us from Melbourne that you were coming. I'm Rose Bradley.'

'Oh.' Somehow, Ryl had not expected to see their neighbour so soon. She had thought she would have to go looking for the Bradleys, even that there might be some kind of hostility in their reception. She had the impression that they had not been treated particularly fairly in their dealings with her father. Mr. Herbert had said something of the sort. But there was nothing but friendliness in Rose Bradley's manner.

'I saw your taxi coming,' she was saying. 'Perry Davis brought you, didn't he? We'd have liked to meet you ourselves, at Mur'bah, but Clem had to take the car to Southport today, bad luck. Anyway, as soon as I saw you coming I put the kettle on, and popped some scones in the oven! It never takes any time to whip up a batch of scones, and they're nice when they're fresh, don't you think? Of course, I knew you wouldn't want to turn round and start cooking food on top of that train trip! I see you've found the shower.'

She talked quickly and seemed not to expect too many answers. Her conversation was hastily flung together.

'Yes,' put in Ryl. 'It's very kind—'

'Now we want you both,' cried Rose Bradley, 'Clem and I want you both to come to us for anything you might want—anything at all!' With a sudden drop in her voice she said, 'We're both *so* sorry of course, Mr. Merewether, about your son's passing —not that we've seen him since he bought the place, mind, and that's sixteen years ago. Of course he only communicated through the solicitor—well, well, well, it was very sad—*very* sad—' Then, with a crescendo of good cheer, 'We let him know some time ago that Clem wanted to retire to a place of our own. We've bought a small property next door, you know. We'd have liked to buy this farm, but your father wasn't willing to sell—even though he'd hardly seen the place, he wouldn't sell it for love or money.'

'He evidently changed his mind,' cut in Dusty. Rose Bradley shook her head.

41

'Oh, yes, later, the rates got too much altogether—though I don't think he wanted to sell at all, really, he asked the wrong price, for a start. Anyway, Clem, my husband you know, is very clever with cattle, and he wanted to give his whole time to them, and to growing pineapples, he's planted a patch to experiment with, and we still cut the bananas—'

'That's very interesting—' began Dusty. Rose Bradley brushed his remark aside.

'Anyway, we'll show you all over the place tomorrow. And you must bring any washing you have, dear, from your trip, and we'll put it in my washing-machine. The old copper under the house is too much trouble, just for the two of you.'

'What?' said Ryl. 'Washing? Oh— washing!'

'Now, enjoy your tea while it's hot! I won't stay another minute. I know you'd like to get settled. I'll come over in the morning and see how you're making out.'

She headed towards the door.

'It's marvellous, really,' said Ryl, 'to have a meal like this. You're an angel, truly.'

'I've done that trip myself, love, so

I know all about it. You must get to bed early tonight; don't forget now, straight to bed as soon as you've unpacked! Oh, have you got bedding?'

'Yes, thank you kindly,' said Dusty. 'We've got everything.'

'I am tired,' said Ryl, 'and how!'

'Of course, you must be, dog-tired. Now, I'm off. See you in the morning.' She opened the door, then added, 'I was going to tell you about the shower, but you found it. Has a good pressure, hasn't it?'

'Sure has,' said Ryl. 'Is the rake there for anything in particular?'

'Oh, yes, that's for killing snakes! They live in the montys, you know.'

Ryl gave a little shriek. 'Snakes! What are the "montys"—so I can keep away from them?'

'The monsteras at the bottom of the steps. Bye-bye!' and she was gone.

'Well, come on, lass!' grunted Dusty. It was the most comradely speech he had made to her. Already the thought of food was making him mellow. 'Come on like she says; drink the tea while it's hot. Then I'll tackle this snake-infested shower meself, and see what I make of it.'

Mrs. Bradley's cooking was evidently as profuse as her conversation. As well as the pot of tea, the tray held fresh scones, tossed salad with corned beef, fruit salad with cream. Even eaten from the chipped china on the shelves—but with the table covered with Rose Bradley's lace cloth—it was a meal which the travellers found delicious.

The canary, Jones, already installed in the flurry of leaves which intruded through the kitchen window, was now preparing for the night. The sun was gone, for even in summer it retreated early behind the crags of Springbrook and Numinbah. Ryl noticed how the days were shorter than in Melbourne. Already, Mount Warning was a purple castle against an indigo sky, and ink-blue shadows were swallowing up the ragged foothills. From a small window in the western wall of the kitchen close to the bathroom, the old man and the girl watched a grave and lovely night coming down from the mountains to the sea.

They sat on, too tired to move or talk. From Jones's window, the lights of Coolangatta came out like stars among the jacaranda branches, and to the east, drifting through Ryl's room, and from

43

the french windows at the end of the living-room, came a faint, far murmur of the night tide. A living light moved slowly across the dark seascape as a ship passed by. Through the long side of windows that faced south-east, a rhythmic flash and flicker marked the light beacon at Brunswick Heads.

'Well, this won't get us anywhere.' At last Dusty stood up and began to collect the dishes and pile them haphazardly into the stained enamel sink. He looked out the nearest window.

'What a place, by golly! What a view! I'd clean forgot it, mind you, for fifty years. But now it all comes back, that it does. It all comes back. And not so changed. Not it.'

'I suppose the *view* is all very well,' sneered Ryl; 'but you could still have that if you were a black fellow living in a hollow log—or whatever they live in. And you might as well live in a hollow log as in this dump.'

'That's all right about that! I've lived in worse houses than this one, and been thankful for 'em, too. Many would be glad to have this roof over their heads tonight. Why, this house is all right—even better than it was fifty years ago! Kind of pulled in a bit here, and pushed out a bit there, but by and large, better than ever.'

'Huh,' said Ryl rudely, 'I'd hate to have seen it then!'

Without any suggestion that she might help with the dishes, she wandered off to her own room, still muttering, 'A shocking dump. Impossible to live in the place. Best to put a match to it.'

'I'll be turnin' in, too,' called Dusty after her. 'G'night.'

In her own room, and sighing with the effort, Ryl began to open the box containing her bedding. She tossed sheets and blankets on to the bed. They were fine sheets with candy-striped borders, and soft blankets checked in pink, lemon and blue. They gave a touch of luxury to the rough little room, with its timber floor, worn and weathered to the colour of driftwood.

Now the hard mattress was well camouflaged. In fifteen minutes she had found her pyjamas, tossing out more contents of her suitcase while looking for them, and was in bed. She tried to adjust her spine to the lumps in the flock mattress, which was about as comfortable as a bed of old golf balls. She wriggled, then gave it up and lay on the lumps, looking up and out, at the stars above the sea.

44

She would never sleep on this thing, she thought. Never. What a lot of stars. Four—seven—eleven—they were infinite.

From outside came strange tramplings and trumpetings combined with a beating of water, which told of Dusty's brave encounter with the pressure in the snake-pit—Ryl's mental name for the shower—by the light of his torch. Something small and quick scuttered across the roof. Several mosquitoes made noisy reconnaissance above her head. But in spite of everything, she was soon sound asleep.

# VI

The sun woke her.

She lay among the tumbled sheets, her eyes exploring the ceiling and far corners of the room. There was a cupboard in one corner. In this room alone the walls were lined. Cupboard and walls were of plywood, which was faded to a soft grey by the sunlight. Walls and floor were quite clean, showing the zealous neighbourliness of Rose Bradley. The ceiling had been freshly whitewashed. Her open luggage made a bright litter on the floor. She had to admit that in its own primitive way, the room was not unattractive. She found herself, even now, mentally choosing curtains for the windows.

Rising on her elbow, she looked out through the old-fashioned half-glass door, across the morning sea. It was a rippling cloth of silver, ruling a line against the sky, ending to the right in the jutting finger of Brunswick Heads, and to the left in the sheer ramparts of Point Danger. Beyond were the sea, the dunes, and closer in, the glittering river, where already she could trace the course of a tiny red speed-boat by its chalk-white wash. Where the Tweed made its channelled delta, a fishing-boat tacked past Fingal.

Between river and house was a long, gentle slope of pink grass —rosy as a sunset and bowing into a wave of silver before the wind. Ryl's eyes were incredulous, unbelieving, as she saw the pink pasture. Green, yes—like the dairy farms of Kilsyth or Gippsland—that she could credit. But whoever heard of pink-grassed pastures, crested with silver?

And there among the fanciful pasture was a fanciful bird, long-legged, grave and contemplative, viewing the wind ruffles that stroked and sleeked the verdure about him with silver highlights and poppy shadings. His head was tonsured with white. Dark blue glowed iridescently on his breast beneath his blue-grey wings. His long bill pointed towards his toes, and he seemed to sway a little, like a long-stemmed flower.

46

Ryl kicked aside the sheet and swung her legs to the floor. The warm air gave a feeling of lightness and luxury. She did not bother about slippers and brunch-coat, but pattered down the high steps. A swath of grass had been closely mown around the house—probably by Clem Bradley, she thought—and islands of tangled foliage sprang from it, paw-paw-trees, thorny bush lemons, the monsteras and a few clusters of bananas. This, too—this wealth of growth, was a kind of luxury. The grass felt rough and clean beneath her feet. She almost ran to the rusty barbed-wire fence of the paddock where the pink matel-grass began, then moved stealthily towards the long-legged bird. She was twenty feet from him when he stretched out his neck and wings and rose, gliding and soundless, to skim away over the paddocks, over a southerly wind-break of tall old sugar-cane and so out of sight.

Her head tilted, her black hair polished-silver like the grass and the bird's dark breast in the early sun, she stretched out her thin bare arms and stood poised, as though herself ready for flight, young and transient. A Never Bird from some nest of childhood, resting before its long flight.

To the left, beyond one of the great fig-trees, was a milking-shed and now there were muffled sounds as a red cow came from it, closely followed by Dusty who carried a milk bucket.

Ryl, forgetting her usual aloof manner, turned to him with animation in her face.

'Hey!' she called to him. 'Did you see that bird?'

'Bird?' Dusty put down his bucket. 'A bird, was there? By gee, look at this, you wouldn't think a feller my age would still remember how to milk after all this time, would you?'

'No. Why, do you?'

'Well, Clem gave me a bit of a hand, but I milked the majority of it meself. The majority of it.'

The girl's mouth twitched. It was a reluctant smile given with niggardly measure. But enough to make the dimple show.

'Who's Clem? You mean the Bradley man? Are you and he friends already?'

'Yes, he's all right, that feller. We're to use what milk we want and give the rest to the calf. Clem's going to do the milking at night. Nice little calf, too. Come and have a look at her.'

'I'm not really interested in calves,' said Ryl loftily.

Nevertheless, she climbed over the fence and picked her way along the narrow path into the cow-yard, where cattle had worn a parting through the grass with their cloven feet.

To the left side of the pink pastures were the stock-yards and the milking-shed set against a crazy fence. She leaned on the rails and peered over at the soft-eyed brown child of the red cow. The mother still lingered dotingly near her offspring, with the fence between them. Through the bent wire and splintery railings, the two exchanged raptured expressions of love.

'Stupid things,' said Ryl. 'Doesn't the cow know that if she just walks along the fence there's a great hole, and she can easily come through on to the same side as the calf?'

'Ah,' said Dusty. 'She's a good creature but not a great thinker.'

'Look at them. Frantic. Practically hysterical at being parted. And all they have to do to be together again is walk along the fence to where the hole is.'

'Oh, well. We can't all have higher education.'

The animals, too, made Ryl smile. She had never actually studied a calf before, and was unable to resist its gangling legs and tail, its innocent face, and the mother's comic, doting expression. She stood for a while longer in her short pyjamas, watching the drama of the cow and calf.

'When I was here before, mind,' said Dusty, 'this wasn't a cow paddock. It was the banana patch. And those fields over beside the cane-brake, they're Clem Bradley's now, they used to

48

be cane-fields. Belonged in with this property. Ah, yes, there've been a few minor changes like that. But the river's the same. And the Moreton Bays. And—well, it has the same feel about it.'

'How long have you been out of bed?' asked Ryl.

'An hour or so. Clem Bradley came and knocked on the door. But you were dead to the world. He wanted to have a chat and show me around. He's a good bloke, all right. They're nice people, the Bradleys.'

'I'm hungry,' said Ryl suddenly.

'Hungry, are you? Not the only one. Come on and we'll get something under the belt.'

They walked back through the pink grass and over the shorn grass, among the islands of greenery.

'I'm thinking,' said Ryl, 'what I'll buy today in Murwillumbah.'

Dusty snorted. 'No need to buy anything.'

49

'Well, I don't know, I do sort of like this awful dump, for some reason. I may as well stay here for a few months, anyhow. I've nothing else to do. So I may as well get a few things, just to have some sort of comfort. After all, there's no reason why we shouldn't *try* to be comfortable.'

'There's plenty of people,' grumbled Dusty, 'who'd think this place was like Buckingham Palace to live in. Why spend money?'

'Money's no object; you know we have plenty of money.'

'Money no object!' Dusty was scandalized. 'You wouldn't talk like that if you'd ever had to do without.'

'But we don't have to do without, you see. I'm not going to stay here for months and live like a black fellow! Anyhow, when we sell the place we can sell everything we buy along with it.'

'Sell the place?' Dusty looked around. 'Now that I've come here, I'll not hear any more talk of selling it. I like it.'

'Oh, well—' They went up the steps into the living-room. 'We'll have to talk that over, of course, and decide what to do. Mr. Herbert says it's run down and a dead loss. And from the look of it I must say how right he is.'

Perry was as good as his word and called for Ryl soon after lunch—a strange travesty of a meal, prepared by Dusty. (Ryl in a kitchen could feel no emotion but hopeless panic.) As she and Perry drove, she consulted her shopping list, yet keeping an eye on Mount Warning, ever shifting, yet always present on the sky-line—and the fields of sugar-cane.

As they drew near the town, she asked the boy's advice as to which hardware store to try for her purchases.

'This is Budd's,' he told her, pulling up at the kerb. 'You can buy anything here.'

'Oh, good then, thanks.'

'How are you going home?'

'Is there a bus?'

'One goes at three-fifteen, from the Post Office. Or I'm off at five o'clock. Would that be too late for you? I'd be glad to have your company.'

'Then I'll take you up on that. The bus would be too early. I'm simply going to buy the place out, if Dusty only knew.'

'Great. Then I'll see you here at about five o'clock, all right?'

'All right.'

'Looks like a fare over the street. I'd better get moving. See you later!'

''Bye for now!'

He pulled away to turn his car, and she waved briefly.

Three and a half hours later as he cruised past, there she stood, amid a great muster of parcels and cartons. He slid into a spare space a few cars down and began transferring the results of her shopping spree into the boot. Ryl's face was somewhat flushed; she was not quite so well groomed as usual, but her eyes glowed with the satisfaction of a woman who has been on a spending spree.

'Gosh!' laughed Perry. 'How did you get all this stuff here in the first place?'

'The shop assistants brought it out for me. They're nice, really. I can't see Melbourne salesmen lumping parcels about the streets for the customers. Here—this big squashy one's a rubber mattress for my bed. Shall we have to put it on the back seat?'

'Yes, we'll have to, the boot's full. Golly, I'd love to have had a bird's-eye view of you loading all this on to the bus!'

They laughed, and together stuffed the unwieldy mass through the door. Ryl slid into the front seat of the car. He took his place behind the wheel, and reversed into the tide of traffic, while she checked over her wilted shopping list.

'I simply couldn't live another night without a proper mattress —I'd have died, simply died. And I bought some coloured sheets for Dusty's bed, and a coloured blanket, too. Not that he cares what he has on his bed, but I simply can't stand his old blankets. And I've got an electric frying-pan and kettle—and they're sending out a baby electric stove. And a water-heater, and a bath. And a hand-bowl. And stuff to line the bathroom. And a carpenter. If they can get one. But they mightn't be able to. And they're sending a lot of paint that I ordered. And some kitchen lino. And some cane chairs and a coffee table.'

'G—e—e whizzo! You *have* had yourself a ball! You're settling in all right!'

'Oh, I wouldn't say that! You see, we can sell it all afterwards, when we sell the house. Naturally, it's only common sense that the place will sell better if it has a proper bathroom. No wonder

51

nobody will buy it the way it is! So it's only good business to fix up the bathroom and kitchen.'

'Is your grandad going to see it that way?'

'Who, him? I really couldn't care less! It's my money—and my house, too, just as much as his.'

Perry felt it safer to make no comment on these statements.

He asked, 'Who's going to put on all the paint? I bet you never catch up with a carpenter—they're as scarce as hen's teeth. And won't you want a plumber, to install the bathroom things? And an electrician?'

'Yes. The shop's going to ask them all to call for me. It's some shop! You *can* buy anything there! Just like Myer's in Melbourne —only it doesn't look like Myer's. The whole thing would just about fit into Myer's hat department.'

'Oh yeah, that's country towns for you. Mur'bah is a great little town. As good as they come, and then a bit better, we think!'

He turned his long-lashed eyes towards her for a moment. His throat and jaw made a smooth, clean line, as he guided the car around the crooked road at the foot of the escarpment.

He asked, 'But truly, don't you think you might settle down here? Don't you like it already?'

'Oh—I don't know. But we may stay quite a while—several months, anyway.' She spoke with great aplomb, like a person versed in the handling of real estate as she added, 'It may take some time to dispose of the property.'

Perry probed a little. 'Would it be like my cheek to ask what you do?'

'Do?' She sounded blank.

'Yes, you know—do! You've left school, I take it.' He felt her youth, the puzzling mixture of childishness and sophistication. 'Can I guess? You're a Uni. student?'

At once he felt a tension in her.

'No. Not yet, anyhow. You're right about school. I've finished doing my matric. The results won't be out until mid-January, but I'm pretty sure to have passed—quite well, actually.'

'Good work. I've just done my matric., too. I've put in for a government scholarship with the Commonwealth Sugar Refineries, and I've checked into Brisbane Uni. for next year.'

'Really?' Ryl was surprised. It was the first time she had met

52

a taxi-driver-cum-Uni.-student, and apparently a half-caste one to boot.

'But,' he persisted, 'what are you intending to be, when all's said and done?'

'I don't know. I haven't made up my mind.'

She had a queer feeling of knowing Perry quite well, much longer than the single day that measured their friendship. Even his golden-skinned, bi-racial appearance she could forget. But still her habit of reticence could not let her show him any glimpse of the lonely wilderness that seemed to lie in the years before her. The indecision and self-doubts. There was a riderless horse that galloped within her heart across the empty future. She could not tell him that no one had ever cared or questioned what she should 'do'. Clever and quick as she was, perhaps it was this one small thing—that no one cared what she should 'do'—which made the years ahead seem a meaningless, empty land into which she could not or would not try to see.

For some reason, the very reference to the future made her depressed.

'I don't know,' she said again.

To ease the tension of her thoughts, not the silence between them, Perry said gaily, 'Anyhow, I still think you might end up here as a Tweed Valley farmer, growing sweet badilla!'

Ryl tossed her black head. 'Certainly not! Not likely!'

The uncomfortable moment was gone.

'Just the same,' said Perry, 'you could do worse, you know. One day I'm going to break the record for cane production!'

'Then why go to University?'

'Why, to learn how to do it, girl! I'm going to do agricultural science. It's a stiff course. You have to have maths. and chem. for it.'

This was a new idea entirely to Ryl—that cane-growing should entail any sort of science. 'Anyhow,' she said, 'I've got time to make up my mind. I'm not seventeen yet.'

Now Perry was surprised. 'You only sixteen? Gee! Smart lass!'

Mollified, she smiled. 'But no wonder I got my matric. I've lived at boarding-school all my life. Being young for my forms is simply the result of living at school.'

They were climbing the steep road now and emerging on to the razor-back, with the unpainted cottage in sight.

53

'Well, I'm old for my forms,' said Perry. 'Nineteen. I've always had to work as well as study. I guess being old for your grades is the result of living with black people.'

His statement stunned Ryl. Black people. His queer, crinkly hair—or wool. Of course he was a half-caste. His good looks—no, his beauty—for it was beauty—was born of ignorance, poverty, and—yes, thought Ryl—racial inferiority. It all came very clearly to her snobbish little mind. And she thought she had liked him! How could she have liked him?

The girl felt a flush rising in her sallow cheeks, an anger both against herself and the boy for some indefinable reason. How dared he! How dared he be clean and soft-spoken and quick-witted and comely! A nigger half-caste. She froze away from him.

Perry had expected it. That was why he had said it. To get it over with, to be over the rough stuff and to begin again, possibly on a firmer and more honest footing.

Perry had learned that every problem was better faced squarely. And he, with his fuzzy wool, was a living problem. His own mind and wit had long since taught him that people could accept him more easily if they knew that he had accepted himself.

And in this girl he had a core of faith. He sensed that she had a background which would make it hard for her to include him, even harder than for most. But he felt her independence from the crowd, and something gallant about her. He sensed that here was one to 'lay the crazy lance in rest, and tilt at windmills, under a wild sky'.

In silence they drew up at the tipsy gate of the old farm. Dusty came towards them from the flagged porch. The weather-grey house with its habiliments of green made a setting for him.

'Help Perry unload the stuff, will you?' said Ryl. She turned a stiff, cold face to him, with eyes of hard opal.

'Thanks for the ride,' she told the boy. Then she fled over the mown path, banging the door behind her.

'Huh!' Dusty looked after her. 'Miss Hoity-Toity's on her high horse, I see.'

Perry smiled.

'She's probably hungry,' he said.

54

# VII

Ryl, in spite of her brave, even foolhardy attitude towards Dusty's money-saving principles, could not but recognize in her heart that a crisis could well be at hand. Out on the front porch was a pile of gleaming, new household goods—and Dusty. They went ill together. She waited in the living-room for the storm to break. It did, with Dusty's explosion through the doorway.

'What in tarnation,' he shouted, 'have you been buying?'

Ryl felt quite calm.

'Things,' she said.

'I can see they're things! Enough things to start up a furniture and hardware shop of your own! Whatever in the name of the three wise monkeys made you go and get all those things? You aren't fit to be trusted out of sight, and that's a fact! You can't have any more sense than a monkey! Buying all those fal-der-rals!'

'But a very intelligent monkey,' said Ryl. 'After all, not every monkey can pass its matric., hoping for three honours subjects—'

'You can take it all back, that's what you can do!' spluttered Dusty. 'Take it all back and no nonsense—'

'Actually,' said Ryl, 'this is only the start, tomorrow there's stuff coming to fix up the bathroom, and—'

Dusty was quite purple in the face.

'But if you reckon you're only staying for a month or two, whatever's got into you, to be buying—'

'Well, it's adding value to the property,' she explained reasonably. 'The place has been on the market for ages; right? And no one will buy it; right? And why would anyone buy the dump, when you can't even have a bath in it? So, if we spend some money and do it up a little, we've lots more chance of selling it—and at a better price, too! That's business!'

Even to Dusty it sounded reasonable. He rubbed his chin.

'Anyhow,' he grumbled, 'I don't want to sell it. Not now. So it's a waste of money.'

'But you can only keep it if I want to keep it, too, and I can't stay here another minute without a bathroom, and so on! And gee, I'm hungry; is there anything to eat?'

Dusty prepared to fly off his perch once more.

'Eat! Eat! And why ask me! All day I've been studyin' the situation here with Clem Bradley while you've been off gallivantin' and spendin' money with a shovel—and you come home and straight away expect to be fed like a calf. You'd better cook yourself—'

A knock sounded at the door, which was immediately opened from the outside without any pause for the occupants' consent. A head was thrust around the opening—a longish head covered in hair which had once been red and was now a mixture of salt-and-pepper, topping a face, very brown, with a wide mouth and twinkling slit eyes. The face was followed at a leisurely pace by a long, angular person whose legs seemed endless, as they insinuated themselves into the room.

'Ah.' Dusty looked somewhat abashed, then suddenly recovered his temper, and made the introductions.

'Ryl, this is Mr. Bradley. Clem—meet me grand-daughter.'

'Good to know you!' The visitor held out a large, hard paw. 'You'd better call me Clem, everyone does. There are a few families of Bradleys about, and it helps to avoid confusion.'

He looked the soul of good humour and kindliness, in spite of his somewhat overwhelming size.

'How do you do?' said Ryl.

'I've been wondering when I'd meet you!' he told her. 'Anyhow, I've been sent over by the boss to ask you to come and have dinner with us. And it's ready now.'

Ryl and Dusty gave each other a sneaky look.

'But,' said Ryl, 'you fed us last night. We can't make a habit of it. It's awfully kind of you, of course.'

'We'd take it kindly if you'd come,' said Clem Bradley. 'Rose does like an excuse to cook a good meal. She's an artist, you know, when it comes to cooking. And she only has me to feed, now that the kids are grown and gone to homes of their own. If you'll come and let her show off a bit you'll be doing us a favour.'

He looked at the pile of goods at his feet.

'You've been making a start,' he said. 'That's the spirit.'

Ryl threw Dusty another private look—this time one of triumph.

56

Dusty turned his eyes to his toes and cleared his throat.

'Then if you're sure we won't be a trouble,' he said.

Ryl showed her dimple.

'We'd love to come, Clem,' she said, 'if you really look at it that way.'

She took a shower in the snake-pit before going to the Bradleys'. This time, necessity prompted her to take a leaf from Dusty's housekeeping book. As she went down the high steps to the garden shower-room, she noticed that several branches of the Moreton Bay fig-trees were bedecked with what were apparently Dusty's newly-washed underclothes. They were a strange collection. Blue pyjamas, the coat patched roughly with some quite foreign material, evidently once part of a shirt. The new shirt was there, wet and woebegone, and some yellowed singlets and drawers. When the girl entered the shower-room she found a large tin dish and a piece of yellow soap, and guessed that Dusty had combined his washing day with a shower. So, standing beneath the icy cold water, she also rinsed out her underwear—a different matter from Dusty's, but still needful of the same treatment. She remembered Rose Bradley's offer of the use of her washing-machine, and decided that she would ask for her help with the laundry in the future. Underclothes, at a pinch, she could cope with. But when it came to sheets and towels—well, thought Ryl—when in doubt, panic!

Dinner with the Bradleys was a happy meal. Clem had an easy manner, was full of knowledge of the place and its people, ever ready with wit and a lazy smile. Rose, under her endless chatter, was shrewd and kind. Though the two took care not to show it, they had resolved that the Merewethers would be their especial care.

'It's so nice to have you in the old house, dear,' said Rose Bradley, over chocolate ice-cream cake and coffee. 'We've been sort of sad about it being on the market. We're fond of the old place, and we dreaded seeing anyone buy it. It would be such a sad day if it were ever cut up and sold as building blocks.'

'Do you know,' said Clem, 'I don't think Robert Merewether wanted to sell it, either. I think he was kind of hoping no one would buy it. If he'd really wanted to see it sold, surely he would

57

have sent me word to carry out a few repairs, and spend a bit of money on the house? He couldn't expect to sell it the way it is, not at the price he asked.'

Ryl shot Dusty a look of triumph.

58

'Possibly,' said Rose, 'he meant to come back and live here some time. I always felt that. But when the rates got so high and the place wasn't showing any profit I suppose he thought he'd better at least make a show of putting it on the market.'

59

She looked at Dusty for confirmation.

'I wouldn't know,' he said.

'Anyway,' said Ryl, 'I'm going to try to make the place more habitable, even if just for our own comfort. That shop in Murwillumbah is going to get the local electrician for me, and a plumber. They said they'd probably be out in a day or so. I shall have to find someone to put up lining in the bathroom.'

'Well, I'm not too busy right now,' said Clem. 'I'm only picking bananas twice a week. I always pick yours too, of course. There's been no one else to do it, and I couldn't just see them rot. So perhaps I can help you out there.'

'If there are bananas to pick,' said Dusty, 'just show me where they are and I'll soon pick them. I can pick ours, and yours too, just to get even. And then you'd have more time to spend on this useless bathroom that she's set her heart on.'

'Right you are,' agreed Clem. 'That's fair enough. I'm not such a bad carpenter. Built most of this house myself.'

'Of course, we will pay you,' said Ryl, becoming business-like.

'Well, as to that,' said Clem, 'I'm a great man for a trade, especially with neighbours. Why don't we, your grandad and I, work a trade of some sort? If he picks bananas, I'll do your bathroom. That's the kind of deal that suits me.'

Dusty's eyes were twinkling with pleasure.

'You're a man after my own heart!' he cried.

'I've bought a lot of paint, too,' said Ryl. 'Would you have time—?'

'Mmm.' Clem was dubious. 'I don't know if my time would stretch that far. And it's hard to get an odd-job man for that kind of thing.'

Ryl wriggled and frowned. The initial steps taken, her fingers were now itching to make some kind of impression on the house of the pink pastures. She felt in her bones that as soon as the paint arrived on the carrier's truck, nothing would satisfy her but to see it applied to the walls of the kitchen and bathroom.

'Maybe I could paint,' she suggested uncertainly. 'That's if you could show me how.'

Clem grinned. 'Good idea! Do you have some old clothes?'

She did not. Not a garment.

60

'Never mind,' Rose assured her. 'We'll find you some sort of painting rig-out.'

This was how it happened that three days later, Clem Bradley could have been found helping Amaryllis Merewether to mix paint. She was almost unrecognizable in one of his own tartan work shirts and a pair of Rose's blue jeans, much too baggy and kept up with a large safety-pin. The shirt hung around her slim figure in confusing folds, and it took her some time to learn how to keep the sleeves out of the way. A smear of blue paint embellished her nose. It was a smear that was to become Ryl's trademark.

She was very earnest, and very happy.

# VIII

'You know what we need?' said Ryl. 'We need an address.'

Superficially, it was surprising that these two people, opposed in every way from age to outlook, had accepted one another. Possibly a student of genetics may not have found it so remarkable. Dusty and Ryl were worlds apart and yet somehow similar. The same carelessness, even scorn, for the opinions of others, the same slight touch of eccentricity, developed in the man, as yet unobtrusive in the girl. Perhaps the same hidden vein of gallantry which Perry had divined.

Now, after three weeks in the house of the pink pastures, both seemed somehow to belong to their surroundings. Dusty, being old, had long since learned to lay in a stock of memories left over from the realities of youth. And the present reality had come so close to the memories that he was almost a youth again. For the girl, this warm, unreal place with its quaint leaves, its flamboyant flowers, its pink grass where a blue bird alighted at dawn, was an island of rest. Here the past was dead, the future quiescent in its pre-birth. She and the long-legged bird were kin, dreaming in the improbable meadows between season and season, night and day.

'Now she wants an address,' remarked Dusty to the freshly-painted kitchen walls. He turned his eyes to them, for unreasonable witness to this unreasonable girl.

'She's spent a fortune,' he continued, addressing the new blue linoleum. 'She's spent money with a shovel and spade, got everything wealth can buy. But is she satisfied? No.'

Ryl's dimple showed. Perhaps Dusty had given her the greatest gift of all. He had tickled into life a dormant sense of humour.

'Well,' she said, 'we should have one. To put on letters when we write them, and when people write to us.'

She rose from her yellow-painted chair at the kitchen table and

62

went to stand in the doorway of the transformed bathroom, feasting her eyes on it. Never had she thought that the appearance of a bathroom could give her such pleasure. The slab walls were covered with blue laminated sheets, the ceiling was painted white, and now its roughness was pleasing. The floor was painted with red-paving paint and had a large round mat of white rubber between the new white bath and new white hand-bowl. The small window was covered with blue muslin curtains. It was really a bathroom she could love.

'And who are you going to write to?' asked Dusty.

'Well—why—' The implication was just. How often at school she had said to herself, looking at teachers, or even girls she had called friends—girls who had homes to go to and mothers who fussed over them and taught them their prayers—how often had she thought, 'I hate them! I hate them, and really, they hate me. Because I've no one of my own they think I'm a drag, an embarrassment. When I leave school I'll never see them again. They won't care, and neither will I.'

She answered, 'Mr. Herbert writes.' It was a statement in self-defence.

'He don't mind sending letters care of the Post Office,' said Dusty.

'But you'll have to write letters when you pay the rates and taxes and things,' said wise Ryl. 'I'm under age. They'll be your headache!'

'What?' Dusty was shocked. 'Me pay rates and taxes? At my age? I'm on the pension!'

'You won't be any more, when the will's fixed up. And anyhow, when we sell the place we'll need a proper address for people to come to, or they'll never find us!'

Dusty glowered. 'You still talking about selling? You keep on and on, you do.'

She looked about uncertainly. It was true that even to her the cottage was oddly engaging. She had gained a lot of unexpected pleasure from her house-decorating. The truth was she had a flair for such work. She had a love for textures. She had instinctively left as they were the silky, age-bleached boards of the living-room floor, only adding a large white rug to hold her bamboo-and-glass coffee table and a group of bamboo chairs. She had a taste for simplicity which prevented her from detracting from the old

63

house's atmosphere. Only utilitarian things had come under her paint-brush, such as the kitchen and bathroom.

'I've been thinking,' said Dusty. 'An old chap like me can't get a pension if he has money. But he can if he owns a house; that's as long as it's not too valuable. This place isn't too valuable.'

'Hardly,' hooted Ryl.

'That's as long as you don't keep improving it!' Dusty eyed her sourly. 'Now if I owned this house, and none of the money, I could live here and still get me pension. Or even if I owned it jointly along with you. You're welcome to everything else Robert left and good luck to you. But this house—well—I sorter hanker for it.' He sounded almost humble. Almost pleading.

Ryl for the first time felt a sympathy for the old fellow. She could see how much he was in earnest. Again she let her eyes wander over the room.

'It's just a dump,' she said again. 'Really, whatever anyone did to it, it would still be the end.'

'It suits me,' he growled, in his wheezing, hoarse old voice, half comic and half engaging. 'I started my days in this place, on this very spot, and here's where I've a wish to end 'em. It's all right, this place.'

Again for the first time, he felt a receptive audience in the girl. Settling back in his chair, he launched into reminiscences. He took a pipe from his pocket. It was a new one, the only luxury he had sought since 'coming into a fortune', as he put it.

'When I was a boy,' he began, 'the slopes of this ridge, and right around to Banora Point, in toward the hills—it was all in cane-fields. Now they only have the river flats into cane. They put bananas on the slopes. I reckon some of it's gone back into bush. Some of it's grazing land, and folk run cattle on it. A lot of properties near the highway have been cut up into building blocks. Looks like this place and the Bradleys' are the only farming properties left in Bundoora. But it was all cane-fields when I was a lad.'

He rolled a piece of tobacco lovingly between his dry palms. It was some years since he had been so well-to-do as the smell of that pungent smoke would measure in Dusty's mind.

'Course,' he said, 'they can't grow the cane they did, on account of not having any cheap labour.'

'What cheap labour?' asked Ryl.

64

'Niggers.'

'You mean aboriginals.'

'No, no—blackbirds. Islanders. Big, woolly-haired coves from Fiji and the Solomons and New Guinea—and the Hebrides and Melanesia—all the islands.'

'Oh?' Ryl was interested. 'I didn't know that.'

'Oh, yes. Slave labour it was, more or less, you see. They called 'em "blackbirds". Though they was well treated, mind you. And they used to have Hindu overseers. Fine looking they was, in their white turbans. Ah, yes. It was quite a thing to see the heathens driving the bullock teams up the hill roads through the sweet badilla, while the "blackbirds" cut the cane and loaded it on to the jinkers. They used to shout at the bullocks in their own language, and d'you know, the unpatriotic durned critters would understand it, too!'

'But,' asked Ryl, 'what happened to them? Where did they go?'

'Ah, you see, the gov'mint put a stop to it. White Australia and all. Stopped 'em from bringin' in the blacks. Made all the cane-growers get rid of 'em—only it was called "setting 'em free". The Indian Hindus, too. But they were all pretty well off, they'd been paid good wages. So they took themselves back to where they came from. There are probably still a few Indian families around, of course. But the "blackbirds", they'd not been given any money, and so they had no way of getting back to their islands. So they stayed where they were. When I was a lad they lived in villages, keeping to their own race, pretty well. As far as I know they still do. They marry among themselves. I reckon the old generation would all be gone now. But their children and grandchildren would still be in their same humpies in their same villages.'

Ryl thought of a boy with woolly hair, of great beauty, with finely sculptured throat and jaw. But woolly hair.

'Why didn't they simply get aboriginals to look after their old cane-fields for them?' she asked.

Dusty blew smoke-rings. 'An abo, now, he likes to please himself, and then he knows he's pleased someone. He works if he's in the mood. Only he's not in the mood very often. Nobody makes slave labour out of the abos.'

'But that's silly! A slave is someone who's made to work. Well,

65

can't they be made to work, just the same as the Island black people?'

But Dusty shook his head. 'If an abo's happy, he sits in the sun and sleeps. If he's not he lies down and dies on you. He can die any time he likes, can an abo. It's a talent they have. But work he won't. So you can't win.'

'Maybe,' suggested Ryl, with a twinkle, 'if they were just a little bit uncomfortable? Just enough to keep them awake, but not enough to make them decide to die?'

'Can't be done,' insisted Dusty. 'Anyhow, they wouldn't have been strong like the niggers I was telling of. Great big fine men. And they wasn't treated so bad, you know. They was only slaves inasmuch as they had no money. Well, I've had no money for some considerable time, and I'm not even black. So they was no worse off than a lot of white people.'

'I'll make a cup of tea,' said Ryl. She was tired of the subject. To date, making tea, apart from interior decorating, was her only domestic art. She filled the new electric kettle from the water-heater over the bath, stood it on the draining-board of the sink, and plugged it into the brand-new power point, recently installed by the electrician from Kingscliff.

'I think I'd better get a new sink, too,' she said. 'This is a nasty messy old thing.'

Dusty caught the indirect hint of permanence in her statement.

'No,' he answered—as though she had voiced the thought—'you'll never get me back to Melbourne now. Can't keep chopping and changing at my age.'

'But,' Ryl reminded him, 'it's not just a matter of living here, we'd have to farm the place, too, don't forget. Unless you want to sell the land and just keep the old house—and there's no point in that.'

'I wouldn't sell an inch of it,' Dusty declared. 'I could look after it well enough. It's only a matter of a few cows and a banana patch. I'd find someone to help me run it.'

Ryl screwed up her forehead. 'Us—or you, anyhow—run a farm? Why, if you're too old to pay taxes—'

Dusty interrupted her, his ear cocked.

'Is that a truck pulling up outside?'

A truck door banged and footfalls approached, muffled on the grassy path. Ryl went to the door, now painted yellow with

66

enamel left over from the kitchen chairs. She ushered in a man wearing the standard local dress of shorts and long socks. He carried a heavy carton, with a large parcel balanced on top of it.

'Oh—hullo, Mr. Biggs. Here, put it on the floor, will you? Thanks.' Ryl had become well acquainted with the Murwillumbah carrier.

'There you are!' He grinned at Dusty, and winked cheerfully at the girl. 'You'll get some sewing done now! Lovely weather we're having, isn't it?'

'Strike me handsome!' Dusty began to bristle at sight of the goods. 'What have you been and bought now?'

The carrier knew domestic trouble when he saw it coming, and felt it safest to go without delay.

'Well, I'd better be on me way,' he said. 'I've got a lot of deliveries to make with Christmas so close. Be seeing you.'

'Thanks, Mr. Biggs, 'bye for now.' Ryl saw him out. She had quite forgotten that Christmas was near. It had never meant much to her. She would casually buy a handful of Christmas cards to distribute among teachers, a handkerchief and card for Mr. Herbert, who always gave her a box of chocolates, and something rather more lavish for whichever classmate seemed most likely to provide a holiday away from school.

'Christmas, oh yeah,' said Dusty. To him it had meant less than nothing. Only that the shops were closed and so he had to take in extra tea, bread, and bird-seed.

'I bought a whole dozen handkerchiefs for Mr. Herbert,' said Ryl rather hurriedly. 'He's been so kind and helpful. I must post them.'

'Well, there's more than handkerchiefs in *those* parcels!' Dusty waved his pipe accusingly. 'Come on, let's have it—what have you bought now?'

Ryl's chin came up and her eyes glinted with the light of battle.

'It's material to make into curtains. I'll make them, I'll borrow Rose Bradley's sewing-machine. My goodness, anyone would think it was your money I'd spent!'

She began to unwrap acres of brown paper. She unearthed gaily striped denim to make curtains for Dusty's room, and sprigged nylon for her own.

'Look,' she said, her interest in the project bringing a grudging return of friendliness. 'See—for the kitchen and living-room! It's

67

glazed cotton. Don't you like it? A cream background, with lovely red strawberries on it, and a few leaves and flowers. Don't you think Jones will like that for his window? I think it's fabulous!'

In spite of himself, Dusty felt a sneaking admiration for the girl. He considered in his mind that she did have a way of fixing a place nice. Not that she could cook, though. Not that she'd even try! But she could do other things. And she'd always have a go.

'Have you got rods to hang 'em on when you've made 'em? Did you think to get hooks and screws?'

She looked crestfallen. 'Golly, no. I forgot you had to have those.'

She felt keen disappointment. 'I—I've never sewn anything before. But curtains should be so easy. And there didn't seem to be any other way to get them but to make them myself. But perhaps it's not so easy after all.'

'Did you measure the windows?'

'M—m—, well, yes. I measured them with my belt.'

'Good grief, what a way to go about a job!' Dusty clicked his tongue impatiently. But his real anger had evaporated. He said, 'I'll get a steel measuring-tape from Clem. Then I can measure 'em up properly. I'd better go into Murwillumbah on the bus tomorrow, and buy the rods and hooks and screws. You need a lot of fittings for curtains.'

'And I've just remembered, I haven't any scissors,' said Ryl. She sounded quite humble. 'Only my nail scissors. Perhaps—they wouldn't do?'

Dusty's explosive snort was all the answer she needed. Plainly, nail scissors would not do!

'Finish your cup of tea,' said Dusty, 'and we'll go over and see the Bradleys. Rose Bradley will soon set you right!'

Later, they crossed the wire fence that divided the jungle-garden from the pink pastures of matel-grass. Ryl climbed over the fence, and Dusty went under, with much grunting and complaining. They walked around the curved cow track that followed the contour of the hill-side towards their neighbour's boundary—in Indian file, for the track was narrow.

As they walked, Ryl murmured, 'I'm going to find a name for the house, anyway. Just so that we'll have an address.'

68

# IX

Clem Bradley rode his big chestnut gelding up to the fence of the matel-grass paddock, and shouted—'Hey there!'

Dusty put his head through the window among the jacaranda leaves. 'Be with you in a shake,' he said hoarsely.

It was very early. River, land and sea were drained of colour and still with sleep. Only the mountain wall of Numinbah and the crags around Springbrook showed deep blues and mauves against a lemon-coloured sky. The horse's hocks were dark with dew. The cow Betsy and her calf dozed by the rickety shed, the cow's bulk exuding a warm, animal smell of comfort.

A white cat from parts unknown crouched at the edge of the monsteras, observing the dawn with narrow, watchful eyes. Ryl's head showed itself above her window-sill.

'What are you shouting about in the middle of the night, Clem?'

The horseman called back: 'We're going to dip the cattle. Why don't you come too, seeing you're awake? Come on, we could do with your help.'

Ryl groaned, but he continued with his persuasion.

'I'll saddle up the Palomino while you get dressed. After all, he's your horse. He goes with the farm, and you've never even ridden him!'

'So what?'

'So be a sport! Come on, there's the girl!'

She rested her chin on the hard sill and yawned.

'Oh, for gosh' sake, really. For crying in the night! I'm not a drover!'

'It's not too late to learn!'

'Whatever help do you think I'd be?'

'You'd be a big help. Everyone's a help. Pal's a nice little horse, too. You'll like him once you get on him.'

'It's the middle of the night.'

'Nonsense, it's five o'clock!'

'Same thing.'

'Chicken!'

'Oh, all right!' she said. 'You've bulldozed me into it. And on Christmas eve, too!'

Dusty walked past, heading for the shed to collect Ginger's saddle and bridle, while Clem went back through the dew-wet paddock between the two houses. By the time Dusty had saddled the brown horse that waited as patiently as a dog and ate the crust of bread which he offered, Clem was back leading the Palomino.

Ryl, in jeans, arrived and climbed into the saddle. She had ridden a little, but could not regard herself as a horsewoman.

'Look,' she breathed, gesturing to where the long-legged blue bird stood again, wrapped in its customary thoughts in the midst of the pink pastures. 'Look—there's that bird again. What is it, Clem?'

'What? That? Oh, that's a blue crane, a sort of heron.'

'Isn't it beautiful!'

As they watched, it rose, legs trailing like the stalks of a flower, and went winging into the gold-washed east above the river. They saw it pass over the swathed sugar-cane fields and the far sand dunes, and so out of sight.

The riders circled around the thirty head of cattle that Clem kept in his paddock above the river. The creatures made low moaning sounds and Darkie, the kelpie cattle dog, ran at their heels, full of importance, his pink tongue lolling and a swagger to his hind quarters. Clem and Dusty both admonished the herd with shouts, so that the voices of men and animals made silver slivers and splinters of sound in the gathering prism of the day. The Palomino moved like a dancer, his small hooves shod with quicksilver on the loose stones of the Ridge Road.

To the left, a steep side road, very rough, turned sharply down towards the river and the flats. With much barking, shouting and lowing, the cavalcade straggled into it.

'Head 'em in there, Ryl!' yelled Clem. 'Git after 'em!'

Then to her surprise she found herself cantering on the flank of the herd, even shouting herself, 'Get back there, you silly things!' Darkie the cattle dog rushed to her help and the cattle wheeled unwillingly down the incline. Once on the downward road they

70

had little chance to digress, for a sheer bank rose to the right, mossy and fern-hung, with cotton-trees and sally-wattle springing from each shallow pocket of red soil. To the left, the cliff fell away under a veil of greenery. Far below lay a pirate's map of the river, coloured tawnily in the morning sun, with its channels and islands. An isthmus of swamp-land edged with mangroves, and with a few dead gums stretching their white bones high, reached out into its waters. A pair of pelicans rode at anchor in mid-stream and looked almost close enough to hit with a thrown pebble.

The party clattered down through the pressing walls of jungle —more cotton-trees, fig- and bean-trees, lillipilly, and tall, ancient palms, all bound together with lianas—until the way became level down the centre of the isthmus. A dank, gloomy swamp had crept to the margin of the road. A pair of brolgas fled clumsily before the intruders and a spoonbill turned a wary eye from his fishing. Huge green frogs stared, panting, from the twisted boughs. Ryl gave a little cry of shock as she passed one.

'Gosh!' she said to Clem. 'He gave me a fright! He looked just like my old maths. teacher, and he was going to say "boo!"'

'Talking of frights,' said Clem, 'don't look now or you'll get a worse one.'

Of course she at once followed his glance—in time to see a slim brown snake oiling its way into the undergrowth, silent, small, and carrying an aura of evil.

'My spine's crawling,' she shuddered. 'I won't get off this horse—nothing will induce me!'

'Ah, that's nothing,' said Clem. 'The place is full of 'em. All sorts. Tree snakes, black snakes, copperheads, whitebellies—have your choice. You name 'em, we've got 'em. You need to watch where you tread. Still, the cattle usually scare 'em away.'

'Oh, they do, do they!' Ryl took a firmer grip with her knees on Pal's dependable sides. 'Well, I'll stay up here, thank you very much!'

They came to the cattle dip. Jungle gave way to swampy green meadows laced with mangroves, and here were the stock-yards, like a Chinese puzzle with a race of water at its centre. Clem assigned the girl a position where she was enjoined to yell if the cattle tried to break; for the rest of the time she was to keep out of the way. The men, she thought, were enjoying themselves thoroughly—especially Dusty, nuggety but straight on his stout

71

little horse. The dog Darkie worked hardest, taking a pride in his skill, urging the stock through the race and into the evil-smelling dip, which was to keep them free of ticks. 'Everyone enjoying himself but the cattle,' thought Ryl. 'And me. I can't possibly be enjoying myself! But I must say I don't really mind it as much as I thought I would.'

It was quickly over. Already as the party retraced their steps up the steep narrow road, the sun was lifting white vapours from the haunt of brolga and spoonbill, warming the girl's bare arms, and making the horses damp and harassed. They ambled out on to the Ridge Road, the beasts glad to have their heads towards home. Now the sea and river were a dazzling glitter of silver. They entered the familiar paddocks. Ryl slid from her mount, legs rubbery and unstable after the unaccustomed strain of the ride. Rose Bradley waved to them from her garden, which surrounded the new brick house.

'Ryl and Dusty! Come on in to breakfast! It's all cooked!'

Dusty looked pleased. 'But I gotta milk Betsy,' he demurred.

Clem was slipping the saddle from his horse. 'She's been milked later than this before. Do her afterwards. Come on in and be neighbourly!'

Unable to think of a suitable excuse, Ryl headed the procession into the Bradleys' kitchen.

72

'I look awful,' she complained to Rose. 'I feel all horsy. I haven't even had a shower in the snake-pit yet.'

She referred to it derisively as the snake-pit, but strangely, had come to enjoy its cool seclusion each morning, under the branches of the trees. No snake had as yet discomfited her with its presence. She took the precaution of singing, and otherwise making as much noise as possible, to scare them away.

Rose Bradley covered her in a cloak of friendliness.

'Then you run in and wash your hands while I make the tea. Not that you don't look all right, dear. You look sweet and pretty as usual. The door on the left—that's the bathroom—and there's a clean towel on the edge of the bath.'

The men came in. Clem washed in the laundry and Dusty followed him, and in a few moments they were all eating cereal and pineapple slices while Rose turned fried eggs on to warmed plates. She soon seated herself, and began to talk in her quick way.

'Have you put up your Christmas cards, Ryl? Look at ours—I always string them over the windows and around the walls. Aren't they pretty? You'd never think there could be such a variety, would you?'

'Golly, what a lot!' exclaimed Ryl. 'Where do they all come from?'

'Just friends and relations, you know.'

Ryl and Dusty had a very insignificant pile of cards tucked behind the teapot and had never thought of displaying them. It would be better not to try to compete with Rose and her gala stringsful of bright colour.

'And how are the curtains going?' Rose went on. 'Will you have them done for Christmas? I could come over later today and give you a hand with them, and between us they'd take no time.'

'Wouldn't they just, though,' mourned Ryl. 'I've only cut out about half of them. I never dreamed what a huge job it would be. Such a bore. I don't mind painting, but I can see I'm not the sewing type.'

'Then you should have told me before! Gracious, I'd have been over in a minute to help you, if you'd have just said!'

'That's awfully kind. But anyhow it doesn't matter about them. I thought I might go into Coolangatta and have a swim today. I haven't been near the beach yet.'

'That's the shot,' said Clem. 'Have a bit of fun at your age. And

73

as long as you're going into Coolangatta, would you mind doing a bit of an errand for me? Take my camera along to Dynon's, the chemist shop. It's on the next corner to the Imperial Hotel. You'll probably see young Dynon there at the camera counter. Young Glen. If you'd ask him to take the film out in his dark-room. I think it's come adrift somehow. Just tell him it's from Clem Bradley. He'll be apples.'

'Glen's a nice youngster!' said Rose. 'I hear he's going to the Uni. next year, in Brisbane. Of course, the Dynons have plenty of money. He's just working in his father's shop to make a bit of pocket-money for the holidays.'

'That Donovan boy—young Red—he's the one who knows about cameras,' said Clem. 'He used to work at the shop every day after school, and he can do anything with cameras. But he's started up a surf-board hire business for the holidays, I believe.'

'He's a born operator,' said Rose. 'He'll get on, that boy.'

'And what's Glen Dynon going to do at the University?' Clem asked Rose. She was always a mine of information about local affairs.

'I did hear it was some sort of business course. Would it be called a "commerce course"? Ryl, would you know?'

'I expect that would be it,' said Ryl.

Clem asked, 'I suppose you're making plans for the future too, Ryl? You've left school, haven't you? What are you going to do?'

She answered shortly, 'Don't know. I haven't thought.'

Clem's question recalled Perry Davis to her mind.

'Do you know that Perry Davis?' she asked.

Rose nodded brightly. 'Oh, yes, he lives down by the lake.'

'He said he's going to Uni., too. How can he do that? He said something about living with natives!'

Rose clicked her tongue.

'He shouldn't talk like that to people who don't know him! He's a fine boy, is Perry. But he's had what you might call an unfortunate start in life.'

'But he's overcome it.' Clem took up the story. 'You see, his great-grandfather is a Tongan. A real identity, as a matter of fact. He's the only one left of the original "blackbirds". The Islanders, you know.'

Dusty was fascinated. 'Is that so?' He leaned forward. 'I didn't know there was even one left! Well, fancy that!'

74

Clem nodded. 'Yes. He's pretty old, of course. He's the only one left. Perry lives with him. There are just the two of them. They live on a bit of a farm that was left to the old man by the chap who brought him here, seventy years ago.'

'Anyway, that's what everyone assumes,' Clem went on. 'Its former owner died just about six months before Ki went to live there with the baby. The little chap's mother was the old fellow's grand-daughter. She was a half-caste. And she married some white man. A bit of a mystery about that. Nobody seemed to ever find out exactly who it was. It was during the war, of course, when there were a lot of interstate fellows up here with the army unit that was stationed on the border. Anyway, Perry's a quarter-caste. A fine-looking boy. Strange, the way his hair makes him look quite native, otherwise he's not particularly dark-looking.'

'A sort of throw-back,' said Rose. 'Sad about him, really.'

'He seems all right to me,' said Ryl. 'I can't see that he's sad.'

Dusty rose stiffly from his chair, straightening out his back.

'That was a wonderful breakfast, Mrs. Bradley.'

'I wish you'd both call me Rose,' said that lady. 'Everyone does.'

Dusty grinned. 'Right you are, Rose. That was what I call a real breakfast! My word, it's good to taste someone else's cooking for a change! Ryl, why don't you take some lessons from Rose?'

Ryl gave him a pained look.

'I'd better go and milk that cow,' Dusty continued. He made his good-byes and stumped homewards, concerned for the patient Betsy.

Ryl had the grace to stay and help with the dishes, though—and Rose would never for worlds have told the girl she was more of a hindrance than a help. While Rose cleared the table she stood with the salt and pepper shakers in her hand, looking bewildered. Rose must needs walk around her, as though she were some ill-placed piece of furniture. She whipped the plates from the table as quickly as possible, then bundled the cloth into Ryl's arms.

'Here, love, you take it outside and give it a good shake and then fold it up. Fold it where the creases come.'

At least this got the girl out of the way for quite some time. Upon her return, Rose draped a tea-towel over her arm and Ryl found a routine task for herself, where lack of experience was no handicap. Brisk Rose washed dishes very quickly, using much soap and hot water, while Ryl struggled to keep up with her.

75

As they worked, Rose said to her, 'Now, I'll be very hurt if you and your grandad don't come over and have Christmas dinner with us! I'm counting on you. I've got a turkey—we'll have it cold—and avocado pears with french dressing, and stuffed peppers. I really feel inspired over tomorrow's dinner. So you'll be here at twelve sharp, won't you? That's so that we'll have time for a social drink first. Clem doesn't drink as a rule, but he does love a drink with his friends before Christmas dinner! You and Dusty will like to meet our relations, I'm sure. Of course there'll be plenty of fruit-cup for us girls!'

Quite suddenly, Ryl's eyes were bright with tears. In her heart, she had felt lonely and helpless over the matter of Christmas dinner. Used as she was to being richly dined by other responsible cooks, she had felt a bleak foreboding at the prospect of another of Dusty's meals, consisting as usual of boiled potatoes and chops —though in spite of this, she still refused to probe into Rose's proffered cookery book. The prospect of a real Christmas dinner —and not only that, but also the spontaneous, even urgent invitation—touched her cold little heart, possibly more than any other incident since her babyhood. But self-expression was not easy for Ryl. She could be glib over small talk but tongue-tied over the things that mattered.

'Thanks, Rose,' was all she said. 'Gee—thanks.'

Rose, in spite of the fact that she never stopped talking, still managed to be observant. She understood.

76

# X

Carrying the camera and with written instructions for its disposal, Ryl walked back to the house among the trees. Dusty had milked the cow and fed the sweet, silly calf.

Ten minutes later, swinging a bright beach-bag, she went up to the Ridge Road just as the blue bus rattled to a stop.

The worn leather seat was hot on the backs of her legs, bare and turning brown. The bus wended its way high above the river, with the Terranora Lakes lying in the valley to the left, at the foot of the mountain face. Then the Ridge Road joined the Pacific Highway at Oyster Point, and was soon unrolling beside the river, blue now, and divided into shaded patterns of deeps and shallows that flowed and ebbed among the mangrove islands. Flocks of water-birds congregated on sand-banks, sea-gulls and kittiwakes grouped like bunches of white blossom about the feet of the bigger birds. Opposite the river, gay motels, painted in holiday colours, hung out their signs above oleanders, lily-ponds, and petrol pumps. Coloured people trudged on the dusty margin of the highway, and their boys travelled on bicycles, their thin black legs moving piston-wise with the pedals.

The bus rattled through the tick gates, past 'Dick's Garage', where the grease-room was hung with elk-horn ferns. A blonde woman served creamed coffee in the bright dining-room that overlooked the river. On Greenbank Island, opposite the prawning fleet anchorage at Boyd's Bay, an old coloured woman stood fishing in the shallows.

Through the cluttered, noisy streets of Tweed Heads they went and stopped on the Queensland side of the border, by the Old Border Fence in Coolangatta. Ryl climbed down. The streets were full of young people—a town where youth was the order of every day. Girls in shorts and play-suits, boys in cotton slacks, with bare feet—girls and boys in pairs, arms entwined, in the streets where every other shop sold hamburgers and fresh pineapple-juice, and there was always the sound of a jukebox. 'Do they all,'

77

thought Ryl, 'know what they must "do?"' Was she the only one solitary and confused, a traveller with no destination?

It was easy to find Dynon's, with its windows full of cosmetics and sun-tan creams and cameras. Ryl went in. The boy behind the counter must be Glen Dynon, she thought. He looked very clean and scrubbed, with a blond college cut and the usual business man's dress of white shirt and well-tailored shorts with knee-length socks.

'I'm Clem Bradley's new neighbour,' she said. 'He asked me to show you his camera. He wants you to take out the film in your dark-room and see what's the matter with it.'

The boy's eyes took in the picture she made, her slim form framed against the light square of the window.

'Sure, O.K.' He smiled. Taking the camera from her, he excused himself and disappeared with it into the back of the shop. Until his return the girl occupied herself by reading the messages on the postcards that took up a full set of shelves. He was not long.

'The film wasn't gripping properly,' he explained. 'I've fixed it now. Lost a few shots—not too many. How do you like our town?'

'I don't really know yet. I guess it's all right.'

'Are you going to the beach?'

'Yes.'

'Funny thing, I'm taking the day off today. There should be good surf running, the wind's just right for it, and the tide. I was just going to leave, as a matter of fact. Maybe I could drive you down?'

She was tired of being alone. 'All right,' she said.

He looked pleased. 'I'll have to change but it won't take a minute. Would you like to wait in my car? It's the heap outside— the old red M.G.'

'All right.' Ryl went out, and sat in the car. She was impressed. Ancient and battered as the car was, it represented a way of life that was every boy's goal. Glen, it was obvious, had reached the top. Sitting in the M.G., she now viewed the passing youth parade as from a throne. She was not the solitary one any more. She belonged to a group of three. Glen, herself, and the car. It was a personality in its own right. A knight's charger—a pumpkin coach for Cinderella.

78

Then Glen hurried out of the shop and vaulted into the driver's seat. He had changed into a beach shirt and shorts, and carried a gaily-striped towel around his neck.

'Oh, and for the record,' he said, 'I'm Glen Dynon. Sorry. You may have been wondering.'

She showed her dimple. 'I wasn't, actually. You see, I knew all the time. And I'm Ryl Merewether.'

'I knew all the time, too. I've heard of you on the grape-vine.'

'Oh. What grape-vine?'

'Aw, just a sort of bush telegraph we have in a place like this. Do you especially want to go to Greenmount?'

'Greenmount? Which is Greenmount?'

'You don't even know that? Greenmount's the main beach, the long one behind the shopping centre.'

'Is there another?'

'Sure is. There's Rainbow Bay. It's on the other side of the headland. You get the best board surf there this season. All the board-men are going there now. And I'm a board-man.'

He grinned down at her. His skin was perfectly tanned against his white clothes.

'What's a board-man? I don't understand the local dialect.'

'Surf-boards. Okanuis. Pig-boards. Banana-boards. Gee, don't tell me! You're from Melbourne!'

'It so happens! I'm told there's also surf in Melbourne; it just happens that I've not been terribly surf-minded to date. Let's have a look at your Rainbow Bay.'

'Good show.' Glen started the M.G. with a noise like machine-gun fire, and zipped through the hugger-mugger traffic, swooped around the corner by the Queensland Hotel, roared up the steep face of Greenmount Point, making Ryl hold her breath in dizzy fright, then down the other side like a slippery-dip, to curve neatly into a parking area above the crescent of Rainbow Bay. The parking area flanked a forest of campers' tents.

'Here it is. The beach. Help yourself.'

Blue-green breakers rolled in, furrowing the sea as far as the horizon, where a fishing-boat punctuated the straight-ruled sky-line. The waves travelled in curved formation around the rocky headland and out of sight, their distant outposts breaking on Greenmount Beach, while their closer crests flung foam on the golden sickle of sand at their feet. Like a flock of lazy sea-birds,

79

or a drift of brown weed pods on the water, the fleet of surf-boards with their riders rose and fell far out on the tide.

'Yippee!' shouted Glen. 'All the chaps are out today! Look at those waves! Boy, oh boy, they're perfect, just perfect!'

A long, smooth slope of water gathered beneath the miniature fleet and most of the boards seemed to be caught up effortlessly, their occupants kneeling, then standing, to come gliding shorewards before the unbroken swell, each trailing a white streamer in his wake.

'It does look fun,' said Ryl.

As the surf-riders came closer, she saw that most of them wore knee-length pants—pirate style. Their muscles moved beneath their brown skin as they guided their craft slantwise across the swell, agile as dolphins. Then close inshore, the long waves gambolled into froth and curling foam, the board-men sprang lightly into the water and took hold of their spindrift craft. To Glen the call of the surf was stronger than the call of a new friendship.

'Ryl,' he asked, 'will you be all right if I get my board and go out for a while?'

'Sure!'

She dropped to her knees on the friendly sand. Its touch held a spell of warmth and soothing, a compliment to the almost hypnotic sea, in its long, hushed sibilant furrows. Glen laid his towel beside her.

'I'll be back,' he said.

Dragging his T-shirt over his head, he dropped it and ran clean-heeled. Up on the bank a slick Malibou board was propped in the shade of a tent. He raised the long, light thing and carried it on his head down the beach and into the water. In a few moments he had joined the outgoing surf-riders. As he knelt on his board, his neat, square posterior was all that showed above the soles of his feet, receding behind the line of waves.

Ryl spread out her towel, emblazoned with a red sea-horse, and sat on it for a few moments, letting the sun soak into her. Unlike the main beach on the other side of the headland, which was crowded with tourists and shattered with sound from blaring loudspeakers, this place was sparsely scattered with sunbathers, coloured umbrellas, children and an itinerant dog or two.

Close by was a calico sign strung between two poles driven into

80

the sand, and reading 'Surf-boards for Hire'. Beneath it was a rack, now empty of its load except for one board. It was attended by a freckled youth in a straw hat.

Several small boys were engaged in a game of shuttlecock, while on the banks above, two lads were absorbed in the task of painting a surf-board with a mixture of fibreglass. Its pungent smell mingled with the overall tang of salt and seaweed, and a subtle suggestion that somewhere in one of the tents fish was frying.

Ryl shed her shorts and overtop, like a cicada in the sun splitting out of its old self. She lay on the warm towel, burying her face in her arms. Gentle bite of sun on bare skin—murmur of waves—voices of holidaymakers—Glen's towel to mind. She never noticed it, but this spelt peace.

Twenty minutes later she felt a tentative tug at her hair. She opened one eye and looked up at Glen.

'Are you tired of your Malibar—or-whatever-it-is—already?' she said.

'Come on in before you're burned to a crisp. I'll show you how to ride it.'

She sat up. As she did, Glen waved to someone behind her.

'Hi!' he called.

Ryl looked round. It was Perry Davis. He walked towards them with a board balanced on his head. She saw that his skin was a dusky brown, not with the golden tonings of Glen's. It went well with his red pirate pants. He and Glen seemed old friends.

'How's the surf?' Perry called.

'Mighty!' Glen told him.

Perry smiled at Ryl.

'Hullo. Been on the boards yet?'

'I'm going any minute, Glen's going to teach me.'

'Famous last words! Well, I'll see you both in the drink!'

He continued on his way.

'You know him, do you?' commented Ryl.

'Sure, everyone knows everyone here. He's a good chap, Perry.'

'Oh?'

'Great. A few days ago I was very glad to have him around. The shark flag went up just after I'd taken a toss in the deep sea, and

my board got away from me. It came into shore without me. Happens sometimes. There you are, out in the drink, and your board riding merrily in on its own, half a mile away. And this time it wasn't just me in the water, it was me and a Grey Nurse shark about ten feet long.'

'Oh—o—o—! And you're planning to get *me* out there! Why aren't you all eaten up and digested by now?'

He laughed. 'Look,' he said, 'it's safer than walking across the street. There's always a look-out on the hill there, watching for sharks. When they see any they run up a red flag.'

'And a lot of good that would do the boys out on the sea. I suppose you all race for shore, hoping for the best?'

'No, we don't. That's the way to get caught. We bunch together. That way the shark's scared of us. We hope. Only I admit it's not much fun when you happen to have lost your board! But Perry saw me in the water, that time. He paddled over and I climbed up behind him. We made it in with the others—slowly, though. The fleet comes in together, you see. They all slowed down to give us an escort.'

'What a horrible experience.'

'Oh, it was all right.'

'And what happened to the shark?'

'Nothing, unfortunately. They sent for the speargun fisherman, but it got away. They usually do!' he added cheerfully.

82

'I don't feel nearly so dead keen about learning to ride that board,' said Ryl.

'Oh, come on, don't be chicken.'

Glen sprang to his feet and pulled her after him.

'Here we go. Lesson Number One. Surf-riding Without Tears.'

Perry was almost right, in that Ryl did find that surf-riding was not so effortless as it looked, but with great striving she did make progress. When they left the water, the boys persuaded her that it was time for lunch. She met Red, the boy with 'Surf-boards for Hire', and his red-headed sister, Dodi. Ryl took to her immediately, which was not hard, for the freckle-faced girl was extremely likeable.

'Come and have fish and chips with us,' Dodi invited her.

'But I'm going to be terribly sunburned. I really think I'd better go home.'

'We can eat under Red's umbrella,' Dodi pointed out. Red, a salesman born, had marked his beach-stand with a red umbrella whose distinctive colour made it easy to locate.

'Then,' said Perry, 'if you're getting burned, you could come home with me; I have to go about two o'clock. I have to drive the taxi later on.'

'But I'm burned right now.'

'Oh, that's not burned! That could be worse, and probably will

be! Have a shower and wash off the salt while we buy the food.'

'And I'll oil you,' offered Dodi. 'The thing is to have someone baste you like a Christmas turkey.'

Persuaded, Ryl went to the shower block. It seemed well patronized with women from the camping ground and their small children. The air buzzed with snippets of a dozen conversations, and as she showered, Ryl tried to unscramble them. 'Say, anyone got any talcum? I forgot my talcum! . . . Here you, Hazel, have mine—Mary, love, take this talcum to Hazel . . . throw it over the wall . . . did you hear our primus blow up last night? Bits of bacon and egg all over the roof! Laugh! . . . and he said, "she's a middle weight, her weight's all in the middle" . . . so I forgot to put any sugar in it, but we made it into Yorkshire pudding. . . .'

Ryl thought of the family who had shared the train carriage with herself and Dusty on their trip from Casino. She wondered if they ever came here. She could imagine how they would like the place.

Showered, Ryl combed her hair, sticky with salt. She rejoined the others under the umbrella, and Dodi took some bottle of brew from her beach-bag and 'basted' her victim. Now the surf-board rack was full, for the riders were all in for lunch. The tide had risen and the waves flattened, so that the boys pronounced the surf past its best, tame and uninteresting. Dodi chattered to Ryl of her own school-days, now finished as were Ryl's. They were a carefree group and it was wonderful to be with people of her own age. Finally Perry looked at his watch.

'I'll have to rush off,' he said.

'Then I'll come too,' Ryl told him. 'Oh, I meant to do some shopping. I forgot.'

'There's still time. What sort of shopping was it?'

'Food for over Christmas. Not really my line at all. I've hardly seen food in its native state.'

'Bad luck! A potato is so hard to recognize with its skin on. But I can tell them all apart, the different edibles. I'll help you.'

'Perry's the Boy Scout type,' said Glen. 'He could always get a job of housekeeping if he smashed up the taxi.'

'Quiet, mug,' said Perry.

They left the surf-riders and made their way through the camp ground to where an old Austin utility was parked. This was Perry's personal property nicknamed 'The Bomb'. It was fitted with a frame on top, and to this Perry tied his surf-board.

84

'About five of us chaps chipped in to make the frame,' he explained. 'It's a group project, but it's usually on my Bomb because it carries the most.'

Glen ran after them and drew Ryl aside.

'There's always a dance in Coolangatta on Christmas night,' he said, 'at the Surf Club. Would you care to come to it with me?'

'A—dance? Golly, I've only been to school ones before. What would it be like? What would I wear?'

'Oh, anything. Shorts—slacks—town dress—sun-dress—anything! You'll like it, truly. And they'll like you, that's certain.'

'Is Dodi going?'

'Of course!'

So they arranged it.

As Perry drove back to the shopping centre, Ryl wondered how it had happened that in a few short hours she seemed to have made more friends than in all the thirteen years of school life. 'Perhaps it's the climate,' she thought. Certainly the warmth did seem to do something for people. Everyone here seemed more relaxed, and ready to accept any stranger. She was still quiet, pondering the matter, as Perry swung into a parking lot next to an open-fronted building which bore the legend 'Kev's Diner. Come in and Eat Before we Both Starve.'

'Now!' Perry got out of the Bomb, and opened the door for her. She had to admit that his manners were not only as good as those of any college boy, but rather better. 'Now, what do you want me to buy?'

'Oh dear, must I think?' she grumbled plaintively. 'Honestly, I don't know. I suppose, vegetables, and salad things. Whatever they have in the shop.'

Perry laughed. 'You're a dream, Ryl!' he said. 'Say, I'm not a bad cook, actually. So I'll get everything I think I'd get if it were me. Just tell me what you particularly *don't* want!'

'I don't know what I don't want.'

'Maybe you don't like carrots or something? Or already have some things at home?'

'I don't know.'

'What sort of meal do you want tonight? Hot or cold?'

'Hot, I suppose. Dusty always cooks chops and potatoes. Oh, yes, that's what I don't want! I'm going to try to cook dinner myself, because I simply will die if I have to face another chop.'

85

'Well, I'll get you some nice things to cook, and on the way home I'll advise you as to how you deal with them.'

'Then I'll go to the butcher's and buy something that isn't chops, while you get fruit and vegetables.'

In twenty minutes they were both back at the utility, loaded with parcels. Perry turned the Bomb towards the country, while Ryl rummaged through their purchases.

'Look, Perry, there was a place where gorgeous roast chickens were in a glass oven thing, turning and turning before my very eyes! So I bought one! It's already cooked, what a break!'

'Yes, this place is a sort of Roast Chicken Paradise. Don't take it out of the tin foil, just heat it again without unwrapping it. And I've got you some tiny carrots, and some frozen peas, and three packets of potato crisps that you can heat in the oven. And you can fry some bananas with all that. See? No trouble at all!'

'It sounds marvellous. I hope I'm clever enough to carry it through.'

'Of course you can do it. Any girl who can get her matric. can cook a dinner! Say, do you mind if I drive around the lake and call in at my place for a minute? I just want to see that my great-grandad's all right.'

'Oh yes, of course.'

She remembered what the Bradleys had said about Perry's great-grandfather. She looked at the boy from the corners of her eyes, wondering if he would be embarrassed to take her to his home and to meet his only relative. But he seemed not to be.

'You've heard, I expect, that he's from Tonga. His name's Kianoko. But everyone calls him Ki.'

'Oh.'

'I call him Grandad. I'm more respectful to my grandfather than you are to yours.' He spoke teasingly.

'You mean the way I call my grandfather "Dusty". Well, you see, I've only known him for about five weeks. I just sort of didn't think of him as "Grandfather". But he seems quite satisfied with the arrangement.'

'Only known him for five weeks? That's odd.'

'We're a bit odd,' she sighed.

It was on the tip of her tongue to tell Perry about herself, to pour out her history to this other person whose story was different from the rest. She felt so at ease with Perry. Even the sight of his

86

woolly hair no longer disturbed her. But it was her habit of reticence that stopped her from speaking—and perhaps, a little, his background. She could not quite reconcile her mind to the reality of this well-mannered boy, and the knowledge that his great-grandfather was an old black Islander who had once been a slave.

On the lake shore a dusty road followed the water, almost parallel with the Ridge Road but on a lower level, close to the mangrove islands of Terranora Lakes. Perry drew up in the shade of a huge poinciana-tree, the largest she had seen, massed with brilliant flowers. Well back from the road stood a weather-board cottage, grey and paintless, not unlike her own house. Exploring the lie of the land with her eyes, she suspected what she later found to be true—that her own farm was directly above this one at the top of the same hill slope. Nothing separated the two cottages but the long hill-side of banana plantation.

A large white cat with blue eyes sat majestically on the door-sill, in the shade of a wonderful climbing begonia. He looked quite familiar. Of course—he was the cat who liked to bask in the morning sunshine in her own monstera!

'Coming in?' asked Perry.

The snobbish core of her mind felt duty bound to say to itself—'Well, this is the bottom of the barrel! A half-caste's house!' But another part was agog with curiosity.

'Oh—all right.'

They walked up the narrow earth pathway scattered with red flowers from the poinciana. The white cat rose and bowed them in with stiff, formal tail.

# XI

There was a clean, bare living-room with yellow duck curtains, rather faded, an old couch covered with a bright navajo rug, a battered bookcase filled to overflowing, a tangle of radio pick-up equipment, and a quite tidy desk.

'Why,' said Ryl, 'it's not too bad!'

Perry laughed. 'Did you expect to find a *gunyah* furnished with empty beer-cans? Come on and meet Ki.'

They went through an open door, across the living-room and on to a back verandah. Here, on a shabby cane lounge, lay a wizened old man, a study in black and white like a photographic negative. Black face, white hair and beard against a white pillow. His frame hardly raised the level of the faded quilt with which he was covered. There was a banana case at his side, holding a milk-bottle full of water, a covered plate, a pipe and tin of tobacco. On his other side was an old radio cabinet, long-legged and uneasy in its surroundings. At their approach the man opened his eyes. Perry automatically took up the pipe and began to fill it. Ki turned his gaze to her. His eyes were deeply sunken and seemed to show a great deal of white around the pupils. Ryl thought of a sick old spaniel she had once seen taken up by the dog-cart in Melbourne. But the eyes brightened as the mind behind them registered their presence. Ryl saw that Perry's face bending over the couch was tender, as his fingers deftly tamped the pipe. She could see very clearly at that moment the grace of the boy's figure, of the long fingers, the ears set neatly against the skull. It was not a European cast of features that bent over the old man, but it was one that would appeal to any artist or sculptor.

'Hullo, Grandad!' he said. 'Are you all right?'

She noticed his voice, too. It had a quality of lightness and yet husky depth. It was the calypso voice that belongs to those who have grown mellow in the sun ever since islands were first bequeathed to the dark peoples.

88

'They're very fond of each other,' she thought to herself. 'They really are.'

The very old eyes of the man had crinkled into a smile.

'Yes. Yes. I all right.' He added though, slightly querulously, 'The wireless don't work. Battery flat again, maybe.'

'Say, Grandad,' said Perry, 'I bet you've been going to sleep and forgetting to turn it off again!' He drew Ryl forward. 'Grandad. This is Ryl. A friend of mine.'

The old eyes judged her. 'Hullo, girlie.'

Perry went on, 'Ryl lives up the Ridge Road, in the old Masterton place. We've been surfing.'

'Yeah?'

For a few moments Perry chattered to the old man as one would to amuse a child. Then he said good-bye.

'We must go now, Grandad; I've got to go to work, and Ryl has things to do. You be O.K. while I'm gone?'

To Ryl he said, 'You can go back to the Bomb if you like, I'll be with you in a minute. I'd better put him back in bed before I go.'

She returned to the car. He soon followed her out.

'I must tell Sandy Mason about his wireless,' he said. 'There's probably not a thing wrong with it. If there were I could fix it as well as anyone. But he uses it as an excuse to get Sandy out to talk to him. Not that he has much to say, not that he even listens to the wireless much. But it's company for him—like having Sandy call. He just likes to have someone near-by, or even a voice on the radio.'

'Oh?' Ryl murmured.

'He gets mighty lonely, poor old chap. Just stop and think about it. His mates are all gone. That's the time when any old feller knows it's got to be his turn next. But take into consideration that this old feller's a different colour from most. He still feels a stranger in the land, even though he's lived here seventy-odd years. In fact, it gets worse. Because his memory's not so good, and he seems to remember his early life as an Islander better than he remembers his later life in Australia.'

Ryl said, 'But there are lots of coloured people about, aren't there? Don't they visit him?'

Perry shook his head. 'He doesn't see much of any of them. He's grown away from all the other coloured people. Doesn't even make them welcome.'

89

They bounced up the steep road, walled in by a green jungle of banana leaves.

'I suppose your own grandad is a bit lonely,' said Perry. 'I gather he's only got you, and he's among strangers.'

'Oh, he's happy as a lark. He lived here when he was young, and he's so tickled to be back he never has time to be sorry for himself.'

Actually, it was the first time that her attention had been drawn to the fact that Dusty would have his own set of feelings.

'You don't need to be old to be lonely,' she said.

And as they drove slowly over the bumps, following the banana plantation, she found herself outlining her own past to Perry, and its years of loneliness.

'Well,' he told her when she stopped speaking, 'you're only young. You've got lots of time to make friends and do anything you want to do. Anyone can do anything they want, if they want it hard enough. But your grandad's been through a longer stint of loneliness than you, I expect. Now's your chance to make it up to him as much as you can.'

'Don't you preach!' said Ryl. 'If you ever wore a collar I bet you'd put it on back to front!'

90

They drew up outside her house, and she stepped out.

'Yes, I'm a bit of a pain in the neck, aren't I?' Perry agreed. 'I'll just dump your things—then I'll have to go like a bat out of hell.'

He tumbled her shopping into her arms and drove off at a great pace, for once without any consideration for the gears of his Bomb. The last she saw of him was a cloud of dust, as he called out, 'I'm so late I'm nearly in time for work tomorrow!'

She looked after him, thinking of his many talents—cooking, nursing invalid grandfathers, driving a taxi, winning scholarships.

Her parcels were slipping from beneath her elbows and between her hands. A pineapple was prickling under her chin. Clinging desperately to her roast chicken she walked down the path, and with one foot pushed open the door of the living-room.

The room was almost unrecognizable. Suddenly the two walls of windows were dressed gaily in strawberry-patterned curtains. It was the material which for two weeks had been lying in its wrapping-paper, still unmade, on top of Rose's borrowed machine. Dusty and Rose Bradley were in the room, looking self-satisfied as they basked in the glow of the new curtains. Dusty was still clutching a hammer, while Rose was folding away a section of the festive cloth. Ryl walked slowly down the room, admiring the windows as she went.

'But it's terrific!' she cried. 'It's just simply terrific! Really! Isn't it!'

'We just finished in time!' Rose gloated. 'We thought we'd give you a surprise.'

'And you certainly did! A marvellous surprise!' The girl had never known such satisfying pleasure as the new curtains gave her.

'Oh, Rose, how *could* you be so nice! Sewing all those miles and miles of curtain! You're superhuman, you really are! I'd have taken years to do all that!'

'But I enjoyed it! They're pretty all right. It's a pattern I'd never have thought of buying myself. But it's that pretty, now it's up!'

Ryl hugged Dusty's arm. 'Thanks a million, Dusty!'

He looked down over his portly stomach at the new white rug.

'Huh! It was a good thing to get the stuff out of the way.'

91

Perhaps his mind was turning back to some long-ago day when he had worked about another house—or even this same one—and been thanked and praised and made much of.

'We thought you'd like them up for Christmas,' Rose said. 'But they really ought to be lined, you know, love.'

'They're just fabulous the way they are. I don't want to shut out every bit of sunshine. I love both the sunshine and the curtains.'

Rose patted the bundle she was holding. 'And you bought more than you needed. You could almost use what's over to cover a chair, or make some cushions.'

Dusty muttered, 'You've got a mighty hazy idea of measuring things, my girl.'

'Anyway,' Rose defended her, 'better too much than too little, I always say.'

They preened themselves for some moments more on their day's handiwork. Then Rose, in her usual bustling way, took her departure and was off across the pink pastures to 'start Clem's tea', and to decorate the Christmas cake.

As they watched her through the strawberry-wreathed windows, Ryl said, 'Isn't she nice?'

She did not know it, but it was the first time in her life that the phrase had sprung to her lips.

'I'm going to cook dinner tonight,' she announced. 'And it won't be chops, either! It's going to be Chicken Maryland—I hope.'

'And how do you know so much about cookin', all of a sudden?'

'Perry told me what to do.'

'What, that young feller with the taxi? And who told him?'

'Search me.'

She thoughtfully surveyed the picture framed in the window—cattle pastures, river, cane-fields, and the distant sea.

'I've been looking for a name for this dump. I think we'll call it "Geebin". O.K.?'

'Call it anything you like, only don't call me late for dinner. "Geebin", hey? Where did you get hold of that?'

'It's an aboriginal name; it means "bird". Nice and short—and well, it sort of sounds the way this place looks, wouldn't you say?'

92

'Huh. "Bird". After Jones, I suppose?'

'Well, no—with all due respect to him. After the big bird that comes to the pink paddock. You know him? He was here the very first day we woke up in this house. Let's name it for him.'

'Oh, him. The blue crane. Yeah.' Dusty took out his pipe. 'Probably born in this same paddock, that bird was. Probably comes back every year, when he's tired of travelling. Has his bit of a spell here. Refreshes his spirit, as you might say. Probably come back here to end his days, that bird will. Queer creatures. Like to die where they originated. Something in their blood that brings them back.'

'Well, I like him,' said Ryl. 'Or her, as the case may be.'

'They always used to say,' said Dusty, 'that anyone who finds a dog or a cat—once he gives it a name, he'll end up keeping it.'

'So what?'

'So you might be coming to my way of thinking about this place. And then there'll be no more talk of selling it. You see, you don't have to live here, just because we don't let Mr. Herbert sell it. But I may as well live here if I want to.'

'Oh, yes, I suppose you may as well. Anyhow, we've got an address, as from this day: "Geebin, Ridge Road, Bundoora".'

'Sounds like somewhere, doesn't it?' acknowledged Dusty. 'I might even go so far as to paint it on the gate, if it makes you happy.'

'You'd have to mend the gate first. But it might be easier to make a new one. If you do, I'll paint it.'

'All right. You're the painting expert. I'll make a gate, and you can paint it.'

'Beaut. We'll do that after Christmas. Are you sure you can make a gate?'

Dusty was incensed.

'Can I make a gate? Can I—? Love-a-duck, what a question! Didn't I help Clem Bradley line the bathroom? I'll make you as good a gate as you'll ever see!'

'What will you make it out of? Will you buy some timber?'

'No, that I won't! I'll knock down a wall of the old cowshed, and use that. Plenty of useful timber in it.'

Certainly, the paddocks around the cattle-yard and house were full of piles of joists and timber cuttings, pieces of board and wire-netting. Dusty was thinking about it.

93

'There's enough stuff lying about this place to make a good fowl-house. I think I'll do that. We can raise our own eggs.'

'But the gate first.'

Ryl gave him her cat-like smile with the dimple showing.

# XII

Rose Bradley's Christmas turkey was a far cry from Ryl's Chicken Maryland of the night before.

Not that the girl's cooking attempt had been *quite* a hopeless failure—but, as Dusty said, 'It's as near as damnit.'

'It would have been all right'—Ryl had held a post-mortem on the meal—'if I'd remembered to heat the chicken, and not burned up the carrots and potato chips, and if I'd cooked the frozen peas —but how was I to know that they'd not melt for ages? Anyhow, the fried bananas were very successful. I can cook them every day.'

'I've never heard such nonsense as fried bananas!' growled Dusty.

'They were delicious!'

Dusty groaned. 'I'll skin that Perry,' he said. 'Him and those fried bananas!'

But Rose's Christmas dinner made up for everything.

It was eaten on a trestle table under the great Moreton Bay fig-trees at the edge of Clem's lawn that were twins to those at Geebin. Clem's new brick house was not large and would never have contained the eighteen diners whom they managed, without any trouble, to muster. These included two very old aunts, a married daughter with three small children, the married daughter's husband and parents-in-law, Clem's father—who was about Dusty's age and universally known as Butch Bradley—and various other people claiming connexion. This assortment of people seemed to enjoy each other's company with gusto, drawing the new-comers into their circle as though they, too, were part of the country and its life.

The meal was such a major affair that it trailed on well into the afternoon, finally merging into a cold tea. Then for Ryl came her appointment with Glen.

He called for her in his distinguished rattletrap, the red M.G.

95

After consulting Rose Bradley, Ryl had finally decided to wear a dress—a straight one in shining mango pink, that went well with her dark hair. Glen's eyes lit up with pride in her appearance, as he saw her running towards him from the doorway.

For himself, Glen was nothing if not a smart dresser. He affected a man-about-town style, and his mother had been known to complain that most of the contents of her husband's chemist shop were to be found on Glen's bathroom shelf, a Mecca for every new kind of shaving lotion, skin astringent, shampoo, and odd toilet luxury. Glen's face and hair were as highly polished as his blarney.

Still, even to him, Ryl looked something special as he went to meet her.

'Hullo, Ryl there! Boy, are you looking like a dream!'

Ryl was cool and collected in the face of his compliments.

'Thank you, thank you. If you wish to show appreciation don't bother to clap, just fill in a form and forward it with stamped and addressed envelope to above address: Geebin, Ridge Road, Bundoora.'

Glen's voice was gay as he answered, 'How can anyone be so beautiful and yet so loopy?'

They parked the car in a back street of Tweed Heads and, hand in hand, wandered along the main street among the parti-coloured crowd and the harlequin fun-fair, blossoming with gay lights beneath the Norfolk Island pine-trees which lined the river front and curved around the river's estuary towards Point Danger and the Porpoise Pool.

There were girls in shorts, boys with bare feet, mingling with lovely black people of the Islands with their statuesque, Gauguin charm. An old black man stood on the side lines, white-bearded, dressed in a bright blue suit, with a tiny black-and-white bundle in his arms. He smiled benignly, proud of his baby-sitting cares, while the child's young parents hurtled overhead on the ferris wheel, or shot at medicine bottles in the ramshackle shooting gallery of the side-shows. Children were everywhere . . . parents looking for children . . . young people in close-knit couples—the pageant of the people, outwondering and outshining the pageant of the Christmas Fair.

'This place,' said Ryl, 'it just can't be true. It's all done with

96

mirrors, I'm sure.' The warmth and colour excited her. She had a wonderful time.

On Boxing Day, Clem Bradley took Dusty in his car to Cudgen Head on a visit to Butch. Butch lived with his two maiden sisters in a neat old house, in a state of awful hygienic subordination, from which Clem would rescue him from time to time. They usually went fishing.

Perry dropped by to ask Ryl, 'Come down to Rainbow Bay and crack a few waves?'

She stood in the doorway to speak to him.

'Golly, that's a good idea! Rose Bradley's here, making the beds in some terribly technical way with the corners folded in. She says I have to learn to do it. And she's saying that I ought to boil the tea-towel, and criticizing our housekeeping in general. It seems just the very moment to go surfing.'

'She's a bit hard, isn't she, on Boxing Day?'

'Well, it's just luck; she came over to ask us to tea tonight, and when she saw the muddle here she just sort of had canniptions.'

'What are canniptions?'

'Things Rose has when she looks in our house! I'll admit it *is* kind of confusing, but I can't see what's to be done about it. But at least we have beautiful curtains! Do come in and look at my curtains!'

She took him in, and he duly admired the strawberry pattern.

'The place looks great!' he said. 'Apart from a certain kind of surface muddle, as you say. Hullo, Mrs. Bradley.'

'Happy Christmas, Perry. How's Ki?'

'About the same. Ryl's been willing with her paintbrush, hasn't she? Are you going to paint this room, too, Ryl?'

'Oh, I wasn't going to bother. It seems silly if I'm only going to be here for a few months. But now the curtains look so nice, I hate to disappoint them!'

'Yes, they do show up the rest, don't they? That's the trouble, one thing leads to another!'

'I suppose I might paint it. Do you think I should, Rose?'

'It would be a real cosy room with a lick of paint, now that you've got some chairs and curtains!' said Rose. 'It used to look quite nice when I lived here—though in a rough way. We never

97

spent much on it, we were always saving up to build our own home, I'm afraid!'

'But that was natural enough!'

'I think,' said Ryl, 'that the main wall ought to be bleached wood. Because it'd have an attractive grain if it were cleaned up.'

'And how do you bleach wood?'

'I'll find out,' said Ryl gamely. 'I'll bleach it myself, of course!'

'Funny thing,' said Rose, 'the things you'll do, young lady—just as long as they're not regular housework or cooking!'

'What if it turns out a mess?' asked Perry.

'Oh, well—with a house like this you've nothing to lose! After all, it can only change for the better!'

They went to Rainbow Bay in the Bomb, after Rose had bustled off down the high steps laden with a bundle of sheets for her

98

washing-machine, and an injunction to Ryl not to get sunburned.

'So this is Christmas,' mused Ryl. 'Do you know, I'm having the time of my life. Maybe I'll have better times. But this is the best I can remember.'

'That's nice for you.'

'Did you have a lovely day yesterday?'

'Not exactly "lovely", but it was all right. I just stayed home with Ki. He's alone so much you know, and he doesn't have me about very often, not for a whole day at a time. So he appreciated it.'

'Oh. Didn't you go to the beach or anything?'

'Oh, no. I just mooned around and played some records, and read out loud to Ki from the paper—and so on.'

'Wouldn't you have rather gone out, to the dance or somewhere?'

99

'Oh, I don't know. I have to watch the pound notes, you know, and try to keep them together. Even with the scholarship I'm not exactly loaded.'

For some reason Ryl felt a little guilty. She seemed to have so much.

'Never mind, no worries,' said Perry. 'I'll take a night out on New Year's Eve. Will you help me?'

'All right. I'd like to do that.'

The beach was noisy with the same bunch of surf-riders, Glen, Dodi and Red, and another younger boy to stand guard over the 'Surf-boards for Hire' business while Red was in the water. There were others, too, who were now familiar to Ryl. They spent the day lazing beneath the red umbrella, and riding the waves. Ryl was making progress on the surf-board. She and Dodi stayed together, while the boys went farther out. Dodi said she had no wish to be shark-bait and Ryl replied, 'I just couldn't agree more.'

When Perry drove her home along the Ridge Road, the shadows were lengthening. She was rather stiff from her efforts on Red's smallest board, had several bruises, aching knees, the skin off one toe where the board rubbed, and was considerably sunburned.

'You're looking like a real surfie,' said Perry. 'You're quite successful.'

'After this, whenever I see anyone with bruises on their knees and skin off their toes, I'll give them the big salute!'

'And I'll come up for you on New Year's Eve at about seven o'clock.'

'What will we do, though? That's too early to dance or see a movie.'

'Well, we can look in at the skating rink, and have some coffee, and go to the Bongo Room and see if the "instant-artist" chap there will draw a picture of you. We'll be sure to run into other board-men. You'll find we can do plenty. And last thing on New Year's Eve there's always a great rag. Last year we tidied up the main street in Coolangatta, just out of sheer public spirit, you know. We piled all the Holden cars on to a freighter-trailer that was in the street and someone drove it over into Tweed Heads.'

'And did the owners thank you for your trouble?'

'Ah, no, we were like the fairies, we just piled 'em up, and silently stole away; we didn't wait to have them thank us.'

'I'd have liked to have heard you being silent about a thing like that!'

'Oh, yeah, the silence could be heard for miles. In fact, chunks of silence were floating down the river for weeks afterwards.'

'Anyhow, Mack-the-Knife, I have no intention of spending the night in the local lock-up, not when I've just bought a nice new rubber mattress. And to think I took you for a preacher!'

'There, there, keep your hair on! You won't end up in the jug! No one minds. It's just Coolangatta on New Year's Eve. You'll learn.'

Which she did. It turned out as Perry had said. New Year's Eve in Coolangatta was a time when the whole town turned out to share one impromptu party, with dancing in the streets, several bands playing different kinds of jazz at once, streamers and balloons and devil-may-care. Dusty spent it with the Bradleys and old Butch, and various other Bradley relations, Ryl—with Perry, and a lot of people just as crazy.

A time had come of sun and peace and friendship. Ryl was one of a group, for the first time. Perhaps it was that in this warm and feckless place, the youngsters had one thing at least in common, and that was a streak of non-conformity. The beach seemed to touch them all with vagabondage. The beach group were individuals to a man.

One was Tom Hurst, the roving photographer, an especial friend of Red Donovan's. He was, of course, older than Glen, Dodi, and the others, but forgot it on his surf-board. There were two brothers who fished for shark, several girls who owned their own balsa-wood craft, and always, Perry and Glen.

In mid-January, Ryl had the results of her matriculation, as did the other beachcombers. She bought a Melbourne paper every day and at last picked out her own number and school. She had passed in six subjects, three with honours.

Now was a time when the surf-board gang compared notes as they lay on their stomachs on the hot sand below the camping ground. All had passed their exam except Red. Fortunately, he was quite cheerful about it. Perry had indeed won his scholarship. This would enable him to live in Brisbane and study Agricultural

101

Science. One day they discussed their futures, for the hundredth time.

'It's a commerce course for me,' said Glen. 'My old man's got me over a barrel, and I can't get free.'

'Where are you going to live, Glen?'

'Oh, with a dear aunt, so help me. They can't let me out of their sight. The old duck lives at Santa Lucia quite close to the varsity, so there's no getting out of it.'

'I'm going to Brisbane next week to look for lodging,' said Perry. 'I don't have any aunts. Never mind. The world's full of potential ones.'

'Wot, no aunts?' murmured Glen. 'All those great families of Kanakas chivvying each other for standing room in their shacks, and not one of 'em an aunt to old Perry?'

It was said teasingly. But Ryl felt her face flush with anger and embarrassment for Perry, and the silence could be cut with a knife. Perry himself continued to turn a statuesque, closed-eyed face to the sun—a carved face where not a muscle moved. He could have failed to hear. But Ryl knew he had not failed.

Dodi was the one to come to the rescue with easy cheer.

'I've signed on for an arts course. I'm going to board with Rita Hollis in South Brisbane. I bet we have us a ball.'

'Sweetheart, I can't wait to get you down in my address book,' ragged Glen, unabashed.

Tom Hurst, the roving photographer, often joined the group of youngsters and listened indulgently to their wisecracks and chatter. He was there now.

'And what will you do, Amaryllis Jane?' he said. 'With this great intellect of yours? I suppose you'll board with the dean himself, and study nuclear fishin', huh, skinny?'

He flicked Ryl's foot with his camera strap. She kicked out, but gently, and tucked her foot into the sand.

'Will everyone kindly stop badgering me about what I should "do"?' she said.

Red smoothed his towel, and prepared to do a headstand on it.

'Thank the Lord I only know enough to come in out of the wet,' he said. 'I'm going to buy me a real good camera with some of me surf-board hire money, and Tom, here, is going to give me a leg-up in the photography game, aren't you, Tom?'

'That's what I said in a weak moment,' acknowledged Tom.

102

'But you'll never get to be a big society type unless you learn to speak the Queen's English instead of gobbledy-gook.'

'Ah, that's all right, I'll probably be a millionaire before any of yous.' Red was now waving his airborne feet about their ears rather dangerously for his friends. But Red himself could talk his particular gobbledy-gook just as well with either end up. His sister Dodi moved to a safe distance.

'Big deal!' she jeered.

'He might at that,' said Tom. 'He may be illiterate but he's a financial wizard, is our red-hot-headed boy.'

'In other words he's Shylock, the spitting image,' said Dodi.

'Shylock who?' asked the innocent Red. As Dodi pushed sand into the pockets of his shorts he went on dreamily:

'You wait until I've made me pile. I'll give television interviews and all, saying money isn't everything, and how poor people have true happiness.'

'Only if they pay you through the nose to have you do it,' said Dodi. Red ignored her sisterly comments.

'And Ryl is good at putting on that snooty, million-dollar sort of expression, so she can be my model,' he said. 'In fact I might marry her if she turns out good-lookin'.'

'Oh, thanks,' said Ryl. 'You're too generous.'

'Your first proposal, Ryl?' asked Tom. 'You should write it down and get him to sign it with his own X.'

'Why don't you just quietly break his neck, Ryl?' asked Dodi mildly.

Ryl pulled Perry's straw hat over her face. 'I would,' she said, 'only I can't be bothered.'

Later, Perry drove Ryl home, and she sat at his side, strangely quiet and preoccupied.

'What you thinking about?' he asked softly.

It was a moment before she answered.

'Perry,—Glen was rather horrid to you, today, wasn't he? I'm —I'm—thinking about that.'

'Don't,' he advised her. 'I don't. It doesn't pay.' But had she not been too preoccupied to notice, the look he turned on her profile, long and speculative, would have surprised her. It was a probing look, and in it was something strangely curious.

'Perry,' she went on, 'I used to be a frightful snob. I mean—

103

well, I was an intellectual snob, I suppose. I would have treated you—well—badly—when I first met you—if I hadn't quickly found out that you're—it's hard to say it—that you're a gentleman! There! It's said, and doesn't it sound silly? There were a few dark girls at school—girls from Malaya and India—and they were—well—ladies! I never felt snobbish towards them. What I'm trying to say is this—I used to feel superior to any person, black, brown or white—who was stupid, or well, not my equal! But why should Glen be horrid to you, when he knows perfectly well that you are *not* stupid, or in any way his inferior? It makes me mad!'

'He's not usually like that,' said Perry. 'You see, I've had good reason to study this problem. And I've found that folk like Glen are not—"snobby", as you put it—to me, in particular—as long as I don't get in their way. Glen and I have always been the best of friends. So, it seems to me, if old Glen has suddenly decided that I'm more Kanaka than white man, it must be because I'm getting in his way somehow.'

'How would you be getting in his way?'

'Do you suppose,' he suggested gently, 'that it might have anything to do with—well—with you?'

'Me! Why me?' She looked puzzled.

'Well—to be blunt—it could be that he resents the fact that you and I are such good friends.'

'Oh, that's too stupid!' she cried.

Again Perry peered deeply into her face, as he murmured, 'Yes, indeed. And maybe it's even more stupid than *you* think!'

'How do you mean? However can it be that?'

But Perry seemed to have lost interest in the conversation. He pursed his mouth, and began to whistle.

'Perry! Here I'm trying to talk seriously, and you make that noise! Stop it, and talk to me!'

'All right, all right—what do you want me to say?'

'Oh, you are annoying! Tell me—don't you want to hit Glen when he makes those horrid cracks about your colour? Just as if you aren't *both* University students, and *both* Australian! What more does he want!'

Perry exchanged his whistling for a song, in his liquid baritone voice.

104

'Like some ragged owlet With its wings expanded,
Nailed to some garden gate or boardin'
Thus will I by some men All my life be branded,
Never was it true, this side of Jordan.'

Ryl sighed. It was plain that he would not talk any more, so for
the rest of the ride she huddled with her feet tucked under her,
listening to his snatches of song.

March came and it was almost the end of the long summer. A
sense of restlessness, lately dormant, came to invade her spirit.
She knew that soon the careless young people with their spirit of
carousel would be gone from the beach, the birds of summer flown.
All but she. The past days of warmth and companionship would
be as a happy day remembered, and night coming down from the
stars.

Sometimes in the dark, as she lay in her driftwood room beneath
the expensive sheets with their candy-striped borders, with the
warm, wind-moved night all around and the rhinestone coast-
lights showing through her window—then she would weep softly.
They were the tears of her age. Partly of self-pity, partly of confusion.

Dusty painted a nameboard, and hung it on the new gate he had
made from the old timber:

### GEEBIN

Then he went to work on his hen-house. He felt full of importance.

But the long-legged bird was seen no more, and the pink flush
had faded from the sloping pastures, as the new year lengthened.

'Your bird's gone, the dear knows where,' said Dusty to Ryl.
'Maybe south, or out west to the riverlands, the billabongs—the
swamp country. They're tramps, them birds. He'll be back though.
He'll come back next winter to his home paddock.'

105

# XIII

Dusty seemed to grow inches taller, in the light of his new interests. Another cow had calved and he supervised its upbringing carefully. He was all the time industrious, pottering endlessly—helping Clem Bradley to mend fences, learning to drive their neighbour's tractor, picking and packing bananas from the old worked-out patch that stretched down the hill-side towards Perry's lakeside cottage, cutting grass with Clem's power mower. He became a great crony of Butch Bradley's, the old gentleman from Cudgen Head. The two would squat on empty fruit-boxes in the shade of the monsteras smoking their pipes and discussing the weather, the crops, and the fishing. His clothes were a thorn in Ryl's side, and she complained to Rose about them.

'I've tried to tidy him up a bit, goodness knows I've tried! But where can you start? He's such a funny shape, nothing fits him! Apart from the fit he throws if you try to get him into something respectable! I've tried to buy him neat shirts. But if they're big enough to meet across his tummy, he doesn't need any pants, because they come down to his toes, anyway!'

'Oh, well,' smiled Rose, 'he looks sort of comfortable the way he is.'

'He won't wear shoes! He insists on boots, all the time! He loves that pair of scruffy desert boots that Clem gave him, because he thought they were worn out! I do believe he's terrified of anything new!'

'Anyhow, he's an old honey,' said Rose. 'It doesn't matter two hoots what he wears, we still think he's an old honey.'

Ryl thought about this as she returned to Geebin, across the cow pastures. It seemed that everyone liked Dusty. They all conceived a fondness for him, and took it for granted that she did, too. 'Am I fond of him?' she asked herself. 'Yes, I suppose I am really. Is he a honey? M—m—m, yes, I expect he is!'

106

It was in this way that a mystery was revealed to Ryl. Walking across the cow pastures on a still, autumn evening, it came to her. Her bare arms had lost their city pallor and turned brown. The skin was peeling a little across the bridge of her nose. That was how she looked on the gentle evening when she saw her first revelation of love.

She saw life, that evening, as a bowl to fill. She saw again in her mind a picture of a Roman water-clock in a book she had studied at school. It was a clock comprised of two vessels, one stone chalice slowly emptying into its fellow, only to turn on its own weight, and repeat its task into infinity. She, young and empty of emotion and experience, could be replenished, and in turn replenishing. She thought of the life force, the grace, which flowed like the clear water of the clock of antiquity, from vessel to vessel. And she saw as her giver and receiver of grace this odd, tubby little man who was her grandfather.

Coming to the stock-yard slip-rails, damp and streaming with a smell of mud and new milk, she was in time to encounter the two cows which were now in Dusty's care, as they stumbled from the captivity of the milking bail. Dusty emerged from behind them with his full bucket. She took hold of one side of the handle and fell into step with him as best she could.

'Dusty,' she said, strangely shy, yet full of her revelation. 'Dusty—gee, I'm glad you're here. Are you—are you glad I'm here?'

He gave a time-blurred version of her own slanting look.

Suddenly he too felt in the long-arid and empty chalice of his heart a welling of some force which he had long since fancied gone.

'Ah,' he said. 'I reckon I am.'

To any stranger, watching the slow-moving figures from the edge of the monstera jungle, they would have looked as always— a tall, reed-like girl, a stumpy old man, and an awkwardly-held milk bucket. But Ryl knew that this was not so. They were a work of great art, a rare treasure, a Roman water-clock. A pair of balanced vessels, complementary and in unison with each other.

That night they sat at the top of the tall steps, watching the purple skyline that was aglow with lights, red, green, gold and amber, stretching in a half-circle about them from Brunswick Heads to Surfer's Paradise.

'It's that pretty,' said Dusty, 'better than any picture show, Technicolor or no Technicolor. And not all spoiled and cluttered up with actors, either.'

Ryl laughed and took his arm.

'And no sign telling you not to smoke,' she said.

'Funny,' said Dusty, 'how much you look like my girl that I had once. She'd have been your aunt, of course. Queer to think of her that way. Just as queer as if you were someone's aunt. And there's nothing aunt-like about you, is there?'

'Certainly not,' said Ryl. 'I couldn't feel less like an aunt. And was she the one called Ryl? Same as me?'

'That's right. Fancy, your father must have named you after her.'

'Actually,' said Ryl, 'I can't be said to have ever known either of them—aunt or father. You tell me.'

108

Dusty took out his pipe.

'There was only the two of them,' he said. 'My daughter 'Ryllis was a lot younger than Robert. She was killed in a road accident when she was only eighteen.'

Ryl sighed to show her sympathy. She could not feel anything but remote to this loss. She could think of no words.

'Then,' went on the old fellow, 'her mother died the year after that. There was just Robert and me left, out of the four of us. Robert was in the forestry work. The land was in his blood, I suppose. He never had any hankering for an office job. He was a smart boy.'

'But didn't you have any other relations? Look at the Bradleys. They seem to be like rabbits. Relations everywhere. And Dodi and Red—they have relations. And Glen—he has relations. Didn't you have some too, at some stage?'

'Well, your grandmother was an only child. Her people all went a long time ago. I had a brother and a couple of cousins. But they're gone before, as they say. It's just a freak of nature, I reckon—that we don't have any relations.' He puffed at his pipe, and bit on the stem. 'Good thing, too,' he said. 'Nothing causes more trouble than a lot of relations.'

'But then,' probed Ryl, 'what about my mother?'

'No relations there,' said Dusty shortly.

'Well, how come you lost track of my father?'

Dusty seemed to shift uncomfortably on the wooden step.

'Him and me fell out,' he said. 'Matter of fact we never did get on well. He was a wild young devil—no disrespect, of course, to them departed. But he was a wild young devil, just the same. Him and me never did see eye to eye.'

'When did you last see him?'

'Must have been just before he bought this place. But we'd— had words by then. So I never heard any more of him.'

Ryl longed to know why the two had quarrelled, but it was plain that Dusty had no intention of going into this problem. He talked on, steering clear of his quarrel with his son, but throwing light on the years that followed. Of how he had fallen on hard times, and how all friends and distant kith and kin had dropped out of his life. 'When you get to my age,' he said, 'your friends don't seem to last like they did. They drop off, one by one.'

Yesterday she would have listened to the story and heard only

109

the words, and those with impatience. But this evening her mind made pictures of them. And she saw them blending into one picture, the one which the old man tried to conceal—of a life whose end was failure. It came to her that Dusty was one who could look back and say, 'What have I to show for my journeyings?'

And the answer would be: 'Nothing.'

And now the banner that Perry had divined in her cold heart, her banner began to fly, raising its sign of errantry. Here was a windmill for her tilting lance. Dusty.

She would make him a success. Better late than never. At the age of seventy-four he would, under her guidance, be set on the road to achievement.

Sitting beside him on the worn wooden step in the lime-scented night, Ryl made up her mind about it, and became filled with resolve. Dusty would make good.

# XIV

After 'the evening of the Roman water-clock' (for so she remembered it), Ryl's solitary hours of the mind were too busy for brooding and tears. Now she thought and planned.

And at last she could do so. After years, some mental block had been removed and she could find pleasure in the future and the building of dreams.

Only—and perhaps this was the secret of the change—she did not see it as simply her own future. It was Dusty's, too. Now at night she would lie in the dark hatching industrious schemes, discarding and reconstructing them, so that the time until sleep overtook her was hardly long enough. . . .

'First'—she thought on such a night—'first there's this dump. I'll just have to stay here with Dusty, for a while at least. So I really will have to get Rose Bradley to show me how to be tidy and to do housework the way she does. I can paint a house, but I don't seem very good at keeping it tidy. The place always looks sort of peculiar. I know—for a start, I can hammer some nails in the walls, and hang things on them. Yes, that's a good idea. Now I think of it, Rose's house doesn't have heaps of clothes on the floor. And it's a nuisance having my wet towel always mixed up with my nice burnt-orange slacks—and finding shoes in my bed, and stuff like that. What a good idea.'

But her plans ranged far beyond simple housework. For these had to be plans for Dusty. And Dusty and the farm went together. Now, Perry knew all about farming; anyhow, he was doing agricultural science. And he'd said once that he was keen on farming. Didn't he want to grow record sugar crops or something? And he lived just down the hill. So Perry would be useful. The thought of Perry made Ryl feel very confident. Somehow, she felt that, with Perry on the job, anything would be possible. . . .

.    .    .    .

111

She sought out Perry, one evening after he had finished packing for his move to Brisbane, and the University. They strolled out to the lake-side, in front of his cottage, and she laid her plans before him.

'So,' she concluded, 'will you help me, Perry? You'll be coming home from Brisbane at week-ends, won't you? Will you show Dusty and me what needs to be done—and maybe help us to do it?'

Perry was again studying her face covertly, in the last of the daylight.

'You've come quite a way, young Ryl!' he murmured. 'Quite a way!'

'Will you help, or will you just confine yourself to shaking your head like an ancient sage, and—'

'I'll help. Say, 'Ryllis.'

'What?'

'Did you tell me once that your father stayed up here once? That he was posted here with the Army during the war?'

'So I believe. Why, all of a sudden?'

'And you never saw your mother?'

'True, true—and why the cross-examination?'

'Oh—just wondering,' said Perry. He stood up. 'Well, good night. I suppose you know that I drove that taxi for the last time, until two o'clock this morning? And that I have to leave at five in the morning, in order to get to that University in time for the registrar? Owing to the fact that I haven't taken time off to do so, and I don't want to be thrown out of the place before I've even started? So—as I was hinting—'

'As you were hinting, it's time I went home and let you get some sleep! All right, I know when I've worn out my welcome!' She stood up, laughing.

'I'll walk you home, through the bananas,' said Perry.

'You won't at all! I've been thrown out! I'll walk myself home!'

'But you're my buddy, of course! And we're going to farm like anything, aren't we? May I have the pleasure of throwing you out next week-end, too?'

'Yes, yes—unless you come up to Geebin, and then I can throw you out first!' They parted in high spirits. . . .

.        .        .        .

112

By the end of March her beach friends had drifted about their business. The rainy season, pleasingly delayed this year, came at last to disperse the tents and caravans on the camping ground, like laundry hastily gathered in at the first coming shower.

For a few weeks, Ryl prowled about the pastures and rode the Palomino over the river flats near the cattle dip, or took herself for shopping trips to Coolangatta on the blue bus. But she missed the others. It was high time to exchange plans for action. She brought home hooks and screws and a cabinet for the bathroom, a towel rail, brackets for a shelf over the stove. She became expert at hammering nails into the walls and soon made a game of hanging up everything not attached to the floor. She reduced the old house to a state of incredible tidiness, second only to Butch Bradley's home with his elderly sisters.

Then she bought large pots of paint, pushed all the furniture into strange places, and began to paint the living-room. It took her a remarkably short time to turn order into chaos.

Rose came in mid-afternoon. The yellow door stood half open in the sticky heat to catch the breeze from the mountains.

'Yoo-hoo, love! Can I come in?' called Rose.

'Hi! Of course you can!'

Rose sidled through the door with an awkward burden.

'I've got a cup of tea here for you, and a nice hot biscuit.'

She elbowed her way to the coffee table, pushed some magazines and a cushion and ashtray from it, and set down her tea-pot and plate.

'Come on down from up there,' she ordered.

Ryl was standing on a banana-case balanced on the kitchen table, while she painted the ceiling. Her black hair was tied on top of her head with a shoe-string, so that she looked as though she had a handle. She still wore Clem Bradley's shirt, which completely covered her own shorts. The shirt, as she had remarked after painting the kitchen, was 'hardly worth giving back'. But it seemed to Rose that she almost lived in it.

'Come and drink the tea while it's hot,' said Rose, bringing cups from the kitchen. 'I said to myself, I said, "I know that child won't stop for a tea-break if someone doesn't make her". I know you. Once you start painting you're like a bulldozer.'

From the banana-case castle, Ryl could just reach the ceiling with her brush. She was painting it lemon yellow, with wide,

113

white borders. The inner wall of boards she had sandpapered with great effort, and then bleached with white lead, rubbing it into the texture of the timber. She planned to cover the end wall with yellow striped wallpaper. She flexed her arms and climbed down to the floor.

'Gosh, you do bully me, but I love you just the same, Rose sweet!' She took the proffered tea-cup and a gingernut, hot from the oven. 'You're always doing something nice for Dusty and me.'

'Ah, nonsense, we like your company. Where's Dusty? It's a wonder he doesn't want a finger in the pie.'

'He's gone with the Mur'bah carrier out to Cudgen Head. He was going to see if Grandpa Butch Bradley would go fishing with him.'

'Oh, well, that explains it.' Rose nodded. Her father-in-law had become Dusty's boon companion.

'Mind you,' said Ryl, 'he didn't know I was going to do this today, or I don't suppose he'd have gone. I really wanted him out of the way. He's not built for standing on tables.'

She sipped her tea and became expansive. 'Do you know what I've been thinking?'

'Not until you tell me.'

'Well, you know Dusty's mad about this place. So I've been thinking I'd better stay here for twelve months. Just to help him get organized.'

'In other words, until you can organize him?'

Ryl pulled a face and went on. 'And,' she said, 'I'm going to write to the Agricultural School at Brisbane Uni., and ask them to send me some literature about soil, and so on. Perry's going to help me.'

'And what exactly for?'

'Because you know how the soil here *looks* marvellous—all rich and red—but it's just worked out? The cows never get fat on the grass, the bananas just get smaller and smaller?'

Rose nodded. 'It's just worked out,' she said. 'When Clem and I parted company with it we knew it needed to have a lot of money spent on the soil. But of course your father—no offence, love—at the time he owned the place, and he just wouldn't have anything done.'

'Well,' said Ryl, 'I'll spend money on it. Perry says it needs trace elements.'

114

'So it does,' said Rose. 'Plenty.'

'Then it shall have them, bless it. And what's more, I'm going to talk Dusty into making a brand-new banana patch, and turning the cows on to the old one. The little calves will be quite good when they grow up. And they're the apple of his eye, of course. He might even buy some more stock and work up a small dairy herd if he can make the grass richer. And Perry will find out how to do that. And we could hire your tractor. Everything business-like, mind. And we could plough up that bottom paddock—the one by the river—or at least part of it. Plough up that coarse elephant-grass that's no good for cattle feed and plant a better kind. Perry says parra-grass and subterranean clover will take over, and make good cattle food. And everything we make out of the cattle can go back into the soil.'

'My!' Rose stared at her, open mouthed. 'Listen to you! Of all people to be talking sense!'

'Oh yes, wouldn't it?' laughed Ryl. 'I'm making like a farmer!'

'And when you "make like" anything, nothing stops you, not flood, fire, or famine; I've learned that much. Here, have another biscuit!'

Ryl took one.

'The old bananas,' said Rose, 'would probably be all right for the cattle. They'd fatten them up, anyhow. And the bananas don't sell well, and the market's poor anyhow, at the moment.'

'So isn't it exciting?'

'And after twelve months,' said Rose, 'what then?'

'Oh, I'm not sure. Haven't I thought hard enough, without going even farther ahead?'

She looked at the wall she had bleached with such labour. 'But I have had a sort of an idea,' she said. 'If I must do some-thing, maybe I'll go to Uni., and learn interior decorating.'

'It seems to me that would be right up your alley.'

'Then there's architecture,' said Ryl. 'But that would be so like hard work.'

'Oh, not for a smart girl like you.'

'I really will need a car,' said Ryl thoughtfully. 'Perry could teach me to drive. If I ever go to Brisbane Uni. I would need a car, so that I could come home at weeks-ends, and see that Dusty was all right.'

'I suppose you could.' Rose felt half-amused, half touched, at the weighty expression on Ryl's face. 'I notice you've had plenty of advice from Perry.'

'He's so knowledgeable. And seeing he lives so close, why his land touches ours. And he's doing agricultural science! So!'

'All right enough at that.'

'You know old Ki,' said Ryl. 'Sometimes he likes someone to talk to. When he does talk, he knows all sorts of things about this district, and about growing things! He's not so stupid. I talk to him sometimes. But most of the time he's in a kind of dream.'

'Ki has been quite a man in his time,' said Rose.

'Last night, Dusty and I went down and stayed with him for a while until Perry got back from Brisbane. Dusty really enjoyed it. He talked to Ki about the old cane-fields, in the days of the bullock teams. Ki did enjoy himself.'

'Yes,' agreed Rose. 'He would have. Oh yes, you get the odd Islander who has the will to make good, and the brains.'

'And some white people are like that, too,' said Ryl.

Rose went on, 'But most of the Islanders are shiftless. They herd together in their villages, living like wasps in a nest, with no sense of responsibility, and no hygiene. They make good money these days. But they drink the lot, or put it on the dogs, or on their backs. The black girls are better dressed than the whites, as often as not. But whether they've had a bath first, before putting on their finery—well, you wouldn't want to bet on that.'

'So I've heard,' said Ryl. 'But I suppose you can't blame them for having a chip on their shoulder, and sticking together as they do, and sort of feeling that no kind of effort's worthwhile.'

She was remembering Glen's jibes at Perry on the beach. 'Funny,' she said, 'how Ki and Perry seem to be quite on their own.'

Rose changed the subject.

'I saw a white cat in your garden under the montys, as I came through. Did you know you had a cat?'

'Oh yes, he's Perry's. He comes here when Perry's in Brisbane, sometimes, just for a visit. He's a pretty cat, isn't he?' She stood up. 'Well, I'd better press bravely on. Gee, that cup of tea was good.'

'You've certainly got a mess on your hands.' Rose looked around at the pots of paint, the rolls of wallpaper heaped in a corner of the room. 'You're a trick, you are. You always look either like a princess or a hobo, never anything in between.'

116

Ryl climbed on to her castle of banana-crate and table.

'Oh yes, I'm just a mud-pie sort of person really. A bit of an Islander!'

Rose gathered up the tray and turned to the door.

'There's rain coming in on the wind,' she called over her shoulder.

Ryl bent her head a little, so that she could look out the window. She saw a veil over the greying sea.

'There is, too. I can see why they call this "the rainy season".'

'When it starts it makes no bones about it!'

'It's time Dusty came home, unless he wants to be soaked to the skin. I'm going to indoctrinate him about modern farming while he cooks his fish.'

'Can't you cook fish yet, you naughty girl?'

'Well, what would be the use, it would only taste like paint!'

Rose went off to her own house across the cow pastures.

. . .

Ryl hurried to finish painting the ceiling before Dusty's return. She was thinking about Ki and Perry. She had come to this district full of snobbery and prejudice. But she had been forced to see that Perry at least was the superior of many a white boy. She wondered why Ki had been so deserted by his fellow dark people. They were so clannish, as a rule. And he was the oldest of them all, the only one who could remember his first home across the Pacific. Why did the dark people not make much of him, and crowd about him? Was it because of Perry? Had the old man deliberately broken his ties of blood for the sake of his great-grandson? Was his ambition for the boy the knife that had severed the bonds of blood, usually so strong among the Islanders?

The more she thought about it, the more Ryl became convinced that this must be so. She felt a respect for the silent, sick old black man. How at times he must long for the normal noisy confusion of the villages of the dark people. Their homes were always bursting with folk of every age, each doing exactly as he liked, never a care for the future, or of what they should 'do'. Ki's ambition for Perry must have been great indeed, for him to cut himself adrift from this way of life. But, thought Ryl, he would be so proud of Perry. She was sure he felt any sacrifice worthwhile.

# XV

By a happy chance, that afternoon Dusty was discussing Ryl's future with his friend Butch Bradley, at the very time when she was confiding her plans to Rose.

This Border coast, where sub-tropical Queensland merges into temperate New South Wales, is saw-toothed with basalt headlands, pushing through the alluvium of the river plains and sandy wastes flung up by the Pacific Ocean. The dark rock is often split into cubes and geometric shapes by the constant battering of the ocean, sometimes forming precipitous cliff faces, sometimes tumbling like great mounds of lump-sugar into the path of the green combers.

Tourists and holidaymakers in the area of Cudgen Head that afternoon may well have been uneasy at the sight of two stumpy figures seated precariously half-way down such a rocky landfall. From shorewards they presented a pair of broad backs, shoulders rounded, and clad in fusty sweaters against the wind from the sea. The broad well-padded figures seemed to teeter on the sharp-edged boulders, the swirling surf breaking with wicked fury far below. If one old-timer had slipped from his wobbly perch the world would have found itself one old-timer short, or possibly two, for that surf would never have relinquished him. It was as well that neither Ryl nor Rose was there to endure the suspense of it.

But more by good luck than good management, the boulders did not slip beneath their feet, or broad posteriors, and yet another day was safely passed by Dusty and Butch in their pastime of rock fishing. The sea wind blew into their faces, deepening the wrinkles and the leathery tan, their rods hung in their hands as they talked of everything under the sun, and watched the foam sucking back among the basalt sugar-lumps and into the sea's maw.

'She's a girl,' Dusty was saying, 'who has the head for anything. She's that quick, there's nothing she couldn't do if she set her mind to it.'

'Can she cook?' asked Butch. Dusty ignored the question.

'A lot like that in my family. Very intelligent. They can turn their hands to anything.'

'Can she cook?'

'You never think of nothin',' said Dusty, 'but your stomach.'

'This time of year,' said Butch, 'you often see a whale spout. Ever see a whale spout?'

'I reckon,' continued Dusty, 'if I could get her interested in the farm, now—keep her busy on it for, say, twelve months—well, by that time she'd be more mature. She'd have made up her mind about her future.'

'Ah,' said Butch. 'And sometimes you see a waterspout, in the cyclone season.'

'All her mates seem to be going to the University in Brisbane. She's young yet, of course. But next year I'd like to see her go and study there. She could knock spots off all them others.'

'Reckon your line's snagged,' said Butch.

'Snagged be blowed. Just you take care of your own line, I'll see to mine. I'd like to see her with a good calling, when she's got the intelligence and all.'

'She could learn typing,' suggested Butch. Dusty let this go over his head.

'I like to see her with her mates,' he said. 'That's if they're the right kind. It might ha' bin the trouble with my boy, her father that was. P'raps I was too strict on him when he was a kid. And then he went wild. Wouldn't want it to happen to Ryl.'

'Far too much freedom, these modern kids have,' said Butch.

'D'you mean to say you can't win with 'em?'

'She sees too much of that coloured boy,' mumbled Butch.

'What coloured boy?'

'That Perry Davis.'

'Oh, Perry. You call him coloured?'

'Well—isn't he?'

'Ah—I'd say only slightly tinted, not exactly coloured.'

'He's coloured.'

'He's a good boy, that Perry; he's a real white man, no matter about his colour. I see what you mean, of course. Ryl's got too much class to be making friends with everyone she meets.' He looked at Butch from the corners of his eyes. There was something slightly wary in his manner, all of a sudden.

120

After a moment he asked, 'My son Robert was in this district, of course, when he bought Geebin. Did you ever happen to meet him at all?'

Butch's gaze—and attention—were fixed on his line.

'Believe I did, now I think back on it. Yes, that's right. I believe I did. But it was a long time ago, now.'

'Did—did you happen to meet his wife at all?'

'Well, now—I don't believe I did. I wonder why that was. I remember him and Clem talking business together. Clem wanted to try his hand at running a farm, but I was never able to back him up with the money it would have taken to buy one of his own. So that's how he came to go in with your boy. Mind, he'd have never got as far as a place of his own if he hadn't worked at two jobs most of the years. He looked after your son's place, and took on other work as well. He's been a good worker, has Clem.'

'Yes, too true—but the thing is, you never did meet Robert's wife, when all was said and done?'

'Matter of fact, I never thought about him having a wife. Didn't know he was married. Mind, at that time, what with the war and chaps here from all over the country, things was a bit confusing. Lots of the army men were married on the quiet, like, and they didn't even let on.'

'That's right,' said Dusty. 'Hey! I believe I've caught something!'

Dusty's line jerked, and he swayed on the slippery rocks. Had Ryl been there she would have shut her eyes, rather than watch the old gentleman teetering at the edge of the swelling surf. All conversation went by the board. Butch was just as eager as the lucky fisherman with the excitement of the moment.

It did not occur to Butch until months later that that fish had interrupted a conversation which would never occur again. That Dusty was talking about his son, for the first and only time. Dusty played his fish, assisted by terse advice from Butch until he, too, felt a sudden jerk to his line, assuring success. By the time that each fisherman wound in his prize in the form of a good-sized cod, the sun had gone from the water.

Whitecaps were gathering on the expanse of the ocean that turned from blue to dull green and then to grey. Two lonely prawning vessels bravely crossed the river bar below Point Danger on the high tide, and drew out their wake in the direction of the fishing grounds off Brunswick Heads. The sky had slyly become overcast while their attention was engaged, and now Butch made the same observation that his daughter-in-law was about to pronounce from the doorway of Geebin.

'There's rain coming in from the sea.'

'We'd better make tracks,' said Dusty.

As he toiled up the rocky headland encumbered with rod and basket, he wheezed—

'Know something? I'm a younger man than the one that left Melbourne last November.'

They paused to catch their breath, then went slowly on.

'All crippled up with rheumatism, I was,' said Dusty. 'Reckon in this climate a bloke could last for ever.'

They stood on the crest of the headland, looking at the grey curtain of rain drawing across the water and shutting off the distance.

'Even when it rains it's still warm,' said Dusty. 'A bloke could

122

last for ever.' He added, 'Only old Ki don't seem to be pulling it off. He looks bad lately.'

'He don't want to pull it off,' said Butch. 'He'll be glad to go, God rest him. All his old Island mates long gone. Nothing to keep him.'

'Ah,' Dusty turned his back to the wind and hunched his shoulders. 'I might go down and sit with him for a while tomorrow.'

'Might help you do it, if I can get a lift in,' said Butch.

A horn tooted loudly. It was to draw Dusty's attention to Mr. Biggs, the Murwillumbah carrier, with his truck. It was parked at the cluster of shops below the sandy roadway. The driver had seen their figures, tiny against the skyline, and felt that his hitchhiking passenger could be hurried a little. He had become used to dropping the elderly fisherman on his way out, before lunch, then picking him up on his return journey.

The pair stumped forward, pleased with themselves and their catch. . . .

By the time Dusty arrived home, the rain had caught up with the carrier's truck and was splattering against the windshield. Mr. Biggs pulled up on the Ridge Road for Dusty to get down. He picked up his basket, which he had put between his feet on the cabin floor, and the rod which he had rested on the tray of the truck, along with a score of empty grocery boxes and a great tangle of rope.

'You better get inside before you get wet, Mr. Merewether.'

'I'll do that. Thanks for the ride.'

'Don't mention it. Always enjoy your company, Mr. Merewether.'

'Feeling's mutual. So long then.'

The old fellow walked through the wet grass and pushed open the door, which Ryl had closed when the rain started. She had switched on the lights and was still on her make-shift ladder, painting the last, far corner of the ceiling. She glanced brightly down as he came in, brushing a dark strand of hair back from her forehead, and so adding a smudge of paint.

'Oh, hullo! Got a fish?'

He pursed his lips and stood taking in her handiwork.

'So this is what you've been up to, huh?'

123

'Isn't it going to be nice? Don't step in the paint.'

'It was all right before. You've always got to be changing things.'

'That's progress.'

'Ah, be blowed! Always must be mucking about with paint and stuff.'

'Ah, stop your growling.' She smiled down at him.

Vanquished, he still muttered, 'Never happy unless she's spending money with a shovel and spade.'

'I'm just going to finish this bit, and you could be a honey and start picking up the newspapers off the floor.'

'I've got to clean me fish.' Dusty brightened. 'A great whopping cod. What a feed on him!'

He picked up his basket and stumped through to the kitchen. Now the rain was pelting against the window. The view of mountains had been erased by heavy cloud, and from the west, Ryl could see no farther than the cow pastures, and that dimly. The two cows and their calves stood in the shelter of the fig-trees, patiently waiting for Dusty with his bucket and the usual handful of green bananas, which they ate with relish.

Seeing them there, he put on two gunny sacks by way of a raincoat, one over his head like a hood, the other wrapped around his shoulders, and went out to attend to them. The air was wet and warm and he found it quite pleasant to splash through the long grass in the narrow world of rain.

When he came back, Ryl's ceiling was finished, and she was herself picking up the layer of newspaper which she had laid to protect the floor from splashes. Dusty dealt with his fish as she restored the living-room to a modicum of tidiness. Soon there was a gay sound of frying in the kitchen to join the noisy clamour of the rain outside. Ryl put a record on her portable radiogram, recently bought despite much protest from Dusty. In the stormy, gathering darkness the little house seemed a bright, friendly haven.

She moved about the room, talking above the sound of her record, unfolding to Dusty her ideas about farming.

'Perry knows a black boy who'll work for us, and plant out a new banana stand,' she said. 'He lives at Chindera—his name's King Cotton; don't ask me why. Perry will bring him up on Sunday if you think it's a good idea. He could start working quite

124

soon. The ground would have to be prepared and so on, even though they don't plant bananas out until early spring.'

'Where you planning to get your new banana roots from?' asked Dusty. 'Got ideas about that, too?'

'Yes, I certainly have! And it's not "roots"—it's "corms" or "spears",' she corrected him. 'I don't know yet where they're to come from, but we can work on that.'

She swept up a small heap of dust and bent down to brush it into the dustpan. 'It's for you, you know. It's to be your banana patch! And *please* don't fry fish and smoke your smelly old pipe at the same time!'

'It's me new pipe. You've got a grudge against it.'

'I haven't—I just hate smoking, that's all, and pipes in particular. None of the surfies smoke! It's square! And anyhow, I'm allergic to it!'

'In other words, you've got a grudge against me new pipe.'

'And as well as being unreasonable, *don't* burn a hole in your pocket with it! Didn't Clem say you could buy banana spears or corms or whatnot from some place up in the mountains?'

'He could have. I'll ask him about it.'

They sat down to their fish, Ryl remarking, 'We won't have another fish meal for a while if this wind and rain keep up. Unless you catch some silly old mullet in the river. The fishing-boats won't be able to go out.'

'That's right. The wet season's a chancy time for the fishermen. We'd better enjoy our bit of fish while we can.'

The wind blew harder as the night advanced. At bedtime Ryl insisted on tucking the new, striped blankets on Dusty's bed, and covering her own with her mohair rug. It was pleasant to lie snug and warm, feeling the old house quiver in the teeth of the storm, listening to a booming like distant cannon fire from the sea. At times it felt as though the house were being lifted bodily from its foundations by great gusts of wind.

But with sunrise the wind dropped, the rain cleared from sea and mountain. From her window she looked over the dripping garden, heavy with the scent of wild lemon flowers, and beyond, the bright-washed pastures. There once more, standing contemplative and sober among the rain-lit grass, was the blue crane.

125

# XVI

One week-end in April, when all the surf-riders were home, they met at Geebin for a working-bee.

Ryl had already come to an agreement with Dusty, concerning the project she had in mind. They were to cut a doorway in the kitchen wall, close to the sink and stove. By it, the inmates of Geebin would have egress to the grass under the jacaranda-tree near the snake-pit. Here, on a comparatively level patch of ground, Ryl proposed to make a barbecue, with various rusty plough discs and nameless bits of scrap-iron which littered the paddock near the cowsheds.

They came in Perry's Bomb—Red and Dodi, Glen, and Perry himself. Glen alone was dressed in stylish sports clothes; the others wore their oldest things and carried hammers, nail bags, and other purposeful tools. Perry took charge of operations. He assured them that he was born to the carpentry trade and capable of wonders. Glen and Dusty were more or less spectators, Dusty mumbling darkly, Glen prepared to be entertained.

'I will be invaluable, you'll find,' he told the others. 'I also have a very straight eye. I'll tell you when you get it all out of plumb. Also I don't at all mind passing things. I know the difference between a saw and a chisel, more than can be said for the others, I'll bet.'

'I know a chisel,' said Dodi. 'It's that deadly weapon that Dad cut the top off his finger with last year.'

'But we haven't one, so you needn't pass it,' said Perry. He drew a chalk mark on the wall. 'That looks about the right place to start cutting, don't you reckon?'

'I can't bear to watch you,' groaned Dusty. 'I'll go over to the Bradleys and see if they've got a cup of coffee to spare.'

He stumped off.

'What a beaut. thing this is,' said Red. 'To have a house that you can just cut bits out of or add bits on to whenever you feel creative.'

126

Glen agreed wholeheartedly. 'I wish I lived in a house like this,' he said enviously. 'The Dad's place cost him thirteen thousand or something, and he won't even let anyone hang up a darts-board in it. Not even in the garage.'

'This dump has its advantages,' said Ryl. 'Except when it rains like mad and the roof leaks. Mr. Bradley climbed up and took a peek at it and he says it's like the Irishman's gun—it needs a new lock, stock, and barrel. But apart from that it's all right.'

'So what do you do when it rains?' asked Dodi.

'For the present, I stand the pot plants under the leaks. It saves taking them outside or trailing about with a watering-can. Did you see my pot plants?'

'Yes,' Dodi told her. 'What are they? I can tell that one's an African violet. And then you've got a thing with red leaves and whiskers and a thing with stiff leaves and a thing with no leaves—'

'Oh, is that an African violet?' Ryl was delighted. 'I didn't know what it was—and I just said to Mrs. Turner-in-the-Terranora-shop that I'd have *this* and *this* and *this*! *You* know! Fancy it being an African violet!'

'So you don't know what any of them are?'

'No, not a one. But who cares? They do to put under the leaks in the roof.'

'How true. And are you ever going to have it mended?'

'Oh, I don't know. Dusty says the rainy season's nearly over, so why worry.'

'Would you mind?' asked Perry, coming up behind them with a key-hole saw. 'If you stand there, you might have this doorway cut straight under your left shoulder-blade.'

The girls moved hurriedly.

'Wouldn't it be funny,' said Red, 'if the whole place collapsed when old Perry takes the chunk out of the wall?'

Ryl withered him with a look.

'Sort of thing that would amuse you, anyway.'

But Perry soon had them organized—even to Glen, who was given the important job of leaning against the outside of the kitchen, and so helping to shore it up. When the gaping cavity was at last revealed, Dodi discovered a baby possum in the aperture. She and Ryl cooed over it tenderly, until Perry took it from them and kept it in his pocket, 'before it's killed with kindness' as he said.

127

At midday, the girls erected the plough-disc barbecue, and prepared to christen it with several pounds of rump steak.

'The logical thing to call this barbecue,' said Dodi, 'is the Hole in the Wall. We'll be able to have parties at the Hole in the Wall—that's with your permission of course, Ryl.'

'Oh, don't mind me,' said Ryl. 'It's a group project.'

Glen called from the bathroom. 'Hey, Ryl—I'm only trying to wash my hands. Tell me, or is it a secret—how do you make water come out of the tap?'

Ryl stood in the doorway.

'If you want hot water, you turn on the taps over the sink and the bath, and then it comes out in the washbowl. If you only want cold water you just turn it on over the sink.'

He stared at her incredulously. 'And what genius worked that out?'

She shrugged. 'It's just one of nature's wonders, I guess! The electrician who put in the water heater connected up the water as well, just as a special favour. He did say he wasn't a plumber—oh, well, you get used to it.'

By this time the boys had nailed architraves around their Hole in the Wall, so that it looked quite like a doorway, though slightly rakish. They viewed it with pride.

'Your eye wasn't all that straight, Glen baby,' Red commented. 'It's so crazy in fact, how do you think we're ever going to persuade the door to shut?'

'Don't blame me!' cried Glen. 'It must have been the plumb-line, or maybe the spirit level had the wrong sort of spirit in it. Anyhow you can easily plane a bit off the top of the door—and the side—and maybe the bottom.'

'Why not,' asked Red, 'just bend the door?'

Dodi chewed her lip. 'When Dusty comes back, you know what he's going to say? He's going to say we've done the house no good.'

But Ryl was quite satisfied. 'Oh, it's all right,' she said. 'I think we've all been very clever. I'll paint it, and it won't look so bad.'

'If a flying saucer were to land in the pink paddock,' said Dodi, 'Ryl's first thought would be to paint it.'

'I have a talent,' explained Ryl loftily.

It was a happy week-end of working with the surf-riders,

128

talking nonsense together under the trees, sharing in the construction of Ryl's Hole in the Wall.

Dusty returned in time to milk the two cows, and feed his six hens. He had sheltered with the Bradleys from the teenagers for the whole of Sunday. Dodi cooked tea and they all ate it wandering about the living-room and kitchen. The menu consisted of thick toasted sandwiches, milk-shakes and slices of pineapple. Later, the boys drove away in the Bomb, but Dodi stopped for the night, sleeping on Ryl's old mattress on the floor. She assured Ryl that it was just the kind of bed that she liked.

'It's very healthful to lie on something flat and hard,' she said. 'I'm learning yoga at Uni., and we always lie on the floor. The teacher tells us that it's the most comfortable position there is, the most relaxing in the world.'

But next morning when Ryl said, 'Well, was the floor terribly relaxing?' Dodi replied:

'Just between you and me, it was something horrible.'

'Next time you can have the bed and I'll have the healthful, relaxing, world's-most-comfortable-position, just to keep us square.'

'Square—I'm not square after last night, I've got every lump worn away, I'm just elliptical!'

But she laughed as Ryl pulled her into a perpendicular position, 'I'm all right really, you know, and it was good fun, and I'm dying for you to ask me again!'

It was the first time Ryl had entertained a guest, instead of being the guest herself. It was an epoch.

Through the windy months of May and June, while the surf-board gang were grappling with their University studies, Ryl became every inch a farmer.

After the term break in May, Perry bowed out of his taxi-driving job. For the first term he had kept up with some week-end shift driving, for he needed the money. During the week he boarded in Brisbane, but drove home at week-ends, and back to the city before dawn on Monday. He was thinner than ever, for between studying, travelling, and still working, there was small chance of indulging in sleep and rest. During the week Ryl and Dusty took charge of Ki.

Every alternate evening, usually with the white cat for company,

129

Ryl would walk down the boulder-strewn road between the banana leaves to Ki's cottage, carrying food in a covered container. Usually she found the district nurse there, for Perry had commissioned her, too, to call each day. His scholarship covered his own expenses if he budgeted well, while the taxi job provided money to care for the old man.

'The poor old coot ought to be in a home,' the nurse grumbled to Ryl—though kindly, for every district nurse must needs be fortified from an inner spring of kindness and cheer.

'But he'd hate it,' said Ryl. 'They'd be sure to make him feel terribly like a black man. He's happier like this, even if he can't have quite the attention he needs.'

However, Ki was not too badly off for friends these days. Dusty and Butch took to calling every other day, while Sandy the radio man dropped by on their days off. The old Islander was usually companioned by the white cat, except when it shepherded the visitors from Geebin. It would press its warm, purring bulk against his skeleton frame, almost immaterial beneath the faded patchwork quilt. Occasionally some dark-skin man, descendant from Ki's own stock, would pay his respects to the last of the 'blackbirds', but this was infrequent.

Dusty and Butch liked to make quite a picnic of their good deed. For Butch on these occasions, his first step was to thumb a ride in from Cudgen Head to Geebin. This was never difficult, for he was a well-known figure, and every local driver was his friend and ready to give a lift to 'old Butch Bradley'. His white-haired sisters, with their fussy Victorian ways, would sometimes put up a hamper for their brother to take to the invalid. On these

130

days, the food would be of top quality—fresh scones with cream in a jar and home-made jam, cold lobster or chicken nestling in a bower of crisp lettuce, with their secret-recipe mayonnaise ready to put on it, jelly, chocolate-cake—and a flask of fresh coffee.

At other times the food for the day was left to Dusty and Ryl to provide. This, in point of fact, meant that it was left to Dusty. So on those days there was bread and cheese!

From Geebin, the stout old-timers would take up the hamper, or Dusty's paper bag of bread and cheese as the case might be, and set off down the road. They would go, broad-backed and plodding, between the banana leaves. Their pace would be dead slow, their shapeless hats bobbing among the greenery, their toes turned out at a dependable angle, knobbly boots seeking the smooth patches among the boulders.

Once at the cottage under the poinciana-tree they would attend to Ki according to their convictions.

'How are you today, mate?'

Ki seldom answered this question, either feeling that no answer was better than a discouraging one, or that the question was foolish anyway.

'What d'you reckon he'd like, a wash or a cuppa tea?'

'Ah, he don't go much on this washing; after all, he's human. Washing is weakening. That nurse gives him more than enough of it, poor fellow.'

'Yeah, he must be fed up with it.'

'Then we'll pass over the washing business in favour of the cuppa tea. All right, Ki?'

Again, Ki seldom advanced an opinion. But there was no need. The other two were confident of their ability to interpret his wishes. After the cup of tea, or coffee from the flask, there would be the problem of making the invalid's bed. Ryl never forgot to remind them of this chore. If the day was sunny—and now that the rainy season was officially over it usually was—they would carry him, or half-carry him between them, out to the cane lounge on the back verandah. Then, 'while the bed aired', they would set up their chess-board on a banana-case where Ki could see it—'to give us a hand with our moves'—and embark on a long game. It was extremely unlikely that Ki had any knowledge of or interest in chess. But Dusty and Butch constantly deferred to his opinion and included him in their conversation as a kind of sleeping partner. Certainly their presence and deference comforted him, just as an old dog is comforted by the presence of those who esteem him. The sunken black face would take on a serene expression, even when the eyes were closed.

After the chess game, the pair of Good Samaritans would eat lunch, trying to tempt Ki to share it with them and sometimes

132

partially succeeding. Then another game of chess or a yarn, and the project of returning their patient to bed.

'That district nurse,' they'd say, 'will be along soon, and she'll fix the sheets and all. No point in us doing it too.'

Then—'So long, Ki. We gotta go now. See you the day after tomorrow.'

Ki would mutter a little, saying good-bye to them sometimes in English, sometimes in his own language, the tongue of his youth, now long silent from this valley of sugar-cane and falling from no lips but his own.

They would leave him and separate, Butch to wait on the highway for a ride home, and Dusty to plod staunchly back up the hill, to give seed to Jones the canary, feed his six hens and attend to the evening milking.

The youngsters called the whole process 'grandfather-sitting'.

'As long as Dusty goes grandfather-sitting for me,' Perry said to Ryl, 'I can keep my Sundays free to give you a hand with all this farming you've taken up. This new banana patch—there'll be a lot of work, you know, before you even plant it. You must have new ground. It will be cleanest—free from pests and so on—and the easiest to get a permit for.'

'Golly, do we have to have a permit?'

'We do!'

'Oh, well—the sooner we start the better.'

'Never heard any talk of permits in my young day!' grumbled Dusty.

Perry explained: 'It's a precaution against bunchy top, that's a disease bananas get. The ground has to be inspected by an agricultural officer before you can plant. Then you have to get your corms from an approved plantation—and clean and cut them down, and have them treated with chemical.'

'I didn't realize it was such a performance,' said Ryl. 'I thought you just dug some holes and shoved them in.'

'And you can't plant until the ground warms up after the winter, you know.'

'Warms up? But it's never cooled down!'

'You wouldn't say that if you were a banana.'

'I dare say!'

'Plant them about September. But we can be working on it.'

Both Ryl and Dusty liked the way he said 'we'.

133

It was this way, almost unintentionally, that Perry, Dusty and Ryl drifted into a kind of partnership with the new farming project. They agreed that Perry should take all the profits from the first crop as Ryl and Dusty knew he was having a financial struggle. He needed the money to spend on Ki.

Ryl carried out her plan of seeking information from the State Agricultural Department on trace elements for the cattle pastures. To her pleasure, Dusty took possession of the pamphlets which were posted to Geebin and studied them avidly. Each evening he would sit at the kitchen table—a kitchen was home to Dusty—and pore over their pages, which revived for him the forgotten world of the land—but with a difference.

The girl would smile to see the comic expression of concentration that would overspread his chubby face.

With Perry egging him on, Dusty looked to the unused paddocks along the river bank close to the cattle dip. Here he began an enterprise of his own, of stocking some dairy cattle. The days became full of importance, too short for the great changes afoot with the inhabitants of Geebin.

Yet Ryl noted that none of these tasks was beyond Dusty's strength. They seemed to her to be wonderfully 'pottery' ways of amusing a grandfather. Butch Bradley was always about to discuss the various aspects of cattle and banana growing, and like Dusty, seemed spryer and more alert than in the past.

Now that fishing was often ruled out by windy weather and short-lasting, gusty rain, the elderly friends would take themselves strolling about the farm, pipes in mouths, their heads full of wisdom and schemes. Each small incident or task was a project to be savoured. Ryl watched their antics with strangely acute perception for a girl of her age.

She once told Glen: 'Dusty and Butch Bradley—when they do the milking they practically charter a bus and pack their suitcases for it. It takes them so long getting ready, you or I could be there and back while they're finding their boots and their tobacco and their hats, and giving the canary some seed in case he starves to death while they're away! They get just the same sort of kick out of it that we get when we go skating or something.'

'Don't talk about "you or I" when you speak of milking, dear girl,' shuddered Glen. 'Milking a cow would be one place where Glen baby couldn't even keep up with Dusty! The day

I learn to milk, will someone please knock me on the head!'

She smiled. 'Oh well, I'll do it just to oblige! But I've learned to milk, you know. Just for a gag of course! I'd hate to be put to the test, though. It's not my cup of tea. But if Dusty likes it, why spoil his pleasure?'

'You just be careful, dear girl, letting him get all those cows and things sounds a bit ominous to me.' Glen warned her. 'The place won't be safe!'

There was a world of difference between Perry and Glen, not only in their appearance, but also in their attitude to work. Glen had become cool towards Perry. Their old, easy friendship had subtly changed.

# XVII

One wet day Ryl found an Alsatian pup on the doorstep. He huddled shivering on the wet flagstones, a picture of misery. She had never owned a dog, and was nonplussed by his appearance.

'Hey, Dusty!' she called. 'There's a great monstrous animal here. I suppose he's a dog, but there's enough over for a cat as well.'

'What sort of dog?'

'A big one.'

'What breed, I'm asking!'

'Well, how would I know? Come quickly and do something about him; he makes me nervous!'

Dusty came to the doorway.

'Hullo, boy!' he said. He rubbed the pup's ears.

'Whatever will we *do*?' cried Ryl, as though confronted with a crisis.

'Do? Bring him in and give him a feed, of course!'

'Oh, no! You wouldn't bring that animal inside? We'd have to move out!'

'But it's raining! And he's only a pup, you know!'

'You're not telling me he's going to grow *bigger*?'

'Could be.'

'He can't come inside. I'm not going to clean house for a dog!'

'Ah, what's a bit of dirt! You're more scared of dirt than you are of snakes. Downright foolishness.'

'And he'd scare Jones.'

'Jones has more sense than wot you have.'

Ryl sighed. 'I'll find something for him to sit on, a bag or something. And I'll give him some bread and milk. And that's the limit of what I'm prepared to do for any dog.'

All this was done, and Dusty spent some time mooching on the doorstep with the new arrival, until Ryl threatened him with dire rheumatism and the disapproval of neglected cows as well.

136

After she had shooed him off to the milking-shed, she herself sneakingly began to make the pup's acquaintance.

'He's a pet, really,' she decided after a while, as he made tentative dabs at her with a pink tongue. 'He must belong to someone.'

After a while the rain cleared, and watery sunshine began to draw steam from the flagstones. The pup rolled on his back and lovingly chewed her moccasins. His stomach and legs were a soft buff colour like a child's teddy-bear and his face was, as even she guessed, beautifully boned, buff coloured, with dark, lustrous eyes outlined in black like those of a model. His pointed white teeth were infinitely gentle on her light shoe—his touch was a foolish, endearing caress.

'You'd better stay here with us, and we'll advertise for your owner,' she told the puppy.

When Dusty returned from the cowshed it was to find Ryl throwing a section of bamboo for the dog to chase.

'He's a well-bred 'un,' he said.

'I suppose someone's looking for him frantically.'

'Ah, maybe not. Lots of people abandon Alsatians, you know. Not everyone likes them. And he's got no collar, you'll notice.'

'We must advertise that we have him, anyway,' said Ryl.

They did, but they never found any claimants for the stray dog, which settled at Geebin, quickly working his way into the affections of the inmates. They called him Bruno.

'He's smart as paint,' Dusty told Clem and Butch Bradley. 'Of course we keep him away from the cows and hens, but he'd know better than to chase them! He don't even chase the white cat. He probably don't know it's a cat. Nobody's told him.'

'I wouldn't want to tell tales about him,' said Ryl, 'but I do think he knows about cows. I caught him chasing them one day. So I walloped him with a newspaper, and he thought that was like all the fiends of Hell after him. He got the message.'

Within a week she was cheerfully doing housework for the dog, for Bruno wormed his way indoors and became almost a part of the furniture.

Clem never ceased to marvel at the new prosperity which had come to Dusty's cattle. Dusty had bought more stock and turned them to graze on the river flats, for long unused. Learning from

137

his agricultural papers, he had bought products to supplement their natural diet of grasses, a type of salt-lick containing trace minerals, and also cube feeding. They improved in quality fast, and the few he sold brought good market prices. Dusty had persuaded Ryl that they should buy a pedigree bull, and for this purpose Clem drove him to the cattle market at Ipswich. They returned from the inland town in great triumph with a champion bull-calf in the trailer. Privately, Ryl thought him a monstrously ugly fellow. She never liked the cattle, and only tolerated them for Dusty's benefit.

'Look at his great stupid face!' she would say in disgust. 'Look at it, will you? Not a brain in his head! All solid bone. Enough bone to make buttons and knife handles for all the Bradley relations and us, too. The creature's just a bone-head.'

However, Perry had brought his coloured boy to help with the farm-work, and King Cotton was a great admirer of the bull-calf. He and the stock saw a lot of each other. The black boy, like the dog, became a fixture of Geebin.

Perry spent much of his week-end time at Geebin when he was not studying. He toiled on its acres with enthusiasm, directing King Cotton in making ready for the new banana plantation, while Dusty and Butch went grandfather-sitting with Ki. Glen made occasional grumbling Sunday calls. He would appear dressed in immaculate cotton pants, white shirt and modish jerkin, the last to prove, in this mild climate, that it was winter after all.

'Old Glen about this place,' complained Perry, 'stands out like a lily on a dirt heap.'

'Well, like I'm trying to express myself!' said Glen. 'You workers give me an inferiority complex. And I don't have any grandfather to bandy about, either. If I hired one could I join the club?'

'You're just not a joiner, Glen baby. Aren't you lucky?'

'Depends. Look, don't you crazy types ever stop work to consider that the surf's still rolling down at Rainbow Bay?'

'And,' said Ryl, 'a freezing wind's still blowing and the waves are as high as church steeples and the sharks are still biting.'

'Like sour grapes!' observed Glen.

'Just the same,' said Perry, 'it's not the wind or the waves or the sharks that keep me away, old buddy boy, it's the strange interest I have in making money. Since Dusty and Ryl were rash

138

enough to mention a percentage if we can bring home the bananas, they're likely to be stuck with me. But never fear! Next week I'll have cleaned up the weeds in this paddock, and I'll come down to the beach and give that old surf-board a real belting!'

Glen drew Ryl aside. 'Will you come dancing on Wednesday night?'

'But won't you be in Brisbane trying to get an education?'

'Brisbane's a crummy place. The only thing to do with it is leave it alone. I can drive down here after lectures on Wednesday and go back early Thursday morning, I don't have a lecture until ten o'clock.'

'But won't all that driving be more like hard work than weeding bananas?'

'Not for me. The work suits me better.'

King Cotton rattled up the hill on Clem Bradley's tractor which they now hired regularly—on a 'swap' basis, of course! He was pulling an empty spray-tank.

'I'll knock off now,' he grinned. 'Done a good day's work, huh?'

'Not bad, Cotton.' Perry slapped his shoulder.

Cotton's legs were like black clothes-props beneath his disreputable shorts. His T-shirt was stained all over with unsightly black-brown marks of banana sap. But as Glen mentioned, 'It's just the same colour as his face, so it suits him really.' Cotton's teeth were white and square—'tombstones' to the youngsters—and his ears large and fly-away. His expression was that of the eternal optimist, a steady rather vacant grin. Ryl understood that back home at Cotton's place there was a whole shanty full of duplicate copies of their trusty helper—as Glen had once crudely put it, 'chivvying each other for standing room'.

'Come on, Ryl,' urged Glen. 'Come and have a quick swim. You haven't been anywhere with me for ages.'

'I don't want a swim, really. Oh well, if you feel neglected I suppose that's different,' she said. 'Then I'll just have a quick shower and get changed. And feed all the dependants. I have to feed Jones and Bruno and the hens—Dusty can do the calves. Really, this jolly place is just like a Salvation Army soup-kitchen!'

But before she went indoors she called to Perry over her shoulder: 'Perry, I'm sick of work, I'm going swimming with Glen.'

139

'That's the spirit. Do that.'

'You don't think I'm a rat deserting a sinking ship?'

'No, of course not. I'm going home to Ki now.'

'All right.'

She ran up the tall steps. Perry shambled away across the paddocks, and Glen sat on the bottom step waiting for Ryl to change. The blue crane gently touched down to a landing in his home paddock of the pink matel-grass.

'You see a lot of old Perry, don't you?' remarked Glen, as they drove down the Ridge Road.

'Yes. We couldn't get along without him.'

'My dad,' Glen was looking at her face with a curious, furtive air, much as Perry had done at times in the past—'my dad was talking about your dad. A chemist is in a funny position, you know. He's like a doctor. He finds out a lot about people.'

'Yes, really? So did he know my father?'

'He's not sure,' said Glen. 'I don't think he did, myself. I think he must have had some other fellow in mind.'

'Oh? Why? What did he say?'

She turned an eager face to Glen. He took his eyes from the road long enough to watch her squarely for a moment. Then he sighed, and nodded, as though satisfying himself about some point.

'Nothin',' he told her shortly. 'Nothing that mattered! He was thinking of the wrong man—that's obvious!'

'Thinking *what* about the wrong man?'

But Glen changed the subject. 'At Uni.,' he said, 'there's this girl—' There was no stopping him.

140

# XVIII

While Perry's scholarship from Commonwealth Sugar Refineries enabled him to live carefully, he looked forward anxiously to the time when his share-farming venture at Geebin should show a dividend.

There was the Tuesday night when Glen took Ryl to the end-of-term ball at the University. The tickets were five pounds each, but Glen was nonchalant about it. He took the day off from studies in order to drive Ryl to Brisbane and instal her in an hotel near Dodi's boarding place. She was to sleep there overnight. Glen took both girls to dinner before Dodi met her 'date'.

For the occasion Glen sported a new suit of tails. Most of the boys wore dinner-jackets, but Glen was never happier than when overdressed for any occasion. Ryl enjoyed herself and felt flattered that she should have been asked to the function. But she missed Perry. The following week-end, when he appeared at Geebin in his sap-stained T-shirt and half-mast shorts to work on the fences of the cattle pasture, she asked about his absence.

'The ball was terrific. It went on and on, and everyone acted as madly as they liked—why weren't you there, Mack-the-Knife?'

Perry grinned ruefully.

'And where would I have found ten quid to squander on fast living?'

'Ten—? But only five.'

'And what girl would take it as a compliment if a chap told her she could come as his partner if she was prepared to pay for her own ticket?'

'Um—I didn't think of that angle. Anyhow, you could have asked me. I'd have paid for my own ticket. I'd have been glad to. You know how I just love to spend money.'

'But I simply wouldn't have asked you,' he said loftily.

'So what did you do, instead of going to the ball?'

141

'Studied. And it could be that at the end of the year Glen and a few others will wish they'd done likewise.'

He sounded superior. But she knew that it was a case of sour grapes.

'Those cattle on the river flat are doing well,' he told her, to change the subject. 'There'll soon be calves to market.'

'Don't I know,' she sighed. 'Dusty hovers over those cows like a matron in a maternity ward. He never takes his eyes off them.'

Perry said, 'I don't know how I ever could have left Ki as I've done, and gone to University, if it hadn't been for you and Dusty. Truly.'

'Ah, nonsense!'

'Anyway, there it is,' said Perry. It was his last word. He made off towards the pastures before she could gainsay his thanks.

At week-ends, Perry began to give Ryl driving lessons in readiness for the time in October when she would be seventeen. Glen had offered to teach her in the M.G., but she had declined. He still seemed to have endless time to spare, while Perry was always busy. As Dusty said, 'That boy's always on the run, never walks anywhere. He's like a racehorse! He keeps himself poor, running all his fat off.'

But Ryl had begun to feel a gap widening between herself and Glen. He had become unduly sophisticated. He took his studies lightly and never let them intrude upon his pleasures. His life was full of adoring relatives, clothes, and girls. Everyone was his friend. Fortune smiled on Glen Dynon. But beside Perry's soft-spoken presence, it began to strike Ryl as a rather vacuous smile. After the ball she saw less of him and the red M.G.

After one encounter she confided to Rose, 'You know, Glen's grown to simply love himself so much, he just thinks he's God's gift to women! All the girls at that stupid Uni. seem to fall over each other to ride in his precious car. He gets on my nerves, really he does. He was good fun at the ball, but enough's enough.'

'Well,' said Rose, 'I've always thought him a very nice boy.'

'He's a snob. And he's always being rude to Perry. Just because Perry has some Island blood.'

Rose looked uncomfortable.

142

'I'm wondering,' she said, 'if perhaps you're seeing too much of Perry. After all—'

'Now surely *you're* not going to be *like that*!' cried Ryl. She added, 'Thanks for the coffee, Rose dear. I've got to go home now or Dusty will make rice pudding—he's got one of his cooking spells. I have to keep an eye on him when he gets like this! 'Bye, Rose!'

She scurried out of Rose's kitchen, intent on protecting herself from the perils of Dusty's pudding.

Winter in the Tweed Valley and in the wild ranges beyond meant not great cold, but bursts of sudden storm, sweeping with passion from the ever-changing sea, to die away in brief, grey aftermath, until the sun again brought still waters and peace. But for ever the streets of Tweed Heads and Coolangatta, the twin towns of the Border Country, were full of girls wearing shorts and sunsuits; still, when the storms were at bay, the surf-riders trailed their white streamers over the blue roll of Rainbow Bay.

King Cotton worked at week-ends, repairing fences and outbuildings. Often Ryl worked with him. She also drove Clem Bradley's tractor like a veteran, using it to drag away loads of rusty iron, wire-netting and old fence posts, debris of the past decade hidden in the all-enveloping buffalo-grass. She found unexpected pleasure in hammering nails and sawing timber. Clem, in amazement, declared she should be a carpenter.

'I wouldn't mind!' she laughed. Then, seriously, 'I mightn't be too far from it, though, because I really have been thinking about doing a course in architecture. I've even sent away for the prospectus about it. Part of the course takes in interior design. Of course I *could* change my mind, but then again I mightn't!'

'"Amaryllis Merewether",' murmured Clem. '"Designed by Amaryllis Jane Merewether". I'm just thinking how it will look on the foundations of a skyscraper.'

'When you put it like that,' sighed Ryl, 'it seems to sound a bit far-fetched. Perhaps I'll just stop at interior design.'

'Don't let me discourage you, for gosh' sake!' cried Clem. 'By the job you're doing on that tank stand, you could handle a skyscraper before breakfast!'

August went out with a blustering wind from the North that kept the fishing-boats bottled up at their moorings at the river mouth. When a lull came in the stormy weather, a convoy set out from Geebin for the Numinbah Range. There was Ryl warily keeping Glen company in the M.G., and Perry in the Bomb, with Tom the photographer and Dodi as passengers. They were after banana spears for the new plantation. The preparation of the new ground was completed. Dusty claimed it to be so rich with added elements, super-phosphate, and compost that it made his own mouth water! The necessary permits were safe in a kitchen drawer. The time had come when spring was close, the soil warmed, and ready to burgeon.

They went through Murwillumbah and up into the strange, sheer-walled mountains that until now Ryl had only seen in a blue haze of air from the windows of Geebin.

The drive lay first through broad, flat sugar-cane fields at the foot of the mountains, and then up, with many hairpin bends in the narrow, one-way road that followed the sides of cliffs, circling and wheeling over creeks, where vehicles must plough through fords, and the low-slung M.G. was in great danger of getting water in the carburettor. They drove up among the giant's blocks, the tilted formations piled at the edge of the coastal plain—the Numinbah Range.

Here, coming suddenly from among dense and primal jungle, were magnificent plantations, clinging impossibly to the cliff sides. Not another car traversed the overgrown, zigzag road; the youngsters had it all to themselves. Just as well, too, for Glen's driving was of the kind where skill replaces caution. Ryl clung breathlessly to the panic bar as he streaked ahead of the old utility, cutting corners with abandon, swaying on cliff edges, sending showers of loose stones rattling into the depths of apparently bottomless gorges. For Perry's part, he drove as usual with discretion, though, as Glen remarked uncharitably, 'His old Bomb won't do more than thirty-five miles an hour, and at the top of the range I bet it'll be boiling like a Chinese laundry!'

Hidden in dense, steep jungle close to the high State Border gate, they found their destination. It was a plantation which grew almost vertically; its owners used wire 'flying-foxes' to bring down the harvested fruit where no man could carry the bunches, and no vehicle could come. The only living soul they saw on the

144

place was a barefooted black boy of about Perry's age, who, with painful shyness, disappeared with a spade over his shoulder as soon as they arrived. Perry had already made arrangements with the owner, living at Currumbin, that they should help themselves to the quantity of spears they needed.

In misty rain for the most part, they worked with mattock and murderous cane knife, barefooted like the shy boy, gathering the young plants. They were soon covered in rich, red mountain soil and black-staining banana sap. As they worked they sang 'On Ilkley Moor Ba Taat,' in what they fondly called 'harmony'. Indeed the sound, though not exactly musical, was pleasing enough in its own way, mournful in the warm mist.

'Stand still there! I'm shooting!' called Tom. Obligingly, Ryl froze in position. Tom had captured one picture for himself, at least.

A pity she never knew the discussion that picture was to stir up in the staff-room of her old school in Melbourne. It was Miss Blake, the science teacher, who gave the first long, hard look at the pictured girl on her magazine cover as she rode on her work-going bus. She took the journal to school, and passed it around among the teachers over morning coffee.

'Look, Clarice,' she said as she handed it to her friend Miss Frobisher, who took leaving maths. 'Look—does that remind you of anyone?'

'M—m—m—no—yes! It's like—it's *very* like that girl, what was her name, Amaryllis Merewether! She left at the end of last year, didn't she? It is like her! But of course it can't be!'

'Oh, no, of course not, it can't be, but isn't it *like* her?'

'You know, I suppose it couldn't *possibly* be her? I mean, you don't think it could be?'

'Oh, no, of course not! Amaryllis Merewether, dressed in rags, in among a lot of banana palms—or whatever they're called! She was such a fussy little thing, like a cat in wet grass! She'd never get her smallest finger dirty, or wear anything that wasn't designed in Paris or what-have-you!'

'But it's so *like* her!'

The teachers debated the point, putting arguments for and against the case.

In the staff-room the question was never really settled!

145

Up on Numinbah they loaded the Bomb with their spoils, then went to the National Forestry Reserve to eat their lunch of grilled chops and billy tea. They ran headlong down the path leading through the rain forest to the Natural Arch, that strange rock formation that spans the mountain river, and Tom took more pictures. But the gorge of the river, full of exotic trees and ferns and giant lianas, was too dark for success with his camera, except with a flash-bulb.

They headed for home, driving above lush valleys without sign of life. The scenes were as still as painted scenes, in the shadow of Springbrook.

'Gosh,' said Ryl, 'what a lonely place! Who lives here? Anyone?'

'Funny thing,' said Glen. 'This place always seems to be uninhabited. But look—there's a wire 'flying-fox'—and a house—and lots of grazing cattle. Obviously some unseen peasant is just quietly making pots of money out of this back-of-beyond. I think most of the owners live down on the coast. They just have a native caretaker up here, or visit the farms from time to time.'

'It's creepy,' said Ryl. 'D'you know, in a way I'd love to come and stay up here. I'd be terribly sad and write poetry. And finally go out of my mind and jump over some bottomless cliff, or something.'

'Oh, what a wild fling! That's living, huh?'

'Shut up, soulless clod.'

'Wot me, soulless? Crikey, what next! Why, one day you must marry me and I'll bring you here for the honeymoon. We could stay in that cowshed—see—down in the valley?'

'My second proposal,' said Ryl. 'Another boo-boo.'

'Just think of it,' pursued Glen. 'Nights of bliss fighting off the mosquitoes, and every day we could bask in the thin sunshine and search each other for ticks.'

'Ticks! Ticks? Ticks!' Ryl suddenly sprang out in all directions.

'Sure, ticks and leeches—'

'Leeches! Now he tells me! Quick! Take me home! I feel all sort of crawly!'

They arrived home just before the rain started again, a dirty, cheerful lot, to eat tinned soup and Dodi's hamburgers at Geebin and take turns under the cold shower in the snake-pit.

'There's a sore lump on my ear!' complained Ryl, as Dusty was about to flee to the Bradleys.

'Let's have a look,' he told her. Then, 'You've only got a bit of a tick there, that's all.'

Glen put his hands to his ears. 'Wait for the reaction!' he said.

But Ryl was brave as Dusty squeezed the ear with his handkerchief. She even seemed proud of her tick. In fact, Glen was quite disappointed.

'I'm off, now,' said Dusty, his Florence Nightingale act over. 'Now you look after your visitors, Miss, after the work they've done.'

'Poor things,' said Ryl. 'If I were to look after them, that would finish them properly.'

'Don't worry, Mr. Merewether,' said Dodi, 'we love the way we don't get treated like visitors around this place. We can sing, or stand on our heads, or make toffee—no one takes a scrap of notice of us! It's beaut!'

Glen had put a record on Ryl's portable player, and it blared forth with gusto. Tom was making a pot of tea while Perry cut up spring onions. Looking hunted, Dusty retreated to Clem's protection, muttering, 'Pandemonium, pandemonium,' as he went. The banana gatherers were left to shake Geebin to its foundations, rocky as they were.

Next day King Cotton came to help with the intimidating task of trimming and cleaning the spears, ready to be sent to the fumigating rooms at Murwillumbah.

Ryl had pictured banana growing on the lines she also considered that oil-painting should be done—large and lavish, with no tedious detail work—an idyllic form of fruit growing, with no such things as weeding, ploughing, tilling or pruning, and no insect pests—and a harvest where many cases of bananas could be gathered at a time, bunch after bunch. This was the boyhood picture that Dusty had retained in his mind, and passed on to Ryl. As far as both of them knew, bananas grew themselves and needed no sort of encouragement from the happy owner. True, they had noticed that Clem seemed to spray his frequently, but to Dusty, this was pleasure rather than business. However, Ryl at least was fast revising her theories.

'Golly!' she said now, sitting on the ground, covered in red

148

dirt and surrounded by banana corms and spears in various stages of mutilation.

'Golly, we certainly will value any fruit these things eventually produce, if they ever grow after what's happening to them. I'll be

just as proud of this banana plantation as if I'd designed Sydney Harbour Bridge.'

'You can say that again,' agreed Dusty. 'I'll guard this plantation with my life, that I will. No cockroaches had better dare set foot on these bananas. Pity help the cows if they get in and eat them.'

All that week there were great toilings and moilings at Geebin. The following week-end the roots were taken to the pest control rooms at Murwillumbah, and the next again, Perry brought them

149

back again in the Bomb. The sun shone beautifully, drying out the tired-looking plants. Ryl and King Cotton spread them carefully in the home paddock. Then the planting began.

When next Perry came back from Brisbane, Red and Dodi again joined the Geebin syndicate and a noisy and inefficient working-bee scrabbled across the new banana patch. In shorts and sun-top, Ryl and her coerced helpers worked in the early spring sunshine.

Then, three days later, a storm came roaring down from the North.

'It's not cold rain,' said Dusty. 'Reckon it will bring them along—that's if it doesn't wash them all out.'

'I can't be worried,' said Ryl. 'I've done my dash.'

She was now spending time in trying to remove the signs of her farming venture. Soil had dried and cracked her hands, her once-smooth skin was well sprinkled with insect bites, and her nails, in spite of vigorous scrubbing, seemed permanently dirty. She sat on the floor in front of the radiator which she had bought during the winter. Her black hair was swathed in a large towel, her feet were bare, and she worked at her finger-nails with deep concentration. If the new plantation were to be washed away in its first infancy it would be just too bad, thought Ryl—she could do no more.

But the rain cleared, and Dusty was able to breathe again, for the young plants were still in their allotted places. A few were rather the worse for wear, and tilted crazily. King Cotton and Dusty worked for two days straightening the plants and staking those that needed support. But the damage could have been worse.

It was a grey, sultry day when three men came with note-books and a theodolite, and took a survey of the razor-back, tramping back and forth across the paddocks and the road above Geebin. Rather, two men and a boy. There was Mr. Bill Brown, the council surveyor, his assistant Mr. Ferguson, and a cadet surveyor, Spike Harvey.

Ryl saw them when she returned from a shopping trip to Tweed Heads.

'What's going on?' she asked Dusty, as she battled against

150

Bruno's welcome home. As usual it was like horseplay with a hippopotamus.

'I dunno.'

In the living-room she dropped her shopping-bags on the floor and sank into one of the deep cane chairs.

'You know what, Dusty? I'll be seventeen in just a few weeks. Don't you think we should buy a car? I'm not a bad driver, you know. I could drive with "L" plates.'

'Always wanting to spend money with a spade.'

'But the man at the garage by the tick gate comes across some awfully good second-hand cars. And he says now is the time to buy one, before the summer holidays.'

'Now's always the time for you to throw money about.'

'But truly, we do need a car, you know we do. And if I have to live in Brisbane next year—'

'You're setting to work on me, that's what you're doing, my lady. You've thought to yourself that you'll give me the treatment.'

She smiled and patted his arm.

'Well, I've got to work on you, sweet, you're such a tough old proposition. Now the man at the garage—he's got a dear old Ford, and he only wants £150 for it. Perry could check it over. It's such a bargain. I'd call it Hortense.'

'And I dare say,' grumbled Dusty, 'it drinks petrol like an alcoholic.'

'But it's such a nice, big old car—'

'And you figure it could carry a surf-board on top.'

'How did you guess?' She was surprised.

Dusty clicked his tongue. 'I can read you like a book, I can indeed! I know there's more in your head than pumpkin seeds and sawdust. You make a start with a car—then you'll start angling for a surf-board.'

Bruno, full of guilt complex for coming into the house against rules, wriggled towards the girl on his stomach, his tail working like a rudder.

'Oh, what a savage Alsatian!' she chanted. 'Oh, what a savage Alsatian!'

Dusty pursed his lips in disapproval.

'You make that dog as silly as you are,' he complained. 'How can I bring him up right when you fill his head with nonsense?'

'Poor love,' she crooned over the dog. 'Poor love, is Dusty cruel and hard to Ryl's good dog? Oh, nasty Dusty.'

'All right! Fill his head with nonsense, only get him off my feet! Look at that rain coming again, quick as drop your hat!'

Sure enough, a squall came suddenly rattling at the windows with wet fingers. In a few moments there was a knock at the door. Ryl dived under her chair to look for her shoes, then decided against putting them on again, and pattered to the door in her bare feet. She opened it to find the three surveyors standing in the shelter of the porch.

Young Spike Hardy remembered afterwards the picture of the girl in the doorway, with her bare feet, her hand, long, slim and brown on the brass doorknob.

'Afternoon,' smiled Bill Brown. 'Could we have a word with the householder?'

'Certainly,' said Ryl hospitably. 'There are two of us house-holders living here—my grandfather and I. Come in.'

She ushered them into the living-room and then indolently subsided once more into her chair. Dusty stood and registered attention to their wants.

'We've been taking a survey,' said Bill Brown. 'The council's planning to put up a new water-tower, and it has to requisition the highest point of land in the area that it's to serve. It seems you're in luck. The site of this house turns out to be the highest point.'

'Luck?' Dusty blinked at them. 'What sort of luck's that?'

'Luck. This place has been on the market, hasn't it? And it certainly must be hard to sell. Well, the council will take it off your hands.'

Ryl bounded to her feet and stood next to Dusty. Together they presented a solid front. They both looked in amazement at the surveyor.

'But,' said Dusty, 'this is our house! We live here! Hadn't you noticed?'

The surveyor inclined his head politely.

'What, are you afraid you won't get your price?'

'This place is not for sale any more,' Dusty told him. 'Because we don't want to sell it any more—see?'

Mr. Brown took out a handkerchief and wiped the raindrops from the back of his neck.

152

'Then you'll just have to change your minds back again,' he said. 'The council wants it now. They'll give you a fair price. Not that it's worth much, of course, but they'll give you market value.'

# XIX

The surveyor looked around the bright room, which was now filled with an intangible sense of dismay.

'From the outside,' he said, 'it looks as though you should be glad to pay us to pull it down. But I can see you've got it quite comfortable inside. Still the fact remains, it's not a property of any real value, is it?'

During a long silence, Dusty and Ryl struggled to assimilate this new idea. Ryl was the first to speak.

'Do you mean to tell us,' she said, 'that the council wants to pull down Geebin, and build a water-tower on its site?'

Her accent grew more correct and redolent of finishing school, the more her anger rose. She could have been royalty at the very least. Mr. Brown almost wilted under the force of her dignity.

'That's the strength of it, Miss.'

'Preposterous!' declared Ryl.

'Hear, hear!' said Dusty. 'So you blokes can go right back where you came from! We happen to like it here!'

Mr. Brown exchanged hostile looks with his older assistant.

'Sorry,' he said, in a voice rather louder than necessary, 'but there's nothing you or anyone else can do about it. When a council wants to requisition land they have a right to do it, just in case you don't know.'

'That's right,' said the off-sider. 'If they need this bit of ground, you can't stop them taking it!'

'Oh no?' said Ryl. Her voice was the cold little voice of the Melbourne schoolgirl, which had not been heard of late. 'Oh no? And who says so?'

Mr. Brown shrugged his shoulders to cover his annoyance. 'The council has legal rights,' he said. 'And in case of argument, the council always wins.'

'Mind you,' his companion contributed, 'they'll compensate

154

you fairly. They'll only take a chain or two of your land. Then you can build a better house near by!'

'And live right next to a water-tower?' scoffed Ryl. 'And scare away the blue crane—and cut down the montys—and—and —everything?'

'That's progress.'

'Well, I don't hold with progress!' shouted Dusty belligerently. 'Progress! Too much progress is what's ruining the world today! You can keep your progress, and I hope it chokes you!'

'I have a feeling we're not welcome here,' said the second surveyor. 'It's stopped raining. We may as well be off and not take up any more of your time.'

The three men moved to the door, while Ryl and Dusty gave them looks that could almost kill.

'By the way, what name is it?' asked Mr. Brown. 'The council will be writing a letter to you, and they'll want us to get your name.'

'Merewether,' Dusty told him sulkily. 'David Giles. This is my grand-daughter, Amaryllis.'

Mr. Brown repeated the name.

'Merewether? I seem to remember hearing something about a Merewether.'

'My son bought this place about seventeen or eighteen years ago,' mumbled Dusty. 'Perhaps you heard of him.'

Mr. Brown looked at him with more interest.

'That's right. Now I remember. I surveyed the property for him at the time. Mm.'

He looked closely at Ryl.

'And you're his daughter, I suppose? What was his name again?'

'Robert,' grunted Dusty.

'That's right. Robert Merewether. And where is he now? And his wife?'

'Passed on,' said Dusty. 'Both of 'em.'

'Sorry to hear that.' Mr. Brown shook his head. He added, 'She was a pretty thing.' He looked at Ryl. 'But you don't—'

Dusty interrupted: 'Like you said, it's stopped raining. Don't let us keep you!'

There was something final in the way he said it.

The three men began to move once more.

155

'You'll be hearing from the council,' said Mr. Brown. 'Sorry you aren't keen to sell. A pity, that. Oh well. So long.'

Spike Hardy, the young cadet, smiled sympathetically at Ryl as the older men hustled him off.

They turned back to the living-room, Ryl leading Bruno by one arum-lily ear.

'How's their form, huh?' she exploded. 'Why pick on us for their silly old water-tower!'

Dusty looked about him, at the fresh paint, the bleached, pewter-coloured wall, the striped wallpaper, the strawberry curtains.

'Fleece us good and proper they will,' he said. 'Them and their fair deal! I know all about their deals, these councils. And of course you had to do the place up like Buckingham Palace. Spending money—'

'—with a spade!' Ryl finished for him. Her mouth twitched. Somehow even Dusty's gloom was comic.

'But anyhow, they won't get it,' she said. 'They can think again! They won't get our Geebin.'

Dusty had to crow a little over her change of face.

'And who,' he asked, 'wanted to sell it in the first place? Who keeps calling it a dump?'

'It is, too,' said Ryl. 'A dump to end all dumps. But I just like it.'

156

'You do, hey? And how are you going to stop them from taking it?'

'I—I'll—I'll see a lawyer. I'll write to Mr. Herbert. First thing in the morning.'

'Well now, seeing it's the last thing in the evening, how about coming and giving me a hand with the milking?'

'Sheer blackmail. Oh well, I'll be the victim. Come and get it over.'

Each armed with a bucket, they went over the cropped lawn with its islands of verdure and through the fence to the blue crane's pasture. They followed a zigzag path over the pink grass.

'That man,' said Ryl, 'he knew my mother, didn't he? Wasn't he talking about my mother?'

Dusty grunted. Ryl went on:

'He said she was pretty. And then you hustled him off. I wish you'd let him talk a while. Of course, I think he's awful for wanting to take Geebin—but I do wish I could have heard some more about my mother.'

Dusty was silent.

'You've never told me a word about her,' said Ryl carpingly. 'Tell me now.'

Dusty's face was closed.

'Nothin' to tell you. She was just a girl.'

'But that man said she was pretty. Was she pretty?'

'Aw—I can't remember. Maybe she was. In a way.'

'Do I look like her?'

'No, you don't!' he cried sharply. 'You look like a Merewether!'

She glanced at him in surprise.

'All right—keep your hair on!' She inspected him from the corner of her eye. 'Only,' she said, 'you're sort of fair, you've got a fair skin, anyhow—and I'm dark, except that I've got greeny eyes a bit like yours. And you're shortish, and I'm tall—and— well, do you really think—'

'Ah, turn it up!' said Dusty. 'Here, pick up your feet, it'll start raining again soon and we'll get wet.'

'Dusty!' Ryl spoke like an inquisitor. 'Dusty—I don't think you liked my mother. Did you and my father quarrel about her? Tell me. You might just as well.'

'All right!' shouted Dusty. 'All right! Yes, we did, Miss Sticky-nose! So now you know!'

157

They walked on to the clank of metal, and the huff-huff of their own feet on the grass.

'There's Perry's white cat!' Ryl called to it. 'Here, pussy, pussy!'

But the aloof, exotic creature slipped silently past the dairy and disappeared behind the Moreton Bay fig-trees.

Ryl's mind jumped back to the visitors of the afternoon.

'Those surveyors,' she said, 'they'll have to get up early in the morning to push us out of our nice, wobbly old house.'

Privately, Dusty thought with relief that she had lost interest in the subject of her mother and his family quarrel. But if he had only known, she meant to bide her time until a good moment should come, and then prise his secrets from him.

## XX

The week-end came, but no further word from the council, no dread announcement that Geebin had been requisitioned for its proposed civic purpose.

Saturday was bleak and tempestuous after heavy rain and high winds during the night. Though the rain had passed, the surf still ran wild, with house-high boomers pounding beach and headland. At times like these, the many fish-shops were out of trade and the fisher-folk must tighten their belts, while their harvest grounds lay deserted. All the world of the river delta and the border towns was withdrawn into itself. Even the tourists seemed to go softly and hush their holiday voices, in the wet wind-swept streets.

For once like old times, Glen and Perry called together at Geebin soon after lunch.

'Hi, Ryl.'

'Oh, hullo, you chaps.'

Perry said, 'Want to come up to Point Danger and watch the king tide come in?'

'Golly, yes. Amuse the canary for a minute, will you, while I get a pullover.'

Dusty had retired to his bedroom for a cat-nap, and the lunch dishes were piled high in the sink, where they were welcome to stay, for all either he or Ryl cared.

Glen did indeed take it upon himself to whistle to Jones, and move his cage to a brighter spot, while Perry's reflex action was to begin to rinse the plates and stack them more neatly. Ryl soon joined them, dressed in a heavy white sweater and black slacks. They went off chattering rowdily, to squeeze themselves into the M.G.

'Lucky you're skinny,' Perry told her.

'Skinny be blowed! The word is slim! In future, remember.'

'Ouch! That elbow in my ribs—that's not slim, that's skinny.'

'Anyhow, you're no Mr. Universe yourself, Mack-the-Knife. Wot, no muscles? You look like a couple of yards of pump water!

Even Glen baby, who never works hard enough to keep himself awake—at least he's got enough hips to keep his pants up! Yours always look positively dangerous, teetering at half-mast!'

'I keep 'em up with strength of mind. Mind over matter.'

'Obviously. And whose mind do you borrow?'

'Anyhow, in spite of everything, just tell me who does all the work? However Glen got his muscles it couldn't have been through work!'

'Work?' Glen had his say. 'Oh, you mean *work*! My kick is real work, living it up good, man, that's real work, like for real! Fighting off the girls is how I get my muscles! Man, it takes its toll!'

Bickering cosily, they climbed the road to the top of Point Danger, where the cliffs drop away to the churning sea. They got out of the car, and stood leaning on the safety rail. Below, the coast stretched in sullen mood. Huge seas, cliffs of water marbled green and white, rolled and crashed, rolled and crashed at the feet of the headland by the Porpoise Pool. The usually narrow channel where the prawning fleet would glide with swift masts at sundown to coast over the bar on the seventh breaker, was now a wide, swirling, angry race, crashing its waters over the stone dykes of Greenbank Island and covering its low sand-dunes, haunt of snake and sand-crab.

'The native village on the island must be flooded,' said Ryl.

'Clean 'em up a bit,' said Glen. 'The Kanakas need a flood every spring; that's their spring cleaning.'

As he spoke he looked jeeringly at Perry; it seemed to give a personal connotation to his words. As had happened before, Ryl's face flushed; she showed more resentment than Perry at the other boy's tone.

'And what about the good-for-nothing white people,' she asked, 'who live in the shanty town behind the railway station? When do they have a spring cleaning?'

Glen laughed maddeningly. 'I love to get a bite from you, dear girl!' he grinned. 'I notice you've taken King Cotton into your little heart, too! Did they teach you to like Kanakas, at that boarding-school in Melbourne where you learned your lessons?'

'They taught me to like intelligent people,' said Ryl coldly. 'So it's lucky you weren't there, isn't it? King Cotton is just as good a workman as any other young Australian farmer. He was born in

160

this country—he's just the same as young Bert Whatson, who helps take the cattle to market, except that his great-grandfather came from Samoa instead of Blackpool or somewhere.'

'I can't help thinking how funny it would be to see the look on your pretty face,' said Glen, 'if you ever found—'

Suddenly Perry interrupted him.

'Ryl,' he asked—quickly, almost rudely, for Perry—'Ryl, who were the visitors you had the other day, during the rain-storm? I was home on Wednesday night, and I nearly called in, but I saw a car outside Geebin.'

At once she remembered the problem of the water-tower. 'I haven't told you, have I,' she said, 'about these peanuts who came last week and took a survey and told us they're going to build a water-tower where Geebin stands?'

'Come again?' queried Glen blankly.

Perry said, 'What? What did you say?'

'They think they can knock over our house, that's what I said. They think they can do it just like that. And the trouble is, they not only think they can. They know they can.'

'No! Fantastic!'

'You're joking!'

The boys listened while she told her story. At the end she asked, 'Any suggestions?'

'Not a thing you can do about it,' said Perry. 'Not a thing. I've heard of these cases before. They say they'll compensate you, but they don't really make up for the loss. For one thing, it always depreciates the property no end. I think that's a rotten deal for them to hand you, just when we were going along so well!'

'It's worse than that!' growled Glen. 'It's—it's—.' Words failed him.

'Dusty's written to our Melbourne solicitor,' Ryl told them. 'I stood over him and made him write. I'd have done it myself, but he's the senior partner, after all! But nobody's exactly encouraging.'

'I should say your only hope,' said Glen, 'would be to get the council on your side, or at least, the council surveyor. If you could only persuade him not even to mention your property to the council! If only he'd do that. Then it just wouldn't come up!'

'But that would be absolutely impossible! You see, the trouble

161

is—well, actually to tell the truth, Dusty and I were pretty rude to him. I expect we didn't impress them. The main one—Mr. Brown I think the name is—he did start to talk about having met my mother, but Dusty chopped him off at the socks. I don't suppose he'll ever make a friendly overture to us ever again as long as he lives!'

Glen groaned. 'You and your grandfather can't be said to have lashings of tact, can you?'

'Well, don't include me! I said Dusty was rude—oh, I suppose I wasn't much better.'

'The young cadet type,' said Glen. 'I think I may have met him up at Uni. I believe the surveyor bods come along every second week for lectures. I met a chap one lunch-time who said he was assigned for prac. work to Murwillumbah council. His name was —what was it now—Spike. Spike Hardy.'

'I didn't hear his name,' said Ryl, 'but that's probably him.'

'I wish we could do something,' said Perry, 'but there's just nothing.'

'It's getting mighty cold,' said Ryl. 'Let's get some coffee.'

Three evenings later, they heard from their old friend Mr. Herbert. But it was not a hopeful letter, and only repeated the opinions they had already heard so uncomfortably often.

'Well, *he's* not a lot of help!' said Ryl in disgust, as she pushed the single sheet of paper back into its envelope. 'Glen was the only person who could even think of the least little *thing* to do! He said we ought to appeal to the surveyor's better feelings.'

'You'll not convince me there's such a thing as a council surveyor with better feelings!' Dusty growled.

'And Mr. Herbert even seems to think it doesn't matter! Why, from his letter you'd think he was almost pleased about it!'

'Ah.'

'He just doesn't seem to understand that we—we've put all of *ourselves* into this place!'

Dusty sighed. 'They just can't understand!'

His eyes travelled about the room. The strawberry curtains were drawn and the silver-grey floor shone in the lamp light. Bits and pieces of furniture had been added. There was a wrought-iron table holding an orchid in a pot, some magazines, a bookcase which Ryl had picked up at the second-hand furniture shop in

162

Tweed Heads and painted. There was the portable record-player. It was a friendly room.

'This place is all our own work,' said Ryl. 'What cheek! To think that they can compensate us for all our effort!'

'All your effort,' corrected Dusty. 'Give credit where credit's due. You've worked like a good 'un on this place, my lass. I'd never have thought you'd have had it in you!' He added as though to himself, 'Of course, your father was a worker, I'll say that for him. Always doing something. His mother used to say he was creative. That was when he was a little feller of course.'

'Really?' cried Ryl. 'Why, what sort of things did he do?'

'Ah, he used to like painting pictures. He even wanted to learn art, if you please. His mother would have let him, too. I said, "What a lot of rot!" I said there's better ways for a boy to waste his time than messing about with pictures.'

'You should have let him learn!' Ryl told him severely.

'Um. But you see, lass, in those times it hardly seemed respectable, as you might say, for a feller to spend his time messing about with picture paintin'. Anyhow that was the way I looked at it. But maybe I should have humoured him.'

'Maybe you should have. But you'll humour me, won't you? We'll bring each other up very well!'

'Only I dunno how I'm ever to teach you any manners!'

'By setting me a better example! Next time you meet a district surveyor—smile! You were awful, the way you squashed him just when he was beginning to take an interest in—'

Ryl decided that this was the moment she had been waiting for.

'Dusty, pet, why didn't you like my mother?'

Dusty fiddled with his pipe. 'I never said I didn't like her.'

'But you quarrelled with my father about her!'

Dusty was silent.

'So why? Didn't you want him to marry her or something? I bet that was it!'

'Huh.'

'There, you can't deny it! Now, why ever didn't you? When she was a nice pretty girl and everything?'

'I can't remember. I only know that you talk too much! And I'm going to bed!' Dusty stood up and put his pipe in his pocket in the very way that Ryl was always telling him not to. He had

163

burned several holes in his clothes by doing so. He stumped off without a word.

Ryl and Bruno were left alone. They sat in silence, until Bruno found the company too dull and began to relieve the boredom by chewing the fringe on the rug.

Because it was a long week-end, Glen called next day, and asked Ryl to come board-riding. Perry strolled up from the lakeside. He was wearing his patched clothes and carried a cane knife over his shoulder.

'I'm going to cut some stools from the old banana patch,' he said. 'I'll feed them to the milking cows. We're experimenting at the varsity's test farm with carbohydrate feeding, and there are some bananas at just the right stage.'

'Glen wants to go surf-riding. What about it?'

Perry stared at Glen.

'You can't be encouraging this young, helpless female to go surf-riding today! Why, the waves are running like mountains!'

'Aw, it's going down a bit,' Glen told him.

'A bit! It'll be two more days before it's safe to ride! Only a mug would go out today. You want to commit suicide?'

Glen was chipper and undaunted.

'If you don't fancy it, I can look after Ryl, old sport.'

'You'd be too busy in a crisis looking after yourself!'

Glen tried to toss him in a judo hold, but the wiry dark boy slipped out of his grip like an eel.

'Ah, come on, Ryl,' said Glen. 'He's been living with grandfathers too long.'

'Maybe Perry's right,' said Ryl. 'Maybe the surf *is* too high.'

Glen shut his lips and looked at her in a way that pulled her up short. Exasperation—jealousy—what was in his half-closed eyes? She had not known that he could look so grim.

'So?' he said. 'Whose apron strings are you tied to?'

She felt a flush of anger creep up her cheeks. But she was not quite sure against whom it was directed.

'Ryl,' said Perry, 'stay home. There's a good girl.'

He had not chosen his words. They were the first that came to his mind, said in a pleading, conciliatory tone. But if he had tried his hardest, he could not have formed a sentence more likely to decide Ryl to go board-riding that day. For a moment she almost

164

exploded. But she had read somewhere that 'the greatest weapon of the gentlewoman is silence'. She used it.

She turned her back on Perry, and spoke only to Glen.

'I'll get my bathers.'

In five minutes the two of them were driving down the Ridge Road. Perry stood still leaning on his cane knife, looking thoughtfully after them.

The beach at Rainbow Bay was deserted except for one figure with a board on its shoulder, looking disconsolately at the wicked surf. Glen and Ryl carried their boards on their heads and went to stand with him. They all lowered their craft to the sand. Ryl saw with surprise that it was the cadet surveyor.

'Hullo!' he said, recognizing Ryl. 'Fancy seeing you!'

Glen struck up a conversation. 'So you're a board-man?'

'Sometimes, but I don't know about today! Boy, aren't they rolling!'

'Nice board you've got there. Custom job?'

'Yeah. Custom.'

'A lot of banana in it.'

'I like a bit of a curve to her.'

'We could handle it, don't you reckon?' Glen nodded towards the surf.

The three of them watched the great green seas humping their backs far from shore, and crawling nearer, nearer, to raise monstrous heads and fall splintering, shouting, tearing up the sand.

'The beach looks sort of hollowed out,' said Ryl. 'It didn't shelve so steeply before, did it?'

'That's the work of the king tide,' explained Glen. 'The beaches are always changing.'

'By the way,' he suddenly remembered, 'do we all know each other's names? Spike Hardy—Ryl Merewether.'

Spike grinned. He had a nice grin.

'We've met,' he said. 'Though not under very good circumstances.'

They chatted for a while. Then Spike asked:

'Are you two really going to ride the boards?'

Glen spoke for Ryl—which she hated.

'Sure, sure, Ryl's real keen, she can handle 'em.'

165

'I wouldn't have gone in by myself,' said Spike, 'but if there are three of us, that's not such bad odds, is it?'

He and Glen picked up their boards, then Glen put out a hand to take the end of Ryl's as well. But she shied away. The truth was, she was feeling in a most disgruntled mood. She wondered why on earth she had ever come, and the sight of the surf did nothing to reassure her. It looked terrifying. But having come, she now must justify her action. Glen's confidence in her wish to board-ride left her no loophole. But she was mentally blaming him for her predicament, and would never allow herself to show weakness to him.

'I can do it by myself!' she snapped. Very awkwardly she managed to lift the board, too big for her by far, and get it into the water. Tons of water, packed behind the force of the breakers, were crushing about her, already waist-deep, for the beach had been washed into a steep shelf. Ryl knew that if she and her board were under those piles of water, their very weight would prevent her from surfacing before she had smothered. Also, that if they tore the board from her grasp and crashed it down on her head, as could easily happen, she would never regain consciousness. With skill born of fear she waited for a huge wave to break, then pulled out from shore as fast as a dolphin, putting distance between herself and the steep sand before the next boomer should crash to pieces around her. Once past the line of foam, the huge surf carried the riders in comparative safety. Now, unless they lost their boards, they had a better chance of survival. Their greatest danger was close to the shore line.

Even so it was no joy-ride to Ryl's way of thinking. Each swell rose before her like a nightmare slippery-dip, which itself rose and heaved beneath her. She always managed to keep on top of the slope of water, keeping ahead of it before it curled into foam. She lay on her stomach, kicking her heels in the air with the effort of her paddling. Then the wave would slither away beneath her, and there would be a swift fall through space, and she would fly up in the air, too light to stay with her craft. The only way she could be sure of making a spread-eagle landing back on her board was by clinging with her fingertips to its polished edges, and this was desperately difficult. After the seemingly great fall through space, both board and girl would land once more on the water with a resounding blow.

166

'I just know I'm going to be bruised black and blue!' she thought to herself, shutting her eyes tight to keep out the view of heaving water. 'And golly—I do believe it's making me seasick! Oh dear, *why* did I come with that *beastly* Glen?'

At last the fleet of three was far enough from shore, which was a discreetly short distance today! They all sat up on their boards and began to glance over their shoulders for waves to catch. Ryl was justifiably terrified of being separated from her board, for she knew she could never swim back to shore through the surf. As

167

for sharks! They could be in shoals beneath her very feet and no way of telling!

The first wave looked so terrifying that she decided she would never have enough courage to wait for a second! With skill born of fear, she caught it perfectly, and rode its curling crest, running the length of its streaming mane, taming the sea monster, her slim feet stepping daintily on the waxed board as she steered it by touch, as a blind pianist plays. Then as the comber neared the shore, and prepared to be pounded to death on the sand, she slid back behind it. It was a beautiful piece of surf-riding!

But for Ryl, it was enough and to spare. She followed the wave in, making use of the comparative calm left by its passing to splash ashore and pull her board after her. She went up the beach to a safe distance, sat down and put her head between her knees. In a waking nightmare she could still see the wall of running water above her head, and feel the motion of its churning body.

The boys were not so long out themselves. In ten minutes they both came in, blowing the water from their lips, dragging their boards behind them, keels up. They plumped down beside her.

'Gee!' said Spike admiringly. 'You didn't stay out long, but can you ride 'em! You caught the first wave! You caught it just like that! And rode it like a broncho! Can you ever ride 'em!'

Ryl opened one eye.

'Oh, that was nothing, really, just a piece of cake!' she said. Never in a lifetime would she let them know how terrified she had been.

'Why did you get out so soon?' asked Glen.

Her green eyes were inscrutable. She'd never let them know. Here they were, thinking she was the new surfing champion. Why spoil a good show?

'It's rather cold in,' she said.

The boys talked between themselves.

After a while Glen brought up the subject of Geebin. He and Spike talked it over, while Ryl sat remarkably silent.

'It's a pity you don't have any influence in that shire office,' said Glen to Spike. 'It's not much use asking you to use your personality to soften up that Mr. Brown?'

'No,' Spike grinned. 'He doesn't really confide in his cadet staff! I suppose you Merewethers couldn't make it out to be so valuable that they couldn't afford to compensate you?'

168

'Not unless they strike oil there,' admitted Glen, 'and it's a fairly remote possibility!'

'The property on the other side of the Ridge Road,' said Spike, 'the one that runs into the valley where the lakes are—it has one point near the corner of the road that's almost as high as your place, Ryl. It's been marked as an alternative site. I don't suppose you could persuade old Brownie to recommend that instead of your place.'

'Across the road?' said Glen. 'That must be the extreme point of the farm where Perry lives. Gee, you want to work on that, Ryl! Surely if the surveyor knows you don't want to sell, and that the alternative site only belongs to a couple of Kanakas—'

Suddenly, Ryl, her nerves already on edge, felt her self-control ebbing. At that moment she hated Glen, with his smooth manners and jazzy talk. Behind them there were the tiny scruffing sounds of footfalls on the sand. Ryl glanced up. Perry had walked towards them.

'Hullo,' he said dully. Ryl knew he must have heard Glen's words.

Glen, unabashed, cocked an eyebrow.

'So it's the master himself. You got lonely, did you?'

Perry said, 'Lonely, no. Worried, yes.' He looked shyly at Ryl for a second. She knew he must have been worried for her. He said, 'I got to thinking, and the next thing I knew I was just taking a run down to make sure everything was all right.'

Ryl felt the smart of tears behind her eyes. Dear old Perry. She stood up beside the brown boy.

'I'm cold,' she said. 'Perry—let's go home!'

'You do look sort of peaky,' agreed Spike with concern. 'Maybe we shouldn't have let you go out in the drink. Don't go and get a cold or anything.'

'I'm all right,' she said. Her teeth would have been chattering if she had not clenched them. 'I just want to go home.'

Glen stood up. 'I'll take you,' he said. 'I'm your answer!'

Between tears and anger, Ryl finally boiled over.

'You!' she shouted. '*You*, my answer! Ha! You just think you're God's gift to women, don't you? Well you can go back to your beastly surf and you can drown and get eaten by sharks and I'll *laugh*! So there!'

Dramatically, she concluded her bit of dialogue by bursting

169

into tears. Glen sat blinking vacantly. Spike's mouth was twitching at the corners, as he struggled not to laugh. Perry put an arm about her cold, wet shoulders. She picked up her towel and scrubbed her eyes with it, and the two began to beat a retreat.

'By the way.' Perry stopped for a moment, and turned back to the others. 'You may as well know—if Ryl can talk Mr. Brown into using Ki's and my land for the water-tower we'll help if we can. Our farm doesn't mean so much to us as Dusty's does to him. And by the way again—Ki and I, we may be black and brown respectively, but we can still behave more like gentlemen than fools who kid girls into killer surf!'

With chins held high the two presented their backs to the others, and left the beach.

Glen tried to collect his wits, scattered for the moment, and think of something suitable to call after them. But for once, words failed him.

In the Bomb, Perry dragged a bulky old jumper from behind the seat.

'Here,' he said. 'Put that on.'

Ryl huddled it around her. It was far from clean but she did not mind. It felt homy and dependable. Faithful . . . a faithful garment.

'I don't think I'm so cold really,' she said. 'I wasn't actually cold so much as—scared! Golly, I'll have dreams about that surf!'

Perry gave her a sideways grin.

'Well, that shows you're normal!' he grunted. 'If I'd gone out in that surf, I'd be dreaming about it! If those bone-heads weren't scared, it just goes to prove they're bone-heads. Where there's no sense there's no feeling!'

She leaned towards him.

'Thank you for being worried about me, Mack-the-Knife,' she said. 'You were right all the time, as it turned out. And—another thing—don't mind what that Glen creature says. He's a little-minded—a snobby—a—oh, he's just not worth bothering about!'

'Thanks, 'Ryllis. But not to worry! I just couldn't care less what Glen baby or anyone else says or thinks! And anyhow, he doesn't mean it, you know. He just talks that way to impress people! He's all right underneath.'

170

'You don't hate him for calling you a—for saying—what he said? I'd hate him for it if it were me.'

'Ho!' Perry patted her hand. 'It's just water on a duck's back to me. You see, I know jolly well that a day will come when I'll run rings around Glen and the rest of them. You see—I've got something to fight for. And so—brother, I fight! Glen—he's always had it good. He couldn't fight if he wanted to. Couldn't fight his way out of a paper bag.'

'But why has he grown so snooty about you?' said Ryl. 'He wasn't always like that!'

'He's growing up,' said Perry. 'I guess it takes different people in different ways! Pardon my mentioning it—but he could be sort of mixed up about you.'

'How me? You said that once before!' Ryl thought for a moment, then pondered out loud. 'You know, Mack-the-Knife, I think you're a wonderful person. But I don't mean in any of that —that—boy-girl sort of way. I just—well—when I'm with you, I just feel the same as I do when I'm with Dusty and Bruno! Of course, you already know that, don't you?'

'Of course,' said Perry. 'But maybe old Glen doesn't. Or then again—' He stopped, and looked furtively at her as he drove. Then he began again: 'Ryl? Have you really—and I mean *really*—ever decided just what you think of people like me? I mean, people of mixed parentage. Think a moment, and then tell me.'

Ryl thought carefully.

'Well—' she said, 'I suppose they can be the best of two worlds —or they can be the worst. It's just what they make of themselves. And as a matter of fact, when you think about it—every race has to be descended from some other race.'

'Yes,' said Perry. 'But it's all very well being objective about other people. What would you do if *you* were of mixed blood?'

Ryl thought again.

'I'd try to be like you,' she said. 'I'd just try to be a fine citizen of the world—or to narrow it down, of Australia.'

They drove in silence. The conversation had disturbed Ryl. She wondered if, under his brave face, Perry had been brooding.

Home at last, Ryl ran into the kitchen. Dusty was sitting there; he had made himself a cup of tea, his dog and bird for company. For some reason, at the sight of him, Ryl's blues caught up with

171

her. She cast herself upon one of the hard kitchen chairs and began to shed tears, leaning her elbows upon the table. Dusty sighed, then poured her a cup of tea. Bruno went to her and put his large, foolish head against her lap and gazed up with comic sympathy. Even Jones appeared to regard her with his head on one side.

'Ah, youth,' said Dusty, with feeling. 'It's crook. Conflict. Youth has a lot of conflict. Very wearing, it is. You've got to be young to take it. It'd be no good to me, at my age.'

# XXI

Ryl went to Murwillumbah on the bus. She missed her rides with Perry in the Bomb or the empty taxi. She went to the Council Chambers, hoping to find Spike.

She walked down the long corridor, reading the names on massive varnished doors, finally coming to one marked 'DEPARTMENT OF SURVEYING'. Timidly she pushed it open, and found herself confronting a desk at which sat Mr. Brown. There was no sign of Spike. Ryl wished she had asked at the front office, instead of coming herself to search him out. She wanted to sink through the floor, but no hole obligingly opened to receive her. Mr. Brown looked up from his work, and recognition dawned in his face.

'Can I help you?' he asked coldly.

'Oh—no—no, thank you. It doesn't matter, I was just looking —looking for Spike Hardy.'

'He's out on some field work. I'll tell him you called.'

'I'm sorry—I shouldn't have—anyhow, thanks.'

She could see by the surveyor's face that he quite agreed that she should not, indeed, have entered his department uninvited. Then, just as she was about to slink away crushed, he himself rallied to her rescue.

He said, 'I'm sorry that your grandfather doesn't take too kindly to this water-tower proposal—or you, either. But perhaps by now you've thought it over, and realized that the old house isn't worth the holding up of a community's water supply?'

This seemed a golden opportunity, after all, for Ryl to put her powers of persuasion to the test.

'But, Mr. Brown—maybe it's you who doesn't understand. You see—you just *can't* know what that place means to my grandfather! He lived on that property when he was a boy. Then later on he quarrelled with my father—not knowing that he'd bought the place back. And then my father went to New Guinea—and he was

173

killed there in an accident—and then my grandfather found that he had his old home back, the home he hadn't seen since he was a boy—and he found he had a grand-daughter—that's me—and I found I had him—because we hadn't known about each other before, and it was the farm that brought us together. Why, my grandfather can remember such a long way back, and all the rest of the district's changed—all but Geebin! And the next property where Perry Davis lives. But Geebin is still as he remembers it. Well the house isn't exactly original, but it's only changed over the years the way a tree loses its leaves and grows another lot— it's only been changed one weather-board at a time, more or less! So it's *practically* the original house! Why, there's even a bird there, that comes back every year, just because he was born there! Maybe he's not the original bird that was there when my grand-father was a boy, but he's just like it. *Do* leave that house there, so that my grandfather can finish his life there—like the bird!'

Mr. Brown smiled at her earnest face. 'You make it sound as though it ought to be taken over by the Historical Society!'

But although he smiled, he could see how deeply she felt about what she said. Her words painted a vivid picture of what the house meant to her, as well as to the old man. She saw sympathy dawning in his eyes, and pressed her point.

'My grandfather's led a very lonely life, Mr. Brown, for the last twenty years. He's been very poor. Then suddenly he finds he's got back the old home he used to be so fond of. How could you snatch it away again?'

Mr. Brown nodded.

'You've made a point, Miss Merewether.' He looked at her thoughtfully. 'Most young girls like you would be only too glad to have a new house instead of an old one. They wouldn't worry about what their grandfather wanted.'

She turned shy. 'Oh, well. I've come to like it myself. I've painted it, and knocked out walls and hammered in nails, and patched up furniture. It's the first—well—home, I've ever had. I've always lived at boarding-school before.'

'Always lived at boarding-school?'

'Yes. In Melbourne.'

Mr. Brown shook his head. 'What would your mother have thought of that?'

She remembered how she had wished that this man would say

174

more of her mother. But now she could not think of a way to set him talking.

'Did you know my mother well?' she said at last.

'No, not well. I saw her around sometimes, just the way you do with most of the local—people.'

'Why? Did she come from around here?'

His eyes were slightly puzzled—then wary.

'Didn't you know that?'

'No. Tell me—tell me some more about her. Where did she live?'

He was quiet for a long time before he answered.

'On Greenbank Island.'

'But,' said Ryl, 'she couldn't have, there's only a native village there!'

'Do you remember your mother at all?' asked Mr. Brown.

She shook her head. 'No. She died when I was just a baby.'

'And your father sent you to boarding-school as soon as you were big enough?'

She smiled. 'Before that, actually, I lived in kindergarten homes.'

He pursed his lips and whistled tonelessly.

Ryl said, 'Mr. Brown, that alternative site—'

She stopped suddenly. She realized that she was not supposed to know that there *was* an alternative site. She looked confused. But Mr. Brown grinned.

'You've got a real pal in Spike Hardy I see!'

As the truth was now out, she gave him a crooked smile and went on:

'Yes—you could say that—anyhow, the alternative site belongs to Perry Davis and his great-grandfather. And they say they don't mind if it's used as a water-tower.'

'Well,' Mr. Brown told her, 'I'll have to think this over. But don't you worry about it. I promise you I'll think very carefully. You've thrown a different light on the matter. Of course, I can't make any promises.'

'Golly. Thanks anyhow, Mr. Brown!'

When she left the Council Chambers, Ryl carried one hand behind her. The fingers were crossed hard in the folds of her cotton skirt. She was saying to herself, 'I'm going to keep them crossed until I hear from that man again!'

.    .    .    .

175

She finished her shopping in time to catch the bus back along the Ridge Road. Her thoughts, as it bounced along, jumped from the safe keeping of Geebin to the second-hand car, the one she had seen at the tick-gate garage. Maybe, she thought, maybe it was a good buy—or then again, maybe not. Would there be any chance at all of persuading Dusty to buy a new one? Oh, no, of course there wouldn't! The price would send him into a stroke. Look how he just hated anything new, even a new pair of socks! He always darned his own socks, darned and darned them, with all colours of the rainbow. His socks were a marvel to behold.

And Perry was having trouble with the Bomb too. He warned against buying old cars. Perry himself needed something new, to travel back and forth from town. But he hadn't any money. Maybe there'd soon be some more calves to sell, and she and Dusty could make him keep the money. Not an easy thing to do, he was so independent! Only a few weeks to my birthday, she thought. That means we've been here almost a year. She felt a lot older. But she must get that car somehow. Now, what would be the best way to get around Dusty?

So her thoughts chased themselves, as the bus climbed the Ridge Road, high above the river.

At the end of the week, Ryl was putting out mineral-licks for stock in the river pasture near the cattle dip, when she thought of Ki.

'Now, whatever made Ki pop into my head?' she wondered, standing in her old jeans at the edge of a thicket of swamp-oaks.

Before her, stretching back from the river were coarse-grassed, greening pastures filled with lambent sunlight. Behind her the slim native oaks and paper-bark trees stood knee-high in fern, while lone, great fig-trees touched the sky above. A tangle of sally-wattle and lillipillies were in the deeper swamps, bound with lianas. The low-lying ground was full of vines, their leaves trefoil shaped and lush. The sky was chalk-blue and the near hills veiled in smoke from burning-off fires. Farmers were laying their fire-breaks against the coming dry season. Everywhere there was a feeling of lethargy, of underlying sadness, the feeling of weak, winter sap struggling upwards against green wood. Even the cattle as she passed them, turned their white faces towards her and the Palomino pony, too lethargic to take fright.

176

'What's made me think of Ki?' she wondered. Then, 'Maybe it's association of ideas. That must be it. Perry bought the cattle-licks—I'm putting them out, so I think of Ki.'

The lick was a new product to combat the soil deficiency, even though both Perry and Dusty were pleased with the progress of the cattle. King Cotton had ploughed a section of the flats and sown a crop of legumes, to put nitrogen into the soil, while they had planted lucerne in another part. Meanwhile it was Ryl's weekly task to distribute the blocks of lick.

'That's the last,' she told herself, placing the block in its cradle of stones. 'Golly, I'm glad that's done, I thought it never would be. Now come on, Pal. Let's go and look in at Perry's place, seeing we've thought about it.'

Usually, neither she nor Dusty visited Ki on a Friday, as they knew that Perry would arrive home for the week-end in the early evening and take over his own grandfather-sitting. But on an impulse, she rode the indignant pony past the gate of his home paddock and down the opposite hill-side through the banana plantation.

Outside Perry's home she looped the reins over the gate-post and walked up the path under the poinciana. She was in time to meet the district nurse on her way out.

'Hullo, love!' The hardbitten but kind woman paused in her stride. 'Don't know if I should tell you to go in or stay out. The old chap's not looking too good.' She hesitated. 'It's the spring, I suppose. The old folks always go at the turn of the year.'

'Why,' said Ryl, 'isn't the spring supposed to be the time when everything's jumping?'

The nurse smiled. 'Yeah, that's the drill they give you, but there's another side to it. The spring's a time that gives to the strong and takes from the weak. It's a funny thing about the turn of the year. Well, can't stop to chatter, I've got to pick up my feet, as usual. No rest for the wicked and the good don't need any they say! Well, I need it, and it's no secret that I do!' She laughed and slapped Ryl's arm with gusto. 'Well hoo-roo, love!'

Ryl ran up the steps. The white cat came to greet her, tail erect and a picture of poise. She went through the living-room, which was always strangely tidy these days, with no one to disorder it, and into Ki's room.

Its furniture was an old iron bed, a chest of drawers and a chair.

177

Its bareness was not depressing for it was clean, with a silver-grey polished floor like those at Geebin, and the big window made it full of light and air. Now the curtainless window framed a picture of purple and indigo sunset sky behind the mountains. Mount Warning took the centre of the stage, making a picture of weird beauty that was better than any curtains could ever be.

Ki gave an impression of stillness. He seemed of no substance, so thin was his frame, and so quiet as to be hardly breathing. His black face topped with its sparse white fuzz of wool looked as though dusted with a grey bloom.

Ryl sat down in the chair by his bed. The cat, paddy-pawed as though walking on tiptoe, sprang into her lap and sat there, staring narrow-eyed at his old friend. Some subconscious know-

178

ledge spoke within the young girl, telling her that here, in this room, was defeat. A giving up; or rather, surrender. No need for tears or sadness. Only that this soft spring evening, coming across the mountains, must mark for the old Islander the end of a long, long day.

She took his thin, smoke-coloured hand that lay on the nurse's white hygienic bed-sheet and sat there, holding it.

After what must have been a long time, Ki opened his eyes and they moved towards her with the whites upturned, more than ever like an old spaniel's eyes. To her knowledge he seldom spoke. But he did now, in a forced, abrasive whisper.

'Girl,' he said, 'you bin to the graveyard at Chindera? Graveyard of my people?'

She nodded. 'Yes, Ki dear—'

She had been there once.

Driving along the Kingscliff Road with Glen, they had passed a village of the Islanders and come to a stretch of sandy-soiled banksia forest. Underbrush of thorns and bracken fern grew beneath paper-bark-trees, giant banksia and she-oak. It was only by chance that she had noticed a rusted iron railing showing through the grey-green, growing things—a broken marble headstone—a tilted wooden cross.

'Glen!' she had cried. 'Are those—are those gravestones? There, among the bush? Surely they can't be!'

'Heck, yes, that's what they are,' said Glen. 'That's the old native cemetery.'

She had begged him to stop and let her out of the car, to read the almost obliterated inscriptions on the broken and tip-tilted stones. Each bore the name of an Islander and the name of his birth-place. 'Joshua Keoto, Abo Island. Sammy Ekebede, New Hebrides. Hezekia Napo, Samoa.'

Also in the white soil, almost pure sand, were newer graves. These were nameless. Some were surrounded by rough enclosures of saplings nailed together, or even tied with twine. Some were adorned with pickle bottles filled with plastic flowers.

'Why don't these ones have headstones?' she had asked Glen.

'I dunno. S'pose the relatives of the deceased can't afford 'em. The old boys, they may have been kidnapped in the first place, but at least their bosses gave 'em slap-up funerals, by the look of it.

179

The next lot had to jolly well pay for their own.' His voice was cruelly cheerful.

Ryl said, 'You know something? You don't much care for the coloured people, I'm beginning to think.'

'Only beginning? You're slower than I thought!'

'It strikes me that around this district there's no racial conscience.'

'Why pick on us? Who else has a racial conscience, for gosh' sake?'

He laughed and steered her back to the car. . . .

Now, holding Ki's hand, she remembered the graves among the banksias.

'I want,' murmured Ki, 'to be there with my people.'

'Yes, Ki.'

It never occurred to Ryl to argue with him, or to deny that his end was near. She knew that to do so would not be comforting, but a breach of faith. The world had given Ki all it was prepared to give. All that could now prove friendship was the gift of honesty.

'For many years,' he said, 'I stay away from my people. For Perry, you see. Perry's father white. All white. Mother a little colour girl, little bit white. Perry's father all white.' He seemed very proud of this.

'He come from long way,' went on Ki, in his strained, husky voice. 'He fine looking man. Black hair, white skin.'

'Yes?' Ryl gave him her attention. He seemed to want to talk, with the last of his strength.

'He go to my islands,' said Ki. 'He go over the sea. Where I no more go.'

'Over the sea. Fancy.'

'Perry a clever chap,' muttered the old black man. 'Perry fit for make big man. Plenty schooling. I no let him grow up in Kanaka place.'

'He's wonderful,' said Ryl. She knew it would please Ki, but she meant it, too.

'I get him out of Kanaka place.' Ki was difficult to hear. 'He a white boy. But me. I bin away from my people too long.'

He stopped talking. His breath was very shallow. He closed his eyes and she thought him asleep, but they opened again, and roved

180

restlessly about the room. He seemed too weak to speak any more. Yet she felt if only she could soothe his restlessness. His eyes were pained. She could not tell if it were physical pain or if his troubled spirit were pain in itself.

'See out of the window, Ki,' she said. 'See the clouds? See how the colours change on them? They make pictures.'

He seemed to understand. His eyes followed hers to the window, and were steadied, as though the mind behind them had been given an anchor. The slow minutes lengthened into a chain, link by link. She kept talking softly, in short sentences.

'See, Ki? There's a gold cloud like a ship. It's unfurling its sails. It's a fishing-boat, like in the prawning fleet. The soft little clouds are mackerel. Or a shoal of taylor. There's one like a sea-horse, with a curl to its tail.'

The colours changed from rose and gold to deep purple and lemon and green, and the mountains bulked black against the afterglow.

In her mind she kept wondering, 'Why isn't Perry here?'

Over the ridge at Geebin, Dusty was missing her—as she knew he would be.

He went over in his mind all the accidents it would be possible for her to have on her Palomino pony.

He thought to himself, 'Horses are tricky things. You never know with horses. You think you have them figured out, and then they go crazy and shy at a bit of bark or the white on a cow's face. Almost as bad as people, horses are, you can't rely on them. Now where can that girl have got to, for pity's sake?'

After a long time, Ki spoke again. 'I go back,' he muttered. 'Back to my people.' Then he talked in his own language. Ryl guessed that his mind was far away, perhaps in the islands of his youth across the Pacific, far beyond the neglected graves among the banksias.

Soon it was quite dark, and she rose to switch on the light from the single bulb. It was hard and garish, hanging from the centre of the ceiling, so she stood on a chair and improvised a shade for it with a tea-towel and some pins from the nurse's tray of odds and ends. She realized she was ravenously hungry, and thought, like Pinocchio, 'hunger is a terrible illness'. She felt she

181

ought to find something which would tempt Ki to eat, and leaving him, went to the kitchen. In a cupboard were a few packets of dehydrated soup, one of which she made up in the small electric urn. She took a bowl of it to Ki.

'Going to eat some nice soup for me, Ki?'

He looked at her vaguely, without recognition. It was a little eerie in the quiet house with the old black man's uncomprehending eyes, and darkness smothering into loneliness.

'Why ever doesn't Perry come home?' she kept wondering. She felt slightly sick, in spite of her hunger. White Cat brushed comfortingly against her legs. Then from the outer gloom she heard the rattle of Pal's bridle. She had forgotten all about the patient pony, still hitched to the gate-post. The nearness of the animals helped her to take fresh courage. With all her strength she slipped an arm behind the old man's shoulders and raised his head, propping it with an extra pillow. Then taking a spoon, she patiently tried to feed him with the soup. After ten minutes she felt she could do no more.

'Anyhow, he's had some,' she thought.

She found she could not touch the stuff herself. She longed to be home at Geebin, even longed to be sitting down to a meal of Dusty's everlasting chops and potatoes. Ki's face was closed and relaxed. He had sagged even lower in the bed, so that his body seemed like an empty coat falling from a peg, something old and worn and no longer needed.

'He's peacefully asleep,' she thought. 'Really, Perry's *got* to be home soon! I may as well ride back to Geebin and at least tell Dusty where I've been. I can't leave poor Pal standing there any longer. Gosh, what's *happened* to Perry?'

She gave the blankets a last pat, making sure that all was done.

'Ki?' she whispered. His face did not stir. Leaving the light shining, she tip-toed from the house.

Pal greeted her with an impatient whinny, pawing the ground and showing his indignation at having been left for so long. She swung wearily into the saddle and let him find his own way in the dark, trusting him to know better than to tread on a snake. Soon at home, she slipped off his saddle and bridle, and turned him into the home paddock.

There was a light burning in Geebin, but no sign of Dusty, or of

182

any cooking activities. She wandered through the chilly, empty house. Not even Bruno to greet her. A bucket of milk and three eggs stood on the sink, showing that the cows and hens had been attended to, and she unwillingly went about the task of straining the milk and transferring it to the metal can which must be left outside the gate for the dairy Co-op truck to collect in the small hours of the morning.

'I come hot-foot home in case he's worrying about me,' she told herself sullenly, 'and he's not even here. He's off gallivanting on his own account, while I have a horrid time.' She felt suddenly enraged against both Dusty and Perry for their absence at this time.

She made herself a cup of tea and a thick cheese sandwich. The food and hot drink made her feel a little better in spite of herself, for it was seven hours since she had eaten, and at sixteen—or even seventeen—much drama may arise from the simple fact of an empty stomach. She looked at the clock. Nine o'clock.

'Maybe he's over at the Bradleys,' she considered. She was very tired. The afternoon's work had actually been a great strain—and it was not yet over. She walked across the paddocks to the Bradleys' house. This was usually forbidden at night, for there

183

was always the danger of stepping on a grass-snake in the darkness, but tonight she did not even care.

As she walked up the Bradleys' path she noted the fact that Bruno was not waiting on the mat, to rise and come bouncing towards her with a rowdy greeting.

'If Dusty were here,' she thought, 'Bruno would be here, too.'

In answer to her knock and call, Clem came to the door.

'Hullo there, Ryl! Come on in.'

She paused with her foot on the sill. 'First, is Dusty here? No? Then do you know where he is?'

'Could be lookin' for you maybe. He came over before, and asked if we knew where you were. He seemed worried. He thought you might have had some sort of buster off the horse. Said he hadn't seen you since you went to ride round the cattle.'

'Oh dear,' said Ryl. She saw now that she had been too impetuous in her concern for Ki. She should have spoken to Dusty first.

'But he's never worried about me before,' she grumbled. 'Why did he have to start today?'

'Search me! Of course, I don't really know *where* he's gone. We told him not to worry. But I don't know where else he'd be, except looking for you.'

Rose came to the door and looked over Clem's shoulder.

'What's the trouble? Can't you find Dusty? Maybe he's gone down to see Ki.'

'No, I've just come from there,' answered Ryl. 'And Perry still wasn't home, and Ki looked—well, you know what, I think he's dying. I'm not being silly, I mean it.'

She told the Bradleys of her vigil with Ki at sunset in Perry's cottage.

'Perry's sure to be there now, anyway.' Clem was complacent. 'P'raps we ought to ring the doctor and get him to have a look at Ki.'

'But the nurse had just left. She'd have told the doctor, wouldn't she, if there was anything he could do. She might be offended if we went over her head.'

'You're probably imagining things.' Clem rubbed his chin and smiled.

'Maybe I'd better go and take a look at the old chap,' said Rose. 'And, Clem, you help Ryl find Dusty. Can't you see she's worried!'

184

'Ah, just because she's loco, do I have to be loco too? Of course Dusty's all right. He's been looking after himself for a long time!'

'But *I* don't know where he *is*!' cried Ryl petulantly.

'And where would we start looking? He's probably—oh, he could be—well—' Clem's mind seemed to have drawn a blank.

'See! You can't think of a sensible place at all! *I* think the only place to start is the cattle pasture, because that's where he went to look for me! So if he didn't come back he must still be there! That's what you call clear thinking!'

'Nothing clear about that,' scoffed Clem. 'Why, that was hours ago.'

'So there must be a reason! He could have had an accident himself, just as he thought I'd had!'

'His horse is as quiet as a cat, in fact quieter than that.'

Rose broke in: 'You can't talk yourself out of it, Clem! You'll just have to stir your stumps and go!'

Clem sighed and gave in. 'Oh, all right! Good on yer, love. Women!'

'And I'll go down to Ki.'

'Then,' advised Clem, 'go in the car, I won't have you walking down that hill in the dark. I'll catch the horse.'

'That's the way. I'll go and put my cardigan on.'

She disappeared into the house.

'You may as well go home, Ryl,' said Clem. 'You look all in. I'll go and find Dusty if that's all you want! You only have to ask!'

Ryl straightened her shoulders. 'Oh, no, I'm coming too. I'll catch Pal again. Even though he won't like it.'

She wearily retraced her steps to Geebin, in search of a piece of bread to use as a sop to Pal's feelings.

185

# XXII

Ryl and Clem rode off in the direction of the grazing flats by the river. Certainly, unlikely spot as it seemed, they could think of nowhere else to begin their search. Dusty never went out in the evening except to the Bradleys. Also, Clem had found the third horse missing when he caught his own. The missing one was Dusty's elderly Ginger.

'I still reckon you should have stayed home,' Clem grumbled at Ryl. 'There's no sense in your coming out again. And Dusty will probably walk in at any minute.'

'But I've got this feeling, you see! It's woman's intuition, or something.'

'Gr-r-r! I've got a better name for it!'

'Anyhow I've left a note on the table, just in case he does come home while we're gone. Of course, I do hope that you're right and I'm wrong, and thanks awfully for coming. I don't know what I'd do without you.'

At once the grumpy Clem was contrite. 'Ah, it's a pleasure, mate! Think nothing of it!'

But in spite of Clem's cheerful company, Ryl was possessed by a feeling of foreboding as they gave their horses their heads down the dark road. It levelled out at the foot of the escarpment, and the two riders went in Indian file between banks of cane-grass as high as Pal's shoulder, or higher. There was no moon. Stars studded the sky, but did not relieve the thick darkness with their far, reflected light. The two carried torches, and these made straight, narrow causeways of light wherever they cast their beams, which served only to intensify the surrounding gloom.

'Gee, Pal, you're a good fellow,' said Ryl, speaking to the pony. 'You feel so warm and solid and sensible. Clem, don't the horses feel warm and solid and sensible?'

'Yeah,' said Clem, 'as long as they don't shy or put a foot in a

186

rabbit-hole, or walk under a tree and wipe me off with a branch under me chin and send me flying. Which is what Dusty thought must have happened to you!'

'And could easily have happened to him,' added Ryl. In a minute she said, 'If only I had a car. Then I wouldn't have gone to the river pasture on a horse, and then Dusty wouldn't have thought I'd had an accident—'

'It would have probably been worse,' Clem assured her brightly. 'You can do more damage with a car than with a horse, you know. Anyhow, you couldn't drive a car all over the cattle-licks!'

They came to the fence that bounded the pasture, and Clem opened the gate without dismounting. They rode through the great swampy paddock, half marsh along the river bank, half paper-bark scrub, elephant-grass eight feet high, and tangled jungle. The paddock was divided into two sections down the middle by a windbreak of giant bamboo. Here, in the hindering darkness they began their search.

They took opposite sides of the central track, urging their horses into the badlands, hoping their keen senses would enable them to pick their blind steps. Every few steps they called Dusty's name, and listened.

Ryl kept the fingers of her left hand linked in Pal's mane for comfort. It was like holding the hand of a friend. With her right hand she held the reins, and knew her firm pressure on them was a help to the horse, often saving him from a stumble, and giving him, too, contact with a friend. Once both she and the Palomino froze with fright, when a weird dark shape seemed to rise at them out of the tall grass, like some nocturnal monster of the swamp. But it was only the roots of a fallen fig-tree, blown over in some past storm and rearing up unnaturally between the stars. Twice her torch beam picked up a red glare of eyes as some wild, timid thing stared at their centaur form, and once, a low rustle and an evil, sibilant voice from the ground told that a snake had crossed their path.

After a while she heard Clem's 'coo-ee', and answered it. They kept up a series of shouts to each other, guiding them together until she could pick up the flash of his torch and follow it. At last, standing on a level knoll, the depositing place of some mineral-licks that she had left what seemed like an age ago but was only that afternoon when the sun was shining, she saw two horses

187

outlined against the sky, and her heart began to beat fast. Even before Clem spoke she knew what the second horse implied.

'Here's Ginger,' said Clem. 'He's got his saddle half off. He found us, we didn't find him. He came galloping up, pleased as punch to see us. So I'm sorry to say it looks as if you were right, love.'

It took Ryl a long time to reply, for although she had dreaded this and thought herself prepared for it, still her throat tightened into a knot. Clem rode close and patted her hand on the reins.

'Now, not to worry, everything's going to be all right! We're here, now, and we'll find him in two shakes, you see if we don't!'

His words calmed her.

'Then come on,' she said, 'let's get moving.'

Clem told her, 'I'll take Ginger over to the north side, and you take the south. Now, don't worry!'

She tried hard to smile, though in the dark Clem could not see it. Still, the very fact that she tried gave her courage. Clem went off leading Ginger. Ryl kept calling over and over—

'Dusty! Dus—t—y! Dus—ty!' From time to time she whistled, a good, carrying note.

When she was close to the bamboos there came an answering

188

call, very faint, and Bruno's excited barking, from the farthest part of the grazing land.

She rode as quickly as she dared to the central track, and over into Clem's territory, calling to him, and signalling with her torch. Finally its moving light attracted his attention and he came to her, his horse stumbling over the tussocked ground.

'Bruno's over in the far corner,' she said. Her blood ran cold at the thought of what they might find.

As they turned the three horses towards the sound of barking, Clem told her again, 'Mind, nothing much can possibly have happened to him, mate. Not with Bruno there. You've done a real good job so far, so don't go to pieces on me now, there's the girl! There's the warrior!'

So she bit her lips to keep them from trembling, and rode over the dark paddock, being a 'warrior'.

Soon the barking was close at hand, and interspersed with eager and pathetically childish whines. But the big pup made no attempt to rush to meet them. Not until they were almost upon him did he come forward, a bundle of mixed emotions—distress, joy to see them, and like any German shepherd pup, a great story of self-pity. Through Bruno's outpourings came another voice and something stirred on the ground.

It was Dusty, who announced in a weak yet belligerent crackle, 'Well, by cripes, it was about time you got here, too!'

He was prone on the ground, his back resting against a small swamp-oak, in a position that did not look too uncomfortable. Clem and Ryl could hear at once by his voice that he was tired and spent. Ryl slid from the Palomino and knelt beside him, hugging him rather tearfully.

'Now, now.' Dusty leaned on one hand and stroked her hair with his free one. 'No call for these carryings-on.'

'What happened to you, mate?' asked Clem. In the murk of night it was hard to see what damage, if any, had been done to the old gentleman.

'Arah!' Dusty snorted. 'I was looking for Ryl, you know. I was going over the paddock and calling, in the dark, thinking she might have had a spill. In fact, I'd *been* over it, and I was just going home, mind you.'

'Yes—and what happened?'

189

'So and then, if you'll believe it, Ginger goes and puts his foot in a rabbit-hole! He stumbled, you see, real bad he stumbled. He must have just took me off balance. Over his head I went like a sack of potatoes! Would have been real funny if it had happened to someone else!'

'But,' sniffed Ryl, 'you're hurt. Where are you hurt, Dusty?'

'It's my ankle—or my foot—or both.' They saw now by shining their torches on his right foot, that it was twisted at a grotesque angle.

'I reckon it's probably broke,' he rasped. 'Painful too, I can tell you that much.' And to prove it, he fainted.

'Well, now.' Clem slipped the saddle from Ginger's back and eased Dusty's shoulders on to it. 'I'll ride home in double-quick time and get back with the car. And I'll ring Dr. McCarthy and have him standing by. That'll be the quickest way to go about it. You stay here and cheer him up. And Bruno can stay and cheer you up. He's a good fellow and no mistake.'

'Oh dear,' wailed Ryl. 'My poor, poor Dusty!'

'Where's our warrior? Come on, buck up, it might have been a helluva lot worse, I don't mind telling you now! And at his age, too!'

Clem rode off, urging his tall mount recklessly along the comparatively smooth track that ran through the centre of the farm. Ryl was left with the still unconscious Dusty, the two horses standing close with drooping heads and enveloping both man and girl in an atmosphere of patient sympathy.

'At least,' thought Ryl, 'Bruno and the horses will keep any snakes away.'

After a while, Dusty came to himself, but was in too much pain to care for conversation. But Ryl chatted softly, trying to think of anecdotes and snippets that might interest him without requiring to be answered. She told him of her visit to Ki, of how Perry had not returned at his usual time, and how she had been reluctant to leave the old man alone. She did not try to convey to him the eerie feeling of silence in the cottage—the feeling of finality, of work concluded and ends tied.

After twenty-five minutes she heard a car approaching slowly over the rough ground. Clem had brought with him two neighbours, Dan and Herb Pierce. They had a blanket. Like most countrymen they had a working knowledge of first-aid and had

190

soon moved Dusty, on the blanket, to the back seat of the car, Ryl climbed in front with Clem, and Bruno squeezed himself in. too. The neighbours were left with the task of bringing the horses home.

'Doc says to bring him to the Bush Nursing Hospital at 'Gatta,' said Clem. 'He'll have to take X-rays and all that. Dusty will have to stay in hospital for a while, I expect.' He drove gently, trying to nurse the car over the bumps on its springs. 'Say, do we have to take that ruddy dog?'

'Certainly we do, we can't leave him all by himself when he's such a hero and a love. Could you leave him after all he's been through?'

'Yes.'

'Oh, cruel Clem, to the best dog. Oops!' She wiped her eye after Bruno had poked his nose into it, effusive as ever.

'See what I mean?' grunted Clem. 'Keep him away from me for Pete's sake; after all I'm trying to drive!'

He sighed and stepped on the accelerator.

At the small hospital, Dr. McCarthy supervised Dusty's removal into the casualty ward, while Clem made himself useful, and Ryl watched, heavy-eyed.

'You look as though you'll go to sleep on your feet any minute,' the young doctor smiled at her.

'Oh, I'm all right. Did we get you out of bed, or were you just going?'

'Neither—no such luck for me. I'd just got in from a job of work when Clem's phone-call came.'

All this time something else had been worrying away at the back of her mind.

'Have you been out to the Lake, to see Ki?'

He gave her his best professional blank stare.

'We're not supposed to talk shop to the customers, you know.'

'Oh, all right, sorry, I'm sure!'

The doctor retired to the surgery leaving Ryl slightly huffy. He soon reappeared after a quick examination of Dusty.

'I suggest,' he said, 'that you both go home and leave the patient here. You can call round in the morning. By then we'll have more information for you. We'll have to treat him for

191

shock first. So we'll look after him now, and you folk can get some sleep.'

'Sure.' Clem took Ryl's shoulder. 'Can we put our heads around the door and say good night to him?'

They did this. Dusty was drowsy and uninterested when they told him they were leaving. He waved them a weary good-bye and actually seemed glad to see them go.

'He's probably been given a sedative,' murmured Clem.

'Lucky him. Come on then.'

The day had been a long strain for the girl. She sat silent with her head against Bruno as they drove back along the Ridge Road.

'You're going to come over and sleep at our place,' Clem told her.

But Ryl was a force to be reckoned with. 'No I'm not, but thank you, you're a pet really. But I like my own little bed.'

'Now see here, a girl like you can't be all alone in a house.'

'Why not?'

'Well—the gob-il-ins might get you. As well as a few other people.'

'Fooey, I'd put buckshot in the pants of any gob-il-in, and Bruno would eat him without salt. Now do let me be, Clem honey. I'm used to my own bed, and I'll sleep better in it. I like to be by myself—and anyhow I'm not by myself when I've got Bruno.'

'Him, the big lug, any burglar that came 'ud find him under the bed, not beside it.'

'Now don't be hard to get on with. I promise I'll be all right, and I'm so tired I'll sleep like a stone.'

'Aw, have it your way, as usual! Then here we are. Your stop.'

They pulled up at Geebin, and she and Bruno got out.

'Good night, mate,' said Clem. 'Leave a light on, and sing out if you need us.'

'O.K. I'll do that. 'Night.'

Clem drove the last few hundred yards to his home. Ryl fumbled under a loose flagstone for the key—though the windows were never locked, and burglars would have found no trouble in roaming about the cottage at will. With Bruno pressing against her, the two of them entered the living-room.

Sitting on the couch was Perry, slouched with his head against the wall. His drawn features held an emptiness as old as humanity itself.

192

She knew at once why he was here. Showing no surprise, she went to him, and took his hand. His eyes remained closed. In his sweet, husky voice he said—

'Ki's dead.'

There was nothing she could say. After a while he spoke again.

'He did die alone, after all. I wasn't there. I was too late to say so long to him.'

'But he wasn't alone, Perry. Rose Bradley was there—wasn't she?'

'No. You must have been—the last person—to—to see him.'

'Me.'

'I had car trouble. I was held up on the way home with a petrol block or something. When I came in Mrs. Bradley was waiting there—to tell me.'

She sat down beside him. They looked strangely alike, by the single globe of the lamp on the table, which had been burning in the empty house all evening. They sat silent, side by side, their eyes seeing other things.

'I should have stayed,' said Ryl.

Perry shook his head.

'I was too late. Just tonight, of all nights.'

# XXIII

Dusty stayed in hospital for six weeks.

Ryl was rather glad that he was kept away from Ki's funeral, for she was sure that it would distress him to see the last of the old Islanders return to his own. Though he seemed to take the event philosophically enough, in his drowsy, antiseptic room shared with two other men patients.

'And how's Perry getting along?' he asked Ryl, on one of her daily visits, for which she made time among the many chores of the farm. Chores which she had never even known existed when Dusty was about.

'He stayed at Red's place until after the funeral. I expect he'll sleep there most week-ends, too, for a while. But he'll be working a lot at Geebin, when he's not studying. Dodi might keep me company at week-ends, too.'

'You'll need some company,' said Dusty, 'and you'll need plenty of help with them cows. This Dodi, can she milk a cow?'

'Wow, poor Dodi. I won't spring that on her or she mightn't speak to me again!' Ryl laughed. 'We'll let Clem and Perry do the milking, with our compliments!'

Dusty muttered, 'Looks as though you won't have any time for a birthday, lass. Farming like a good 'un, there on your Pat Malone, and trudging here every day to see me.'

'Golly, it's not that bad, honey! I'm enjoying it! I mean I'm sorry you had to break a leg, but still—'

She took a comb from her bag and began to arrange his white curls. 'No worries. Anyhow, I'm not used to birthdays. I can take 'em or leave 'em alone.'

But from his bed Dusty was amusing himself by making plans for this birthday. He discussed it with his visitors—Clem, Perry, and Butch Bradley. It was many a long year since Dusty had been interested in birthdays.

194

In his wily way, he knew that the project which he embarked on from his hospital bed was one which would, as well as pleasing Ryl, help Perry over a difficult adjustment period.

He was speaking to Perry one day, during one such visit.

'Now you'll know what kind she wants? Not some high-flying nonsense of a thing. A good, dependable one, that's all I want her to have. But the kind she wants herself.'

'Sure!' grinned Perry. 'The kind she wants, as long as it's the kind she can have! I'll fix it up. I know just what she wants. We talk about it all the time.'

'I'll sign a cheque and give it to Clem, he's a good feller, he'll not lose it or anything. I suppose I can get some of this money that Ryl's always spending if I sign a cheque. I haven't done it before, but they tell me I can.'

Perry said, 'I wouldn't lose it either, you know.'

But Dusty shook his head.

'I want Clem to go with you. Just in case you get carried away. Two heads are better than one, you know, even if they're only sheep's heads.'

'Well, thanks!'

'And you're sure you can order it at Southport?'

'Sure, I'm sure.'

'And they'll get it out in time for her birthday?'

'Yes. I'll tell you what—how about, on her birthday, if Clem and I drive her to Southport, and she takes delivery of it herself?'

'I wish I could see her face!' Dusty's eyes were glowing. 'I just wish I could see her face!'

So Ryl's birthday present was planned.

A week after Dusty's accident and Ki's death, Glen appeared at Geebin just as Ryl and Bruno were taking themselves across to the Bradleys for dinner. She heard the M.G. before it pulled up at the gate and went out to meet it. She had kept a distance between herself and Glen ever since the day when he had inveigled her into the surf against her better judgment. Though, as Perry pointed out, it was silly to blame Glen because she had not shown character!

Glen, as usual, looked suave and polished. Ryl, on the other hand, still wore the jeans in which she had helped Clem with the milking. Her hair was lank, and without its usual sheen. Without

195

lipstick her face looked colourless under its tan, and possibly a little thinner than a week ago.

'Do ask me in, dear girl!' said Glen.

'Hey.' Ryl looked down at herself. 'Ever see a physical wreck?'

'Pretty yourself up and I'll take you down town for a decent meal. Do you good. We could go skating or something afterwards. You look like a one-woman chain gang.'

'That's for real! But I can't do it. The Bradleys are expecting me for dinner, and anyway, for once I'm too tired. I don't want to skate. I want to sleep.'

She led him into the living-room. 'I never thought,' she flopped into a chair, 'that I'd be slaving away like the original Merry Peasant.'

'You certainly didn't look the type when you first hit these parts.'

'I'm at the beck and call of a lot of cows. And a banana patch. Golly, who got me into this, anyway?'

'Big deal!' Glen crowed. 'I knew something had to give! You and that banana patch just weren't made for each other!'

'Of course,' she assured him, 'it's only while Dusty isn't here! And anyway, I never *said* I'd stick it for more than a year! I'm going to Uni. next March.'

He stretched out a foot and rubbed it against her bare ankle.

'I've missed you lately.'

'Serves you right.' She remembered something else. 'And why weren't you at Ki's funeral? Tom was there, and Red, and his other friends.'

'Couldn't get up from town.'

'Huh! I'll bet you could have if it had suited you. Tell you what: you've gone all colour conscious lately, let's face it. Remember when I first came here? Then *I* was colour-conscious! You talked me into liking Perry! And now you've dropped him like a hot coal!'

He kicked at the corner of the rug. 'Aw . . .' he muttered.

'What,' she asked, 'was the real reason why you didn't even do Perry the kindness of coming to Ki's funeral?'

'Well, if you must know, I just didn't, that's all! Sure—I know, he was a poor old black fellow, made history, been here since the year dot, and all that stuff! I knew the place would be a mass of

196

hysterical Kanakas and maudlin, sentimental whites. None of 'em wanted any part of him when he was alive but they were sure to turn out in force to make a hero out of him once he was dead! Black and white hypocrites! I wasn't going to be numbered among 'em!'

She was thoughtful. There was so much truth in the picture he painted. He went on:

'As to Perry—well, I used to be good friends with him; still am, I suppose. But a chap gets other friends as he gets older.'

'Especially if he's a snob!' said Ryl, standing up. 'I want my dinner!'

Glen stood too. He looked in a teasing mood, and yet belligerent, and whistled between his teeth, always a sign that he was put out.

'Who's talking about snobs? Me! My dear girl, if I were a snob, and colour-conscious and all the rest of it, I would hardly be here now, barneying with a pretty little brown-skin—' He stopped. He even looked slightly ashamed of himself.

'What?' Ryl couldn't see that he was making sense. 'Whatever are you talking about—or don't you know either?'

'Oh yes, honey, I know! The things I know would surprise you! Surprise a lot of people, really they would!'

'Then start by surprising me! What were you saying? What about a brown-skin something or other?'

'Oh, heck—I dunno. Ignore me, dear girl! If you don't know what I was about to say, why take candy from a kid?'

'And *now* what are you raving about? Gee, you're making me mad!'

Glen laughed delightedly. This was probably just what he wanted to do.

'My dear innocent child!' he said. For Ryl, this was the end. She stamped her foot in fury.

'I am not your innocent child!' she shouted. 'Next year at the Uni. I'll be as good as you, and in the meantime you can go and fly in the air! Big Noise Glen! Big deal! Big nothing!'

'Temper, temper!' said Glen.

Ryl stamped out the door, reaching behind him as she did so to bang it shut. She did this with such speed and vigour that he jumped. Then she jog-trotted away in the direction of the Bradleys' house, shouting over her shoulder:

197

'And I'll never speak to you again, never, never, not simply forever!'

He could not resist shouting derisively after her retreating figure:

'I don't want to play in your yard!'

But he went and sat in the M.G. for some time, looking across the pink matel-grass in the direction she had taken. Finally, he got out and strolled over to the Bradley's, knocking on the back door. Ryl had seen him through the window, as they sat over their meal.

'Rose, love,' she said. 'There's Glen Dynon out there, and we've just had a great row and I'm not going to speak to him, so would you mind going out and telling him I hate him and to go away?'

Rose looked up from her steak and chips. 'What's that, dear? Glen, is it? Tell him you hate him and to go away, is that all the message? All right.' She went, quite unperturbed, to carry out her mission.

On the back door step she greeted him.

'Hullo, Glen. Sorry I can't ask you in, but Ryl says she's not speaking to you. She wants me to tell you that she hates you, and to go away.'

'Oh.'

'Of course, I wouldn't want to pry, dear, but it does sound interesting.'

'It's not really. We had a bit of a blue, I forget why. Just one of those things.'

'Well,' said Rose, 'will you please make it up by next Saturday, because it's Ryl's birthday, and we're going to give her a surprise party. Can you make it? I do hope so!'

He brightened at the mention of a party.

'Will I ever! She's sure to have gotten over it by then. She did say she'd never speak to me forever, but surely by next Saturday? Don't you think?'

'Well, if you make it up to her!'

'Oh sure—and shall I bring my portable barbecue to the party? You can't have too many, can you? I'm pretty good on the hamburgers!'

Glen always became executive at the very mention of a party. He and Rose conferred in a pig's whisper for some time, before Rose could return to her half-eaten dinner.

.        .        .        .

198

As they washed the dishes together, Rose could not resist asking Ryl about her quarrel.

'Far be it from me to be a sticky-nose, love, but it would be so interesting to know why you and Glen got so hot and bothered.'

Ryl thought.

'That's funny, I can't remember! We just sort of started calling each other names! Oh, yes, that was it, it was to do with name-calling. He started to say something, and wouldn't finish it. I can't think what on earth he meant.'

She was quiet for some time, thinking as she dried the cups. Then she began:

'Rose. Rose, I wonder just what Glen *was* talking about? And really, it's not just him. He started to say something about "brown-skin"—well, I suppose he was going to say "brown-skin girl". And he could only have meant me! Now whatever did he say that for? And then, I've been thinking—other people have sometimes stopped talking just as soon as they see me coming. And Dusty, too. There's something—I don't know—I have this feeling—is it something about my mother? Rose, if you know, *please* tell me what it means! Please, or I'll go crazy!'

Rose slowly rubbed steel-wool over the base of an already-shining saucepan.

'Perhaps I may as well,' she said uncomfortably. 'Yes. I think it might be best, at that.' She did not go on, just the same, until Ryl gave her another jog.

'Then come on, Rose, *tell* me!'

'Well—it's like this, Ryl. You never knew your mother, did you?'

'No, I never did. But Mr. Brown said she was pretty. What about her?'

'For a long time after you came here,' said Rose, 'no one really placed your parents. A few of us could remember your father. Then bit by bit, Clem's father, Butch, began to recall little things and fit pieces together. And at last they made a story. As it now becomes plain, your father was up here with the armed forces, just at the end of the war. Well, he married a girl here. But he kept it very quiet. When he got leave he took her down to Melbourne. Well, I suppose the marriage must have met with great opposition because she came back and lived with her own people. And by this time there was a baby, too. A little boy. And another on the

199

way. Then, when it was born, in Brisbane, your father came back up here. He bought this farm. And he bought a second, smaller one, under a different name.'

'Whatever for?'

'I'm coming to that. You see, pretty soon he went away again. He took the baby girl with him, and left the mother and little boy here, giving them the second farm. Maybe he told them he'd send for them later. But the mother died, before he ever saw her again —or the little boy. So the little boy was brought up by his old great-grandfather, on the farm that had been given them.'

'I can't believe this nonsense,' said Ryl. 'Why ever would anyone behave like that? Why take a tiny baby girl from its mother, and leave the older child? Or why leave either of them for that matter?'

'You see,' said Rose, very gently, 'the girl—the mother— evidently there'd been very hard feeling about the marriage in the first place. Because the mother—was a coloured girl. And the little boy—he had woolly hair.'

# XXIV

For a long time Ryl stood in front of Rose's kitchen-sink with the tea-towel in her limp hand. She stood there, staring into space. Rose watched her with sympathy. At last the girl said—

'I remember soon after Dusty and I came here, you told us some story about Perry. But I'd forgotten it. Why didn't anyone tell me then?'

'We didn't know,' said Rose. 'Your father had covered his tracks very well. He'd gone to some trouble to keep his affairs to himself. And remember, it all happened seventeen years ago. Not many people would remember it.'

'Then how does Glen know about it? And that surveyor, Mr. Brown. He must have known. I thought that day I talked to him, that he looked sort of queer!'

Rose took her hand.

'Sweetie, I can assure you, very few people would ever even think about it! The surveyor happened to know your father because he did some work for him. Glen's father is the chemist, so he would probably know something of the affairs of many people, just as a doctor does. But what does it matter? You're a girl we've come to love, like one of our own, and nothing can change that.'

Clem called from the doorway.

'Aren't you girls done yet?'

Ryl put down the tea-towel.

'I—I think I want to go home,' she said. 'I want to think.'

'What's been going on here?' asked Clem, looking from Rose's face to Ryl's. 'You both look downright punch-drunk! What's the matter?'

Ryl said, 'You tell him, Rose—I'm going home!' She suddenly gave Rose a quick hug, then disappeared through the door into the night.

'Hey!' Clem made a movement to go after her. 'Ryl! Come on back—!'

But Rose stopped him.

'Let her go, Clem. That girl's got some thinking to do. Leave her be.'

In the living-room at Geebin, Ryl sat hugging Bruno, while her mind grappled with this strange new revelation. She thought of the day when Perry had asked her—'What would you do if *you* were of mixed blood?' At the time she had thought it a purely rhetorical question, but now she added to it a certain awareness of attitude that she connected with Perry. Had he known all the time? Had he been trying to help her, to prepare her for this very moment? Her eyes welled with tears, she hardly knew why. Her life, she realized in this moment of truth, had been one of material luxury—and yet cold, friendless, a life of spiritual poverty. Perry, her brother as she now knew, had known such poverty as had never touched her—and yet, he had always been loved. Loved, and loving. Was that why he had been such a good friend to her, why he had tried to give her the benefit of his own experience? She wished Perry were with her at this time, to give answers to these questions. And Glen. For how long had he known of her parentage, and her relationship to Perry? She guessed now that in all probability Glen had fought against the knowledge, and that would have been a reason for his unreasonable and sudden antagonism to the dark boy.

Ryl sat until the small hours of the morning, turning over this new knowledge in her mind. There were so many aspects of it, it made her head ache. Not the least of them was Dusty's position. She knew now why he had refused to speak of her mother. But she could hardly believe that Dusty could willingly have broken up his son's home, ruined lives, altered destinies. She was impatient for the morning, when she could go to him and put many questions.

'So, old Ki,' she whispered to Bruno, 'was my great-grandfather, too! I wonder if he knew? He said Perry's father was a fine man. He said he went away over the sea, to his islands. I suppose he meant New Guinea! I suppose he thought of any islands as home. I don't think he knew that I was his great-grand-daughter. But Dusty—he must have known!'

202

Then she thought—'After all, I'm no different from before. I'm still me, just as Perry's Perry! I'm just descended from a Samoan, instead of from some Cockney convict! And I'm Australian!'

On this note, she dropped asleep, with Bruno warm beside her. . . .

The next morning, Ryl hurried to the hospital in Coolangatta. Last night she had done a lot of thinking, and her emotions had passed through a wide spectrum. There had been disbelief and doubt—there had been a kind of shame, though not directed against herself. Perhaps it was an abstract kind of shame, against the human race at large, and the unfair arrangement whereby some people were white of skin, some black, and this chance of birth could come before an individual's inner worth, of heart, brain and soul. Then, just before she fell asleep, there had come acceptance.

Ryl was an early visitor, and in a larger hospital, would most certainly not have been admitted to the ward. But at the Cottage Hospital, no one minded the non-observance of regular visiting hours. Dusty's white curls were damp and smoothed, showing signs of hospital discipline. His face looked rosy and scrubbed, shining with soap and water, his eyes bright and noticing as Ryl came into the ward. He had it to himself now, for male patients were few in the small nursing hospital.

Ryl thought as she saw him, 'He looks as if butter wouldn't melt in his mouth! He *can't* have anything to do with it!'

'Good day!' he greeted her. 'You're early, aren't you, my lass?'

She came and sat in the chair by his bed, straight and uncomfortable and uncompromising.

'Yes, indeed I am. And there's a reason for it! A very important reason!'

It was plain to the old man that she meant it. But she gave him no time to ask questions.

'Dusty, last night Glen came along and we had a fight and he said some things that didn't add up—so I badgered Rose, and made her tell me exactly what he'd meant! And she told me the queerest story! About my mother! And I think you know it!'

Dusty sank back against his pillows. His face showed that he did know it.

'So somebody's remembered, have they? And passed on their

203

information. They would. Can't take a fine girl at face value. If she happens to have the least little drop of coloured blood in her veins—sure, they've got to tell her about it! Ah! People make me sick! The lot of them!'

He looked crestfallen and sad. But, thought Ryl, not guilty!

'That's nothing,' she said. 'Rose says it's nothing. I do admit that at first I felt a bit—well—queer! Goodness, if I'd found out when I was at school in Melbourne I'd have died, I'd just have died! But now that I'm used to the idea I don't mind. Especially when Perry gets thrown in with the deal. And I'll tell you this, anyone with Perry for a brother is lucky, no matter if they're all colours of the rainbow!'

Dusty's face was puzzled, as Ryl's had been the night before.

'What's Perry got to do with it?'

She gave him a long, hard look. Then she shook her head.

'No, you don't know! Whew! Am I glad! I didn't want you to be the cause of it all!'

'What in tarnation are you talking about?'

So she told him Rose's story in its complete form.

When she had finished, Dusty lay looking at the ceiling.

'I ought to be hung,' he said. 'Ought to have been hung long ago. I see now what I did when I was so hard on that girl. But I never realized before.'

Ryl took his hand. 'Well,' she said, 'it's done now.'

'You see,' said Dusty, 'as far as I know, it was like this. Robert came up here with the forces, and next thing I knew he'd written down that he was married. Then eighteen months or so later he turned up in Melbourne with this Kanaka wife. You see, he'd never told me in his letters that she was *black*! Anyhow, she was brown! And a dark brown, too! So we had a great row, and I said I never wanted to see either of them again! Which I never did! Where they went to I didn't know—and I used to tell myself I didn't care. You see I'd never got on with Robert. But I'll admit it now, me girl—as the years went by and I was all on my own, I used to get thinking about Robert, and wondering where he was, and what he was doing. But I'd have never given in, not unless he'd given in first! But he never did. Until at last I found out he'd been killed. But believe me, I never knew anything about any children. I see it now. Robert knew I'd make a fuss, I suppose,

204

so he left the little boy behind when they came to Melbourne! He probably thought one shock would be enough for me! That's especially if the baby looked like a native, with woolly hair.'

'Never mind,' said Ryl, after a while. 'I suppose you thought you were doing right.'

'That I did, you can be sure. But now I see that it was me who broke up that family, when you get down to the bottom of it.'

Ryl could think of no comforting words.

'Mind you,' said Dusty, 'I don't think, even then, that Robert was too happy himself, about the marriage he'd made. I noticed that he never introduced the girl to his friends.'

'Poor girl,' said Ryl. 'Poor girl.'

'Anyhow, when the pair of them just disappeared again,' said Dusty, 'I just took it that they were living their own lives somewhere.'

'And you never heard of them again?'

'Never again.'

They were both quiet for a long time. Then Ryl said—

'Some bits of it we'll never know. Like, why did my father take me away from my mother, and take me to New Guinea, when I was such a little thing.'

'Maybe,' said Dusty, 'it was for no other reason than that you look all white. And Perry—doesn't.'

'Perry!' said Ryl. 'We're getting to be an awfully big family, aren't we?'

For some reason a tear began to trickle down beside Ryl's nose.

She said, 'Remember how you looked after Ki? And you never knew that he was—that he was my other grandfather. Or anyhow, great-grandfather. Do you think he knew?'

'No, not him. I wouldn't think so. Don't suppose he ever even heard our surname. He lived such a quiet life. And we never took any real notice of him—I mean, not to talk to him much.'

'That last day,' said Ryl, 'he told me that Perry's father was a fine man, and that he'd gone across the sea, back to his islands. Do you think he was trying to tell me anything?'

'Maybe he was, then. But whatever it was, you know now, don't you.'

They talked all the morning—never giving credit to the forbearance of the nursing staff, who allowed their patient so much freedom. It was late when Ryl left with a promise to bring Perry

205

himself to visit Dusty in the evening, although it meant bringing him, with a telegram, from Brisbane.

As Ryl ran to the bus-stop, she thought with a light heart, 'But I've got a brother! What a lovely birthday present! A brother! And just about the nicest brother in the world, too!'

The Bradleys, and various others, annoyed Ryl by their solicitude. No one could feel easy at the thought of the young girl being alone in Geebin at night, even though she kept assuring them that Bruno was actually another person! She had to be constantly telling people that she liked it this way, and was not lonely.

Ryl was naturally independent, and liked her own company. Through childhood she had developed resources in herself. Then, too, there was a great deal to do on the farm, and the animals had to be cared for. Dodi sometimes stayed with her on Saturday nights, using Dusty's bed, which she reported to be only softer than the floor in places. Apart from these nights of week-end companionship, the little house was very still after dark. But Ryl found something soothing in this, as she lay by the big, starry window in her bed with its mohair rug, with Bruno on the floor at her side.

In the morning after Rose's surprise story, Spike Hardy called.

Ryl and Bruno were at breakfast, which was the only meal she did not eat at the Bradleys' house. Bruno was rudely guzzling bread and milk, and spattering it over the flagstones, while Ryl made herself tea and toast in the kitchen.

'Hullo, there!' she greeted Spike. 'Come and help me drink this pot of tea, it's a pity to waste it!'

'Thanks, I couldn't, I've just had two eggs and chops and all the rest of it. I'm on my way to Mur'bah, but I just dropped by to say how sorry I was to hear about your grandad's accident.'

'Very kind of you, Spike. Do have just an itty-bitty cup of tea.'

'Couldn't!'

'Lucky you called early, I'm going straight in to see Dusty at the hospital.'

'I called once before but you were out.'

She sighed. 'I mostly am.'

He eyed her critically.

206

'Hey, you're looking a bit pooped! Circles under the eyes and all!'

'A *bit* pooped! I'm stove in! Golly, next time I know who'll be smart and break a leg! Dusty's having himself a ball in hospital. He plays chess all day with anyone he can catch, and does cross-word puzzles, and drinks tea from dawn till dark; they're just ruining him. I suspect that he could just as easily be at home, only they know darned well that he'd play up on me! I'd never be able to bully him into looking after himself.'

They laughed.

'Say, how about coming out with me on Saturday night? To a movie or skating?'

She shook her head. 'I'd like to, but I've told the Bradleys that I'll spend the evening with them. They're having some visitors they want me to meet or something, goodness knows why. I bet it's a terrible drag, but I'll have to do it; they've been so good to me I can't very well let them down.'

He nodded sadly. 'Then next week?'

'All right. We'll do that. Hey—have you heard any more about the precious water-tower?'

'No, but I believe Mr. Brown's sent his report in to the council. I hear they'll decide on it next week.'

'I wish they'd hurry up, the suspense is killing me!'

He looked at his watch. 'I've got three minutes to get to work,' he observed.

'Oh, lovely. Seeing it's a fifteen-minute drive to Mur'bah!'

She walked him to the gate and waved him off.

It was ten o'clock that night that Ryl heard the unmistakable sound of the Bomb pulling up outside Geebin. She had waited all day for this moment. Yet, now that it was here, her legs felt too weak to carry her to the door. She thought vaguely—'This must be what they mean when they say someone's suffering from shock! It's odd, because otherwise I feel quite matter-of-fact!'

Perry let himself in, and found her sitting on the cane lounge, staring at him as he came through the door.

'What's up? Are you all right? Why did you want me to come down? Why are you looking at me like that?'

Ryl forced herself to snap back to normal, and patted the seat beside her.

207

'I had to look at you properly,' she said. 'I know I've seen you plenty of times before—but it doesn't seem like it. I'm—I'm looking at you through different eyes.'

He sat down. 'What are you talking about?' he said.

So Ryl told him all she had learned, of the two babies, the man who had bought two farms side by side, the parents who had gone their ways, one keeping a woolly-haired boy, one with a green-eyed girl. He listened, calm and composed, hearing her out.

'You know,' said Perry at last, 'I'm not too surprised. You see—it's hard to explain—but for some reason, right from the first time I saw you—I had a feeling about you. I know it's silly— but—well—I sort of felt that you were going to mean something to me. And then—well—here—give me your hand.'

He took her hand, and held it palm up.

'I noticed your hands,' he said. 'Almost the first time I saw you. See how the palms are much lighter than the backs? It's only a little thing—but somehow, it made me wonder. Then—I found some papers in a box in Ki's room. One was the deed for our farm. And one was a marriage certificate. My mother's.'

'So,' said Ryl, 'you knew? But you never said a word!'

'It wasn't easy.' Perry stroked her hand gently. 'You can see that, can't you? Maybe I would have, eventually. I don't quite know.'

They talked for a long time, back and forth, around and around—it was a strange, a momentous night.

'You'd better get some sleep, Mack-the-Knife,' Ryl said at last, 'if you want to get back to Brisbane in the morning. You'd better sleep in Dusty's bed.'

'I have my first exam tomorrow. The year's almost over at University. The exam isn't until the afternoon, luckily. But I'll probably fail it, you know. Gee, I can't afford to! I can't lose my scholarship!'

'Then get some sleep, and pull yourself together. There's no reason why acquiring a sister should make you fail your exams!'

They both stood up.

'I've never kissed a girl,' said Perry. 'It would be sort of nice, don't you think, if the first girl I kiss were to be my sister?'

They kissed, very shy and solemn.

'Good night, sister,' said Perry.

'Good night, brother!'

208

# XXV

On Ryl's birthday morning she was roused early by Clem and Perry shouting outside her window. She put her head between the curtains and blinked sleepily down at them.

'Happy birthday, Ryl, get up at once!'

'What do you mean, happy-birthday-get-up-at-once? You can't have everything, so make up your minds.'

'You've got to come to Southport. Dusty's orders.'

'Why? ˑ

'Let us in and we'll tell you.'

'But tell me now!'

'Let us in first.'

She yawned. 'Golly, no peace, even on my birthday!' She came and unlocked the front door, assisted by Bruno.

'I'll make you some tea and toast, your favourite things,' offered Perry. 'And you get dressed. That'll speed things up a bit.'

'But where am I going?'

'To Southport—we told you!'

'And why am I going?'

'Because we're all going.'

'Then why are we all going?'

'Because Dusty wants us to!'

'*Why* does he want us to—and *why* are you both being so maddening?'

'We are not! Do get dressed, and hurry up!'

Scowling at all this pushing around and obvious skullduggery, Ryl trailed a towel over her arm to the snake-pit, and soon reappeared, dressed for the day.

'I think I'm awake now,' she said. 'Where's that tea and toast, or did I dream someone said they'd make it?'

While she ate and drank she went back to her theme.

'Did someone say something about Southport? I was asleep before.'

'Oh yes, we're going there.'

'Why did you say we're going there?'

'We didn't say.'

'Anyhow I didn't dream that you're both being low-down swindlers, that's true enough. So now, and I want a straight answer—*why* are we going?'

'Dusty wants us to.'

She sighed. 'So we're back where we started! *Clem, why* are we going?'

'Ask Perry.'

'Don't ask me!' said Perry. 'I thought you knew!'

'Oh, you're mean things, teasing me on my birthday. You're both so silly, Dusty might just as well send Rhony and Bess on his messages.'

Clem nodded. 'They're pretty bright cows, those ones.'

Ryl tossed her head. 'I'll come now that I'm up, but I won't talk to you, you're too silly!'

During the drive through noisy Coolangatta, around the curves of the sea to Kirra—by the bridge at Tallabudgera to Burleigh Heads and along the sand flats to Surfer's Paradise, they teased her abominably.

'Actually we're going to look at a bunyip that a fellow caught up on the Roper River. Dusty wanted you to see it so's you could describe it to him.' He's thinking of buying it.'

'Yeah. It's a big one they say, about twelve or fourteen feet long. One of the smooth-skinned variety.'

'They say that kind's no good for the table.'

'But they're quite intelligent, and make good pets.'

'Yeah, very fond of children they are.'

'And they have a pleasant whistle.'

'You can't teach 'em to talk, but they can be trained to use a cash register.'

'By all accounts,' said Ryl, 'this bunyip must be a cut above you silly types.'

At the edge of Southport shopping centre they parked Clem's utility near the motor show-rooms. They steered Ryl through the big glass doors.

'Why are we going in here? Oh I forgot, it's no use asking you pair of dim-wits, I'll get a better answer from your bunyip!'

Perry spoke to a salesman, who then led them to a side door

opening into the drive-in yard. Here a gleaming, new red Herald stood basking in its own polished glory.

'There!' said Clem. 'What do you think of that for a bunyip?'

'Happy birthday, Ryl!' Perry and Clem both burst into song. 'Happy birthday to Ryl—happy birthday to Ryl—'

Ryl was speechless and bewildered. 'What's the matter, have you two been drinking or something?'

'Ryl,' said Clem, 'happy birthday from Dusty. To you from Dusty, the best bunyip he could find.'

'That—for me? From Dusty? You're a pair of lying hounds!'

'But it's the honest truth! Crikey, how's her form! Talk about a suspicious mind!'

'But—' she quavered, 'Dusty doesn't *like* cars! And he'd never be able to bring himself to pay for one! I mean—I mean—'

'Look,' Perry had to convince her, 'it's your car. See, here are the keys!'

But even after Ryl had personally signed her name on the ownership papers she found it difficult to believe.

'But *Dusty*!' she kept exclaiming. 'Why the old pet! The dear, sweet thing! Golly, I wonder if he hit his head when he fell off that horse!'

'I'll tell him you said that!' threatened Clem.

'Oh Clem, honey, you know I don't mean it—I'm just so excited I don't know what I'm saying! The old pet!'

Clem took his utility home by himself, leaving Perry to hang Ryl's 'L' plates on the new car.

'You'd better drive home,' he said, 'to start getting the feel of it. You must drive it all you can over the week-end, and then go for your licence on Monday.'

'Oh dear, do you think I'll get it?'

'Of course you will, with one hand tied behind you!'

'I bet I wouldn't, not under those conditions. Because the police wouldn't think it was clever!'

She took the driver's seat, her whole being radiating excitement.

'What turns it on?'

With twinkling eyes, Perry pointed out the various switches. She rehearsed the gears.

'Are you really sure that I can drive it, Perry?'

211

'Of course—come on, put it into neutral and turn on the ignition; it won't bite you! You want to drive it to the hospital and show Dusty, don't you? He hasn't seen it yet. He asked Clem and me to buy it for him.'

She finally got the car in motion, and they began to cover the homeward miles.

'Isn't it a honey?' said Perry. 'What do you think of our choice?'

'It's perfect, it's just exactly what I wanted! I just can't get over it! You and Clem were so good and sweet to buy it for me!'

'Dusty wouldn't trust me to buy it on my own, I guess he thought I might end up with some racing job!'

They laughed, thinking of Dusty's mind ticking over so busily as he lay in his hospital bed, in the only room in the building that was never tidy.

An hour later they were there with him. Through the window of his ward, they showed him the car, Ryl showering him with gratitude.

'It's the most terrific, fabulous car in the world! It's the most! It's too much! It's—it's—' What more was there to say of it?

But in a way it was Rose Bradley's surprise party that meant the most to Ryl.

That warm evening of early summer, the Uni. year-end exams were just over, so all the old surfing gang were able to come.

Dodi was there with her flaming red hair, now lacquered into a sleek fashion, and using much eye make-up. Red was there, with quite a polish to his shoes and his manners which had not been there when he did headstands on the beach last autumn. All the others, too, were there. They were all more mature and worldly-wise than in the days when they were last season's beachcombers. Except Tom the photographer. He had come to the party too, to wish Ryl a happy birthday. For him, older than the rest, there was a dash of nostalgia in the occasion. But the others were too busy having fun to feel this. For them, that would come still later. Now they flung themselves into the moment's doings, so that Rose and Clem, not without a sigh of relief, were left restfully in the back-wash as onlookers, while the guests swept past in a whirl of party spirit.

212

As to Ryl herself, in some ways she actually felt younger than she had twelve months ago, but in others, a whole generation older. She tried to remember her last birthday at school in Melbourne. But it seemed unreal and obscured by a mass of time and experience. Surely—that must have been someone else! Surely, thought Ryl, it was just that she had once known a girl who was lonely in a crowd, without friends or family, a girl with but one song in her heart, and that the sad song—'I care nought for nobody, and nobody cares for me.' Tonight in the Bradleys' garden with red and green lights strung from branch to branch of the Moreton Bay fig-trees, that girl was hard for Ryl to remember.

Rose, assisted whether she liked it or not by Glen, had done a wonderful job as usual. For true to his promise, Glen had quickly turned on his full voltage of charm, and mended his quarrel with Ryl.

Large quantities of food were always a challenge to Rose. She had been a little nervous when she had confided to Glen that this was her first 'teenage' party. But he had assured her that teenagers were also human, just as when her own children were in their teens, that they ate the same things as the rest of the race— except that they were particularly fond of barbecues. So, working as a team, Rose arranged lobster-salad on trestle tables, while Glen turned out hamburgers on his portable barbecue. Rose was most relieved to see that Ryl's 'forever' had been so short, and that Glen was forgiven, for he was certainly useful to have at a party.

To Clem's amazement and relief, they danced on the cement patio, rather than on the polished floor of the living-room.

'Spare me days,' he said, watching them, 'and look what they wear on their feet! Rubber-soled shoes, thongs, suede boots— there's a girl with no shoes at all! Remember when we used to dance? We used to wear special patent-leather pumps. And all that kerosene and boracic that we used to put on the floor of the Progress Hall to make it slippery!'

'Do I ever remember!' smiled Rose. 'Didn't we make those floors shine? The floors at Geebin, and in Perry's house, they've all been rubbed with kerosene and boracic in their day; they've all been danced on.'

'And none of the modern floors are the good colour they've come up,' agreed Clem. He went on watching the youngsters.

'Don't they look a lot of hobos? The girls wear dresses like corn sacks. And then they talk about gracious living.'

'Anyhow, it saves the new plastic floor surface,' comforted Rose. 'It'd probably be ruined if it were danced on, it can't take a beating like the old kerosene-and-boracic ones.'

214

At about one-thirty the young people also pleased Rose by collecting the supper things and forming themselves into a dish-washing team. Certainly they defeated their own purpose, for while they were about it they brewed more coffee and ate a great deal more food, though there was still plenty over. Clem complained that he would have to have hamburgers for breakfast.

'But I'll say this for them,' he added, 'the evening's been more or less painless, after all. I was prepared to suffer. But it turned out that it wasn't such an ordeal, comparatively speaking.'

Very late indeed coats were collected and cars started. Voices called good-bye in the moonlight. Glen lingered on, replacing chairs, collecting paper serviettes and limp lettuce leaves, and feeding the remains of the lobster to Perry's white cat which had invited itself to the tail-end of the party.

'Ryl,' he asked, 'can I take you home? Seeing it's all of one hundred yards away, you'll need protection.'

'I might if I went with you!' But there was no malice in her tone.

'Oh, I'm not such a Gay Lothario,' said Glen, 'I'm putting all the bright lights behind me.'

'No! Since when?'

'Since I flunked in political science and the Dad's stopped the allowance!'

She had to laugh at Glen.

'Come on, then. I'm ready for home.' She picked up the cat. Perry was still there, too, lingering on to finish the coffee. 'Perry honey, mind if I take White Cat home? He's nice and warm on my feet.'

'So that's where he sleeps!' said Perry. 'The traitor! Why doesn't Bruno tip him out?'

'Well, at first he was terribly rude to Bruno and spat and swore at him. But he got over it. And Bruno doesn't know he's a cat, so he's safe. Bruno's been taught not to chase the calves and hens. Maybe he thinks White Cat is a sort of hen, and is just waiting for one fine day when he'll lay a real egg.'

'Huh! Well he can go with you. I'm tired, tired. Good night everyone.'

Soon there was a great noise as the Bomb started up.

Impulsively, and for the first time, Ryl kissed Rose and Clem. Her kind neighbours had become closer than parents in the space of a short year. She gave them each a quick peck—for all her life, except to dogs and cats and Dusty, she was to retain her old undemonstrative ways. Then she ran down to Glen's car, with the

216

boy following. As he pulled away they both waved to the pair in the lighted doorway.

'Good night! Thank you for a wonderful time! Thank you!'

'Golly,' said Ryl, as White Cat protested and squirmed in her arms, 'they've been a lot better to me than I've ever deserved. I can hardly believe my luck! To have the Bradleys—and Dusty—and Perry—'

'Perry, huh? All this and Perry, too?'

'You knew about Perry, didn't you?'

'W—e—ll—' admitted Glen, 'I kind of half knew. I didn't want to believe it. You see—it's hard to explain. But really it can't make you any different, the fact that your mother was a coloured girl; after all, you're still you. And Perry's always been a brainy, likeable chap. We were at high school together, and he was always top of the class. It was as though he'd set himself that standard. Not like me. I expect I've always had it too easy. And Perry's had it hard. But he's won through.'

They were already at Geebin. Ryl got out of the car, still hugging White Cat.

'Say,' said Glen, 'Perry's always been called Perry Davis. I suppose that was his mother's name, wasn't it?'

'Yes. But it won't be much longer. Dusty and I are going to adopt him legally. Another headache for our solicitor in Melbourne! But Dusty says that will be the best way to do it. Then Dusty is going to make over his part of my father's money to Perry. He never wanted it, anyway. He hated the thought of parting with his pension!'

'Crazy!'

'Anyhow,' said Ryl, 'I'm too tired to stand around and natter all night! 'Bye, Glen!'

'Good night, dear girl. Be seeing you!'

He drove off, and Ryl and White Cat walked up the grassy path to Geebin.

# XXVI

Dusty was to come home soon. Apart from having his leg in plaster, he was in fine fettle; in fact the rest in bed had done him a world of good. Patients had come and gone from the other beds in the ward, with the usual quick turnover of the modern hospital, but the old gentleman with the white hair and whiskers had become an institution. He and Butch Bradley were able to prolong their games of chess over several visits, and the board was always set up with pieces—a constant irritation to the cleaning staff.

Today they were playing as usual. Dusty had just won, so he was in a particularly good mood. A nurse's aide brought two cups of tea on a tray, and Dusty played Mine Host, making the ward his castle.

'Why don't you break a leg, Butch me boy?' he asked jovially. 'Half the time I'm the only fellow here, you know, and the place is a hive of maternity cases. Last week I had a kid with tonsils in the room with me. Only his tonsils recently gone missing, of course. Well! I'd rather have a dorg for company. But even he got better that quick, it wasn't natural!'

'Too late now—for me to join you, you'll be home next week,' said Butch.

'True enough. Ah, she's all right here, but I'll be glad to get home. Home's a good place. There's nowhere like it.'

'Ah. And now you'll have Perry all the time to look after the farm work.'

'Yes, that's right. He's started his holidays, so he'll have nothing to do but work.'

Butch nodded. They were quite in earnest, and saw nothing odd about the statement.

'Ryl's gone to Mur'bah,' said Dusty. 'She won't be in to see me this afternoon. She's driven the car to Mur'bah all by herself. She's going to try and find out something definite about the water-tower business.'

218

Ryl had indeed passed her driving test and was the owner of a driver's licence—new, clean—still smelling of printer's ink, and carried tenderly in a new wallet in the glove box of the car. At this time, the new car was still like something sacred. Bruno was not allowed within scratching distance and White Cat was discouraged from sleeping under it. Before Ryl started the car, it was necessary for her to dive under it on all fours to make sure the cat was not about to be run over.

She drove carefully and with great respect for the new gears, and parked the car near the shire office. Before entering she stood for a moment watching the busy street of the country town, busy, yet not too busy, with slow-moving crowds, more leisurely than those of the big cities. She looked at the taxi rank, where she half-expected to see Perry's face behind a windscreen, at the red-brick shops, and behind them the purple ramparts of the Numinbah Range, and improbable Mount Warning. She realized for the first time what this small country town had come to mean to her, and what it would always mean.

The door of the building opened and Spike came out.

'Ryl! I was just thinking about you! Come and have a soda.'

They walked across to the opposite side of the street, and to one of the town's two milk-bars.

'I can't stop long,' she told him. 'I've got to get back to those darned cows!'

His eyes twinkled. 'Then you won't mind losing Geebin?'

Her heart turned cold—but only until she looked at his face, with its mischievous expression.

'Yes, I would mind! The cows I've never learned to love, but they're not all of Geebin! Tell me and don't tease; what's happened about the stupid old water-tower and the council meeting?'

'Well, they've had their meeting. Had it last Friday night. I've seen a copy of Brownie's report on the water-tower site—and what do you know?'

'Tell me quickly or I'll scream!'

'Well, old Brownie didn't even mention your Geebin! He just straight-out recommended the place opposite, on the other farm, where the old banana patch is growing!'

'That's Ki's old banana patch! Well, good old Brownie! Bless him! He turned out to be a goodie after all! Whee! Good old Brownie!'

219

'And what's your friend Perry going to say about it?'

'He won't mind. Anyhow he's going to live with us at Geebin soon. We're going to knock out another bit of the kitchen wall and build on another room, next to the bathroom—but coming out farther past the corner of the kitchen—oh well, you'll see it.'

'Why is this Perry going to live at your place?'

'Because—well, it takes a bit of explaining—but—the fact is that he turns out to be my brother. So—' she gave him a slanting look, 'anyone who doesn't like Perry had better not like me!'

'Strike me lucky!' said Spike. 'You are full of surprises! How come?'

'I said it's a long story. Can you just take my word for it?'

'Oh. Then all right.' He thought for a minute, then added, 'That Perry is quite a person, of course. Gee, I'd like to come and help you knock your old house into a new shape. It sounds like fun.'

'Then why don't you come out at week-ends? The more the merrier!'

'Could I? Then I certainly will.'

'Good, you've just joined the club!'

When Spike went back to his desk, she sought out Mr. Brown in his office.

'Hullo,' she smiled at him. 'I've just dropped by to thank you. And I mean it. You don't know how we appreciate what you've done for Geebin.'

'Oh,' he told her kindly, 'that's all right! We suddenly found that the alternative site was four feet higher than our first measurement!'

'Anyhow, if that's your story, you stick to it! But really, we do thank you!'

He waved her away, but kindly. In a few moments she was on her way back to the cows.

Dusty was due home from hospital next day. Ryl was going to mark the occasion with the most noble gesture she could think of. She was going to borrow Rose Bradley's cookery book and personally make a cake. As she drove she steeled herself for the task.

220

# XXVII

Dusty came home in festive November weather.

Perry and Ryl went to fetch him in the new car, after a day of banana cultivating on the new plantation.

Perry and Red had slept at Ki's cottage for the week-end, but apart from that, had lived at Geebin. Perry's University exams were over, so that he was back in his home district, slipping into its old ways. Red, the boy who had never had a flair for studying, was doing quite well with his various business projects, and remained a staunch friend. Perry planned to sell his old farm, for it was worked out. He would concentrate on the rehabilitation of Geebin.

On this late Sunday afternoon, he and Ryl enjoyed each other's company as they made their way to the cottage hospital. As he drove, Perry sang once more his sad folk-song:

> 'Take off your old coat and roll up your sleeves,
> Life is a hard road to travel I believe.'

'Mack-the-Knife,' said Ryl, 'nobody's asked you if you mind having this prefabricated family suddenly on your doorstep! *Do* you mind us?'

He grinned at her.

'Oh, I can stand it,' he said. 'I guess I can stand it!'

She joined him in his song, their voices blending.

The youngsters installed Dusty on the couch near the french windows in the living-room. From here he could see out over the pink pastures of matel-grass, and beyond the river to the sea. It was sundown, and the sturdy boats of the prawning fleet were tacking past Point Danger, to stand by for the seventh boomer that would carry them over the bar, and so across the shining sea to the fishing grounds far out of sight beyond Brunswick Heads.

221

Or if he tired of the river and sea, he could turn his eyes to the room around him, glowing as it was with the feel of life about it. Jones the canary had been brought to sing in the window at his side. By way of celebration he had been given a new cage, which combined with a plant urn. Here he carolled like a tiny minstrel among his setting of begonias.

Perry was doing the evening milking—rather late, as Dusty had remarked querulously. Ryl came to sit near her grandfather on his first night home, and together they watched the oft-repeated journey of the fishing-boats. Seated on a heap of cushions, Ryl told of Mr. Brown's water-tower report, and Geebin's reprieve.

'So,' she concluded, 'he is really a kind person, isn't he? I think he was so kind about it all!'

'Ah,' said Dusty, 'he was got at! You must have got at him!' She laughed. 'Are you glad to be home?'

'That I am! It's as good a home as anyone ever had!'

'It's a dump. But we like it, don't we? Just for the moment I'm tired to death of farming. It almost makes me long to go to Uni. next year! But Perry's here now so he'll take over. And next year, we can travel back and forth to Brisbane together, in the car, and we'll both come home to you, every week-end.'

'I'll have a good feed of chops and potatoes waiting for you,' said Dusty.

'Oh dear, must you? And Dusty—I've made up my mind about what I want to "do"! I'd like to be an architect. And when I've taken my degree, I think I'll specialize in renovating old houses. You see—there's something about an old house! I don't know—an old house has a mind of its own, somehow!'

'And all these boy friends you seem to collect,' said Dusty. 'What are you planning to do with them?'

'Oh, nothing at all—they're quite safe for years and years yet! I hated Glen for a while—but he's turning the corner. Perry always did say he was sound at heart. Then there's Red! He's a dear, but quite nutty! And Spike Hardy's nice, you'll like him, he's coming to tea one night.'

'Does he know about your cooking? Is he going to bring his own fish and chips?'

'He can jolly well eat my cooking, and undergo the test of friendship like all the others!'

222

'Butch ought to be here for our game of chess,' complained Dusty. 'I wonder what's keeping him?'

The sun was dipping bright tentacles into the sea, making a path of light for the fishing-boats to follow.

'Where's our bird?' asked Dusty. 'Where's the blue crane?'

'He was here a few days ago. But it's the time of year that makes him restless. I expect he's gone away.'

'Uh,' said Dusty. 'Gone off on his wanderin' wings, ur? He thinks he's searchin' for something better all the time. He has his ups and downs in the course of his travels, I'll be bound. And when the tarradiddle's all over, back he'll come. His paddock will be here waitin' for him. Back he'll come.'